Zulula

C000225560

By Oliver Strong

ISBN: 978-0-9955188-7-2

Word Count: 73,289

Contents

Chapter One: Kreli's Surrender

A rectangular clothes brush darted left to right, shoulder to cuff, its bristles a blur, zig zagging east to west and back on a southernly path, as did the creature from which it originated, boar country was not far from here.

Its handle was constructed of elephant ivory, the spoils of a separate hunt thousands of miles away on the subcontinent of Asia.

A tall Englishman with thick black hair stood before his manservant, the servant's heritage similar in geography to the alabaster tusked beast. The Englishman's mutton chop side burns met above his stiff upper lip, a clean shaven chin below, grey blue eyes rested beneath dark brows.

A pair of gentlemanly legs stood firm and proud, a powerful figure widening at the chest to stretch his British Army officer's tunic, a scarlet beacon of order and civilization. His sub-continental servant, once finished dutifully dusting his master's tunic, began brushing his trousers.

Lord Chelmsford admired himself in the mirror, adjusting medals and straightening collar, he a civilized Englishman sent forth into savage Africa to shine enlightenment upon the primitive elements of this crude continent.

Lord Frederic Augustus Thesiger, 2nd Baron of Chelmsford was in his early forties, forty one to be exact. A Major General of Queen Victoria's Royal Army and a veteran of more than one campaign, Crimea his first, the Indian Rebellion of 1857 to name a second.

The Empire had rewarded Lord Chelmsford for his loyal service in defeating her enemies and laying the savage low. Promoted in line with his achievements Frederic dwelled within the Cape Colony, modern day South Africa or at least part of what modern day South Africa would eventually become.

Yet on this day Chelmsford inhabited neither town nor city, not even so near as to be within sight of a church steeple on a sunny day. On this day a field tent divided him from the elements, out here in Xhosa country on the

Eastern Cape of South Africa, soon to be absorbed within the British Empire.

The ninth and final war with the Xhosa was to meet its conclusion in a prompt fashion. Many battles lay behind Lord Chelmsford, a tapestry of horror and carnage, its closing threads depicted Kreli's final stand at Kentani against Her Majesty's redcoats.

The African effort failed to impress the British lion; he'd fought savages in the past and when set beside Russians in Crimea they did pale. Today Kreli was to formerly surrender, permitting a smooth transition of his people's tribal estate and full control of the Eastern Cape into the dominion of the British Empire, pushing Her Majesty's borders upwards to meet that of the Zulu.

To the uneducated man or woman it would seem the British Empire had moved in and conquered these people out of a lust for power and wealth.

In truth the British had nothing to do with this war, it was an intertribal conflict brought on by drought and fought between two tribes, the Fengu and the Gcaleka.

Modern day South Africa was yet to be formed, its current map resembled a bag of liquorice allsorts dumped into a frame constructed along lines similar to the nation we recognize today.

A complicated scheme of tribal and ethnic areas rubbing up against one another, the British controlled its southernmost cape area, a modest piece of land compared to the expanse owned by long established African tribes.

Today men in England were to begin work on redrawing that map, for the British long intended on bringing those tribes into a confederation under the banner of Queen Victoria, the Queen of Africa.

A fellow named Henry Bartle Fere had been appointed High Commissioner for South Africa; at his suggestion did these plans of confederation become reality.

So with confederation in mind the British entered the ninth and final Xhosa war on the side of the Fengu. With Lord Chelmsford commanding Her Majesty's Armed Forces the British absorbed more territory into the Empire, crushing the Xhosa at the battle of Kentani and pushing the Queen of Africa's borders against that of Zululand.

Both sides held concern over these fresh living arrangements, but that was an issue for diplomats and men of words.

The order of the day was to accept the Xhosa King's surrender, and ingest his pitiful people as a pride of lions might consume a wildebeest.

The British were always poised to take advantage of any situation in the region, especially drought, for there is an African proverb as old as civilization itself, "Peace is the rain that makes the grass grow … and war the wind that dries it out".

The commissioner for South Africa and the Cape Colony employed this skilfully to attain his dreams, a confederation of states under a single flag, and why not? For he'd achieved the very same in Canada, bringing a mighty landmass full of wild men and creatures alike under the standard of civilization, the union jack; surely these savages couldn't resist the will of civilized men, when before this time white men who opposed the Empire had buckled under imperial pressure.

Besides, who wouldn't want to be part of the greatest civilizing force in the history of mankind? The British had outlawed slavery, marching proudly into the world in a bid to exterminate its blight from the planet, of course that meant many of the African slave states had to be conquered, not that they weren't given the option of changing their ways first.

It was Henry's Christian duty to release men and women from slavery wherever they may be, if that meant the Empire expanded, well, that was a good thing for all involved, was it not?

An Indian manservant unbuttoned epaulettes on his master's scarlet tunic, running two leather straps over the tunic as a man would braces, a third strap stretched diagonally from left shoulder to a belt on Chelmsford's right hip.

This piece of uniform, worn by officers exclusively, was called a sword strap, of course these days it held not just a British cavalry sabre but also the newly issued Adam's revolver MK III. A weapon every British officer found useful fighting savage Africa.

The pistol's double action … that is when you pulled its trigger it served more than a single function. It cocked the firing hammer (rather than having to pull it back with one's thumb), while turning its cylinder and loading a fresh chamber, loading and firing the weapon in a single action. This function permitted rapid fire of all six chambers in quick succession.

The Adam's MK III had entered service only this year, 1878, every officer was issued one, much to native chagrin. For this weapon was of considerable assistance in close combat, where natives excelled. It offered accelerated fire and devastating stopping power, a single shot might drop a 450 pound wildebeest, a charging native had little hope.

The manservant buttoned down his master's epaulettes and fastened a buckle before presenting Lord Chelmsford with his sword, an 1853 pattern cavalry sabre.

Its black leather grip was coursed by a single golden braid wrapped around from end to end, its brass guard a piece of fine intricate work crafted by the most acclaimed sword smith in Birmingham.

A shimmering blade of the finest steel man had ever produced. One of the blade's edges bore faint inscriptions, for this sword had been issued in the Crimea many years ago. It'd seen much use yet he refused to replace it, for sentimental reasons.

Its blade rested inside a beaten old sheathe, also constructed from steel, it was his last line of defence versus the Dark Continent's brutal savagery.

Today Lord Chelmsford awaited his defeated enemy in the province of Natal, a large chunk of land between the now British Cape Colony and KwaZulu or better known to its white neighbours as Zululand.

After checking his master's dress the short Indian fellow nodded his head, "Very good Master."

Chelmsford checked himself in the mirror, noting his manservant's meticulous work, not a speck of dust blemished his fine woollen tunic, a mark of British elite populating the African Cape and the scourge of the Xhosa.

Chelmsford, a tall man at just over six feet marched out of his campaign tent; here at Kentani centuries of Xhosa self-rule was about to come to an end. High Commissioner Bartle was overjoyed; his plans for confederation were going full steam ahead. African savagery found itself wanting when weighed against mankind's most modern military. Often natives were frightened into surrender without a shot being fired, for resisting the British Royal Army's onward march seemed an impossible task.

Inside camp, beneath a tree, Bartle waited on his Major General; as Henry's Alexander exited his tent hot African sun glinted on lacquered boots and the old man arose.

Bartle removed his top hat, grasping it alongside his cane, before dabbing his brow with a handkerchief. The commissioner wasn't dressed for the heat of Africa; he appeared to be straight out of a production of "A Christmas Carol" by Charles Dickens, his forehead reeking with perspiration.

Grey hair and moustache, Bartle was of average height and in his mid-sixties, long face with small beak like nose. Heavy black coat, black top hat, dark cloth trousers and dark leather shoes; an English gentleman pulled out of Dickensian London and plopped on the East Cape of South Africa.

"Is it always so hot here?" stated the Dickensian commissioner whilst dabbing sweat from his brow.

Chelmsford, a typically sombre gentleman, some said he was aloof but that wasn't true, he was a stoic since his days in Crimea, further detaching himself from society after his wife's death three years ago, leaving him no children.

Those who accused him of haughtiness were often men who envied his military achievements, from the Crimea to the Indian Rebellion to the Abyssinian expedition of 1868.

Truth be told Chelmsford envied their families as much as they his prestigious career, in his mind military achievements served as poor recompense for a loving wife and strong children.

Chelmsford approached the commissioner, stood beneath a star chestnut tree, and growled in a stern aristocratic tone, "No commissioner but in times of war natives care little for climate, be it mild or blistering they suffer its ordeal."

Bartle placed a damp handkerchief inside his jacket before returning an uncomfortable top hat to its crown, "A savage people for a savage land, they ought be grateful."

"Perhaps," replied Chelmsford, halting beneath one of the thick trunked fern's low hanging branches, where a cluster of unique fruit in the form of four velvety boat shaped carpels, dangled. Each carpel about five centimetres long with prominent prows arranged in a star pattern. Each boat, when ripe would burst open to reveal black seeds embedded within long hairs.

Chelmsford plucked one from a group hanging at eye level, held its pod between middle finger and thumb while tapping it with his forefinger. Its contents dispensed into the palm of his hand before Chelmsford discarded the empty pod. He offered its dark seeds to Bartle, "Chestnut Commissioner?"

Commissioner Bartle eyed with suspicion a group of seeds in Chelmsford's palm, "Are you sure they're safe to consume?"

Chelmsford picked a seed with his right hand, popped it inside his mouth, chewed and swallowed the fruit, "Commissioner, an entire army with knowledge of this land may move anywhere during any season without the handicap of supplies.

This fern feeds native warriors, fighting men, you can be assured its fruit is harmless yet avoid the long hairs which bind its seeds together, they can be most disagreeable."

Bartle took a single seed popped it inside his mouth and chewed, after swallowing the fruit his brow raised in pleasurable surprise, "Once the crown confederates these savages there'll be no need for war or armies, we'll set them about the proper division of labour, build infrastructure and civilize this brutal place."

Chelmsford looked out at the beautiful Kentani hills, breath taking mountains rising in the distance to meet light cloud huddling around their peaks, "This land is most pleasing to the eye, perhaps it will requite the sensibilities of high society?"

Bartle plucked another seed from Chelmsford's palm, "I don't see why not, peace does often attract aristocracy. Civilized men may no longer experience an aversion to dwelling along these shores."

The grey commissioner chewed on another black berry, its taste and texture pleased his palette, "Tell me Frederic, do you think African life would suit you?"

The usually stoic General produced the tiniest of smiles beneath his thick moustache, "The land is charming yet it shall detain me only as my posting to the Cape Colony requires."

"Detain you?," inquired the commissioner as he returned to his stool, leaning on his walking stick until the seat of his trousers made contact, "I suppose the heat plays its part in your decision?"

"Commissioner, I was stationed in India; the heat of this land is quite mild compared to the blast furnace that is Bombay. No, my father died recently, his estate passed into my hands and awaits my presence."

"Trouble at the manor?"

"Nothing so dramatic, it's expected of the 2nd Baron of Chelmsford. Also ..." his visage became firm and void of expression as he pushed the following words from his chest, as if they were a flock of rebellious sheep herded by a growling dog, "... I must visit Anna's grave."

Lord Chelmsford wallowed in melancholy brought on by the memory of his wife, "Anna passed three years ago."

"Yes, I remember," stated a sombre commissioner.

"Unfortunately, since laying Anna to rest my mother has pressed me to remarry and raise an heir. She has little else to do but compose badgering correspondence.

I imagine the Chelmsford postal service has witnessed lucrative trade this last year."

The grey commissioner finished off his star chestnut seeds, "Forgive me Lieutenant General but your mother is quite right. You're not a young man, find a good woman of age and put your mind to securing the family line."

Lord Chelmsford popped a black seed into his mouth, while chewing his gaze did attach to the grey commissioner as a Nile crocodile would lock it's cold vision upon impala drinking at a river bank, waiting for one of the herd to forget present danger, move in, stretch its neck, providing the crocodile with distance he may cover in a single leap, quick enough to grasp the impala's throat and drag it to the bottom of the river, spinning it around until the creature drowned.

Bartle felt the herpetological gaze of his commanding officer touch his skin, a cold blooded reptilian scrutiny mastered during the Crimean war; the Russian's had taught Lord Chelmsford many dimensions to the art of manhood. Russia had tempered his soul in the furnace of battle, today it was a cold, dark presence, hidden beneath the uniform of a British General, for in war he found the Russian manner to be most productive, added to that, in life, similar outcomes were maintained.

Lord Frederic Augustus Thesiger, 2nd Baron of Chelmsford and Major General of Her Majesty's Royal Army … hold on … Lord Chelmsford spoke to the commissioner in a quizzical tone, "Lieutenant General?"

The grey commissioner grinned, "I'm not supposed to inform you until after Kreli surrenders, you've received a promotion from Major to Lieutenant General. From what I've been informed you'll soon have another medal to keep those beauties company," he gestured with his stick toward medallions decorating Lord Chelmsford's tunic.

The Lord had won many honours on the battlefield, from the Order of the Medjidie placed upon his chest by the Ottoman Emperor himself alongside medals for the Sardinian and Crimean conflict as well as being mentioned in dispatches and his Companion of the order of Bath medal, won during the expedition to Abyssinia.

"Thank you Henry, I'm sure I'll find room."

Lord Chelmsford and Commissioner Bartle had been friends since the time of the Indian rebellion. Henry Bartle, then Governor of Bombay, had the pleasure of promoting Chelmsford to Colonel after he'd dealt with quarrelsome natives; the two quickly became firm friends, a friendship which served them both in India and here on the Cape of Africa.

Henry had been introduced to Frederic's former wife, Lady Anna Chelmsford; a charming yet childless woman … Anna's death was most unfortunate. Henry witnessed its effect on his friend; he no longer carried a sense of joviality for Chelmsford's merry attitude only existed in correlation with Anna's presence.

No longer did Lord Chelmsford appear during social functions since other officers' and officials' wives would accompany them, inducing a morbid recollection of Anna's absence.

Sir Henry Bartle Frere did sense a darkened spirit hang above his friend, casting a Crimean shade onto any trespassers entering his orbit. The majority of society were unable to understand its nature and so believed Lord Chelmsford to be that hard hearted fellow. Henry knew otherwise, Anna's passing permitted this darkness, acquired in Russia, to reach within Frederic's soul. For Anna did repel the forces of darkness, chasing shadows from Chelmsford's psyche upon his return home, yet she no longer walked this earth and so the Devil dispersed her light, causing Frederic to set career before all else.

"I'm certain Wood will press for a celebration of one kind or another, you know how proper he is over military honours and such," stated Bartle.

A rumble commenced throughout the camp, its wave ascending a sea of tents. Lord Chelmsford and Commissioner Bartle moved in tandem as a band of Xhosa at the front of a British column appeared on the crest of a hill.

Men discernible only by their red tunics marched to the sound of the drum and bagpipe, glory and honour preceding a baggage train, making its way toward the British camp. Xhosa emanated defeat, dressed in tribal skins their dark sunken faces and tired eyes superfluous against music playing behind them.

Lord Chelmsford called to his manservant, "Field glass Wallah!"

A turbaned fellow, short and dressed in traditional Indian attire walked quickly from Chelmsford's field tent carrying a cylindrical leather case. On reaching Chelmsford he popped its cap and waited on his master.

The tall General drew his field telescope of bright polished brass and brown leather from within. Chelmsford gripped leather with his right hand extending the short end with his left, drawing out the three piece telescope before placing it to his right eye.

Zooming in on the dark tip of this red spear he noted the captured Chief Kreli, directly behind him marched the men of the 91st Argyllshire Highlanders. Originally drafted to fight Napoleon these Scots traditionally wore the kilt with a fur atop their heads; however conditions were very different from the cold and damp winter climate of Northern France.

Today the 91st Argyllshire Highlanders wore not furs but a pith helmet, each tea stained helmet displayed a brass regimental plate facing directly forwards, as the eyes of Mars upon a Spartan shield.

The scarlet tunic of a British soldier covered the torso with a single thick white leather strap across the chest from left shoulder to right hip intersecting a thick white belt and small white bag carrying ammunition and odd and sods.

Rather than standard black trousers these men displayed tartan colours, one of many changes to the uniform. You see, since the Napoleonic era the British soldier's uniform became quite flamboyant until utility superseded glamour.

Tartan trousers disappeared inside a pair of patent leather boots, a frightening sight to any native army, though to be fair Kreli had played a good game.

The British had a single obvious weakness; they were slow, moving in columns with heavy baggage trains, very much reliant on supply lines. The Xhosa were not so hindered, able to travel fast and free without need for logistical supplies. The Xhosa led British redcoats a merry chase, until with the help of the Fengu, a rival tribe with whom Kreli went to war, the British did bring the Xhosa army to battle and claim victory over them.

Kreli attempted to flee but today he was being brought in chains for the ceremonial transfer of the Natal into imperial hands.

Redcoats each carried a MK II Martini-Henry rifle on their right arm. A sturdy and reliable piece of technology, some would argue unmatched by any other military. It was developed from an American rifle, improvements were added such as a superior loading system wherein its cartridge was automatically ejected, permitting fast firing.

Made of dark wood, bright British steel glinted under African sun where its trigger and firing chamber rested, it was a modern marvel, again, much to native chagrin.

To the right of the column two horses travelled at a leisurely pace, one before the other. The foremost carried Colonel Evelyn Wood, at forty years of age his rank was displayed for all to see via a brass officer's badge beaming out from brown pith helmet, noting his regiment, the 91st Argyllshire Highlanders.

During the Indian rebellion men were issued pith helmets. Although being totally ineffective against a rifle bullet it was lightweight and kept sun from a soldier's head.

During the Indian mutiny soldiers stained their bright white helmets with tea so they might camouflage themselves, Officers rarely did so, yet Wood was the type of insufferable fellow more than ready to get stuck in, a serious career soldier whose judgement his Lieutenant General held in high regard.

Lord Chelmsford's helmet remained bright white, a stubborn and fearless man even in the face of death. Kreli had attempted to target him, yet failed, for redcoats cut tribesmen down in waves of a dozen at a time, MK II rifles firing a 0.45 calibre bullet, enough to drop a rhino.

"What do you see?" inquired Bartle as he rested upon a wooden stool.

"Colonel Wood, he's captured Kreli," replied Chelmsford eyeing the column from a distance.

Lord Chelmsford collapsed his telescope with firm satisfaction and turned his head to view Bartle wiping a sodden brow, "Tea Wallah!"

Frederic's manservant appeared from the servant's tent once more, this time bearing a silver tray carrying two glasses filled with ice, a tea pot and small ceramic pot of milk. Another servant appeared with a small table and two more stools.

Red tunics patrolled the camp, tending to supplies and cleaning armaments. Once the 91st Argyllshire was identified the hustle and bustle quietened to a murmur, a stampede of elephants became a leisurely drink at the river bank.

Chelmsford rested upon a wooden stool beneath a quivering ceiling of layered branches. The star chestnut's leaves diffused a bitter sweet scent, its honey, a dark blood-red colour, was known to natives in this part of Africa as an aphrodisiac.

A table separated the General and commissioner, "Thank you," stated Chelmsford permitting his manservant resume his previous duties, both glasses resided within bright steel frames. A wallah raised the pot of lukewarm tea, made eye contact to which Chelmsford returned a nod allowing Wallah to fill his cup with ice cold tea.

The dark skinned fellow from the sub-continent, curled beard and turban, finished pouring Chelmsford's drink before turning to Bartle. Henry nodded, "Please do," the Indian servant smiled as he poured dark tea into the commissioner's glass. He placed the pot down and inquired in a polite Indian accent, "Milk Mr Commissioner?"

"No thank you," said the perspiring official as he waited for his friend to be served.

The man from Punjab turned to Lord Chelmsford, "Milk Master?"

"Lemon, thank you."

"Yes Master," replied the servant, before he softly called a second wallah, a mere youth rescued from the squalor of Bombay to follow an English Lord on his adventures in Africa.

The young man appeared with a knife and fresh lemon. He sliced the fruit asunder and squeezed its contents, doing his best to retain any pips from plopping out and into the drink.

"That will be all Wallah," stated the English lord sending his servants back to their tent until required.

Bartle took a draught of iced tea, for even beneath the chestnut tree's shade this heat was more than he cared to suffer. While Governor of Bombay Henry had the luxury of servants fanning him night and day, even so the heat was horrendous. Despite having withdrawn from India in 1867 and spending the following twenty years in England, studying at Oxford and journeying to Canada, the memory of that terrible climate failed to escape the mind of Henry Bartle Fere.

He felt iced tea flow through his body, followed by momentary relief from the eye of Helios, until an African climate penetrated his frame once more, "You know old boy, I ask myself every day, why couldn't these natives live in a more agreeable climate?"

Lord Chelmsford, rather than find his statement humorous, for that was his friend's intent, took a sip of lemon tea and fixed his gaze upon the 91st Argyllshire Highlanders, marching down a hill they'd previously been forced to march up, "I pity those poor men Henry, torn from their families, from the cool air of Scotland and forced to march over hills and across dusty plains in drought stricken Africa, all for a miserable ribbon on their chest."

Henry was taken aback, "They should be proud, they fight for the Empire!"

Chelmsford delivered a typically stoic response as he monitored men labour beneath blistering African sun in scarlet tunics, tea stained pith helmets bobbing up and down in synchrony to form a sea of char, "Tell me, what does the Empire do for those poor wretches other than place them in danger?"

"They're paid aren't they?" protested Henry.

"So are you old boy yet that has little influence on your objections to the local climate."

Commissioner Bartle withdrew his protestations; he'd had this discussion more than once with Fredric, it wasn't easy to come off on top when a man of such high honour and lauded achievement in military matters was your opponent, and besides they were friends. Should a man from the lower orders voice a similar opinion Henry would've seen proper correction, as would Lord Chelmsford. In fact both Bartle and General Chelmsford had done so in the past for many of these men were criminals, murderers and rapists, drafted from Her Majesty's Prisons to fight for Queen and country in faraway lands. These convicted criminals often acted up on first arrival, yet after the taste of military reproof they always fell into line, serving as a fine deterrent to fellow scoundrels.

"That may be so, yet it cannot be denied that the flotsam and jetsam are recruited to bolster their ranks, those men are little more than villains!"

Henry referred to the Natal volunteers, young men who existed in the gutters of colonial life, lurking the streets for employment or opportunity in the hope they might coin a few pennies from African tragedy.

When the rumblings of war lifted the African horizon it was music to their ears. They'd take the king's shilling in a mismatch with spears and shields. Imperial food and accommodation, though nothing a man would aspire to, certainly beat what might be scavenged in the gutters of the Cape Colony.

But as far as armies go, the tinned rations apportioned to British troops were nothing to complain about, preserved meat at one end of the tin with a cocoa "supper" at the other.

This meal was intended to sustain a soldier for 36 hours in the field. Then there were biscuit rations which every man kept in that small bag on his right hip. Named "Hardtack biscuits" by the issuer, they were dubbed "Liverpool pantiles" by its beleaguered consumer.

A reference to a specific brand of roof tile for these biscuits resembled them not only in form, down to its dimples, but also in texture.

As the Argyllshire regiment passed the hill's crest Lord Chelmsford expected to see dry grass yet Frederic witnessed a second dark sea. Standing up Frederic snatched his eyepiece from the table, opened it and examined an opaque blob trailing a scarlet snake.

Behind a tiny baggage train, for the 91st had been primarily using supply depots since the British were now firmly entrenched in Natal, followed a white man on a horse with many Africans in chains.

Truly an odd sight, for fifty years ago parliament outlawed slavery in the British Empire, leading to crusades across the planet, fighting the great slave states of Africa, the Middle East and Asia.

These were not prisoners of war for in reality the war ended months previously, this was merely an operation to force the Xhosa chief into an official surrender.

"Soepenberg," muttered Chelmsford.

"Is something the matter?" inquired Bartle as he stood beside Chelmsford.

"Here, take a look, following the 91st," Fredric handed his field glass to Henry, "do you recognise that fellow on horseback?"

The grey commissioner tipped the brim of his hat upwards, so he might scrutinize the column, "I'm afraid my eyes aren't as sharp as yours old boy, are you familiar with him?" replied Bartle.

"Yes, he's a Boer or he was, a rather distasteful fellow."

"Why would he be in possession of ...."

"Slaves?" stated Frederic.

Commissioner Bartle collapsed the field glass and handed it back to Chelmsford.

The British lion drew in a deep breath, African chestnut honey soothed his sensibilities before they clashed with the anticipation of a bitter Boer, "He used to live and operate in Griqualand until the Crown took possession. I had surmised he transferred his illicit trade north, out of our jurisdiction. I have absolutely no idea why he's conducting business in the Natal."

The Crown had taken Griqualand from Boer control last year, outlawing slavery, per British law.

This didn't go down well with the Boers; they were farmers with a lot of money invested in slave labour. The British freed slaves by the hundred but some refused to sacrifice their investments, not without recompense.

Bastijn Klein Soepenberg gave up farming and went into business supplying fellow Boer farmers with fresh labourers. Forced out of Griqualand, Soepenberg followed droves of Boers in a self-imposed exodus, what he was doing south of KwaZulu, in the Natal, was a complete mystery but Lord Chelmsford was about to find out.

When the British took control of the Cape Colony more than three hundred thousand slaves were released from servitude. Boers moved north, until the British marched in and took control. Eventually the only land remaining where Soepenberg might ply his wicked trade was the Transvaal Republic, North of Zululand.

From what Chelmsford observed Soepenberg was presently trading in women, there was always a good supply of the fairer sex bordering Zululand, for King Cetshwayo wasn't popular amongst all the tribes of KwaZulu. Added to that polygamy was a recognised practice and so it was common for women to flee the Zulu King's jurisdiction with lovers in tow; many settling on the now British side of the river separating KwaNatal from KwaZulu.

The column of soldiers reached Chelmsford's camp, a trumpet sounded, announcing the return of victorious warriors. Lieutenant-Colonel Evelyn Wood rode into camp, halted at the star chestnut tree, dismounted and saluted General Chelmsford, "Sir!"

Chelmsford nodded, "As you were Colonel, tell me, how was it?"

"The Chief led us a merry chase but the lads held firm, sir."

"Good work Colonel, now what about this slave trader, what on earth is he doing in your column?"

"We were watering at the Buffalo River and this Afrikaner knave was on the cusp of driving at least fifty men and women over to Zululand."

Chelmsford observed the 91st as they dispersed to their tents, erected by the King's Rifle Corps under Lord Chelmsford's instruction, "Bring Soepenberg to me."

"You know him sir?"

"We've crossed paths, dismissed."

Lieutenant-Colonel Evelyn Wood was a strict military man, he said "Sir" more often than required and followed military code to the letter. Some found him tiresome; Lord Chelmsford was rather pleased to have a man who followed orders without question or complaint.

Wood handed his horse over to a young redcoat before making off towards the detainees. Kreli was escorted to a guarded tent while Soepenberg was separated from a band of chained women and escorted by a sergeant to the chestnut tree.

The blonde haired, former Boer, smiled, "Gooden morgen Mr Chelmsford," he stated in a distinctly Afrikaans accent.

Afrikaans being the language also known as "Cape Dutch" was a language of contact; created when Dutch sailors first met the Khoi and the San on the Cape of South Africa. It is 95% Dutch, the rest a mixture of West Germanic, Malay and local languages. Afrikaans eventually formed its own distinct language spoken by millions in Southern Africa today.

At this time in history it was a language of class, mainly spoken by the lower orders of society. Until around 1870 Afrikaans was a "kitchen language" used by servants and slaves, for obvious reasons Soepenberg was fluent in Afrikaans. After selling his farm he'd slipped down the social order from Boer to Afrikaner.

Commissioner Bartle rose and pointed his stick at the prisoner, "That's LORD Chelmsford."

The slave trader's grin widened, "Ah, so the old man croaked? I guess that makes you a Baron doesn't it? Lucky for some."

Lord Chelmsford's face barely twitched, a stoic lion glared down the wicked Afrikaner, "Despite the climate you'll make no headway Mr Soepenberg, a guttersnipe that trades in human misery is far beneath my threshold. Now let me ask you, what exactly is your purpose in crossing the Buffalo River?"

"These ain't slaves, these are wanted outlaws in KwaZulu. Cetshwayo's offering a hefty reward for some of these women."

"Really Mr Soepenberg?"

"Yeh, really," replied an impetuous slave trader.

"We shall see, Sergeant, put him in the stockade and release those prisoners."

A redcoat with tea stained pith helmet and three golden stripes running down his left arm saluted stiffly, "Yes sir!"

Soepenberg protested, "Aye! You can't put me in the stockade! I ain't done nothing!"

Chelmsford looked down his nose at the vile man, dressed in dusty leather trousers and jacket, dirt stained shirt and leather hat, "Perhaps he might spend his time in the pursuit of the Queen's English, Sergeant?"

"Yes sir!" the sergeant saluted the General.

"Dismissed Sergeant."

A thickly moustached redcoat grasped Soepenberg's arm, "This way sir,"

Soepenberg resisted, feet rooted to African dust in disbelief, "Sir, it would help if you co-operated, we don't want this to get nasty."

Soepenberg looked over in wonder and nodded his head as the sergeant pulled him toward a wooden box on the other side of the camp.

"What should I do with the slaves sir?" inquired Colonel Wood.

"They're no longer slaves, release them forthwith," replied Chelmsford.

Colonel Wood hesitated for a moment.

"Is something amiss Colonel?" inquired Chelmsford.

"You wish me to release them into the country sir?"

"That is correct Colonel; now carry out your orders."

The Colonel saluted, "Yes sir!"

General Chelmsford returned salute and Colonel Wood made his way toward a holding pen usually employed for pack animals on the baggage train. Today it was put aside to hold a largely human population which Soepenberg had rounded up on the British side of the Buffalo River.

Unfortunately for Soepenberg, when he'd captured these exiles of the Zulu kingdom, KwaNatal was under Xhosa ownership or so he believed.

The Xhosa King, Kreli, had no qualms with Soepenberg for he was no ally of the Zulu, quite the opposite in fact. Had the British not intervened in this intertribal conflict Soepenberg would've taken his slaves and been off to Zululand for he'd travelled hundreds of miles in the hope of capturing not only a band of slaves but in search of the daughter of King Cetshwayo kaMpande.

The Buffalo River demarked the lands of Kreli and Cetshwayo and those who were against the rule of Cetshwayo did often seek refuge on the Natal's banks.

One person in particular had rebelled, rather than be married to the King's General, Dabulamanzi kaMpande, her father's half-brother, a man with three wives under his belt.

Nkosazane, daughter of the Zulu King, was living peacefully on the banks of the Buffalo River until Soepenberg appeared, for there was a price on her head and rather than spark a war with his neighbours to the south, Cetshwayo sent bounty hunters such as Soepenberg in search of his daughter; for oddly enough a white man could move around these lands relatively unmolested compared to a native African.

The grey commissioner rose to his feet and eyed a group of penned up Africans, "Bloody shocking!"

"Yes, it's a terrible crime, that someone who purports to be a Christian could bring himself to treat his fellow man with such indignity."

Henry glanced at Chelmsford before returning his gaze to the band of African women, caged alongside pack animals, "Yes of course."

The tall General peered down at his superior, "Oh? What were you thinking old boy?"

"I was taking note of the native dress code, why, some of those women are barely clothed," he pointed his cane at a group of young women in nothing more than grass skirts.

"That cannot be denied," replied Chelmsford, his eye scanning dark flesh. The General's head stopped moving as his vision fell on a single female in particular. She stood out above the rest, somewhat taller than the average man at five foot eleven inches, her African brow towered above redcoat saviours, that is, once they'd removed their pith helmets.

She wore colourful beads, red, green, yellow, white and black; her braided black hair was encircled with a band of beads. She wore a necklace, each band a different colour forming a large choker, its beads seamlessly dropping down to touch the top of her chest.

A top covering her breasts was contrived of the same matter forming ever increasing circles of beads. Tassels plunged from throat to dangle beneath an ethnic brassiere.

Her skirt constructed of the same material, bands of beads, each band alternating between red, yellow, green, white and black, its tassels stroked her knees, allowing thick thighs to excite a man's senses.

Chelmsford was fascinated by her, an odd occurrence, for since landing on this continent all natives appeared as one to his eye, indistinguishable, yet this woman did discern herself from every African creature his gaze had scrutinized, before … or since.

She was unmistakably African, tall strong legs, powerful features; her visage struck him as invulnerable beauty wrestling with a man's fragile sense. For the first time since his assignment to this land he noted a tribal nose and full lips. Chelmsford's eyes dissected her image with greater intent than any man in polite society ought, and in doing so he garnered his subject's attention.

The tribal beauty sensed intensity caress her dark skin, not uncomfortable … but intriguing, as the first rays of sun on a cold winter day. Instinctively she was cognisant of his location, her head moved ninety degrees. The colourful woman's eyes locked his in place as a tempestuous sea takes command of even the greatest battleship, snatching his attention and hitching it to her mystery. Large African opals fixed on the white man ogling her, it felt that a great distance had been bridged, collapsing as the General's field glass.

The enclosure was well away from the officer's tents yet Chelmsford discerned intricate features while her fellow captives remained a blur. Likewise, Nkosazane, while ignoring a multitude of white men felt a pull, her vision cleared around Chelmsford's ivory face and she did separate it clearly from the herd. Her interest caused fortitude to enter her heart for curiosity is a form of bravery in the feminine.

"Fredric, are you feeling under the weather?" inquired Commissioner Bartle.

Lord Chelmsford snapped out of it, though the African woman remained entranced, "I'm quite alright; it's just that girl over there."

"Which one?" inquired the commissioner.

"The one attired in colourful beads."

Henry squinted at the pen, "Yes, I wonder who she stole those from?"

"What brings you to such a conclusion?"

"Well, the last time I saw a native adorned in similar fashion she was royalty."

Chapter Two: Nkosazane

Observing from a distance as a ship's captain might gaze into early morning mist; a sense of trepidation was balanced out by the burden of military analysis, whilst settled on the scales of fate. Lord Chelmsford perceived a beaded African tribeswoman move toward a redcoat, to which the soldier, guarding a lot marked out for beasts of burden, formed a rather odd expression.

A sergeant was called over, he spoke to the young woman, perhaps in her mid-twenties, at least that was the best assertion Chelmsford could form without assistance of his field glass.

For a while the two made conversation. Now unless his sergeant spoke the local language, a highly unlikely scenario since he'd recently departed a steamer from Bristol, but one conclusion did remain ... she spoke the English language, another highly unlikely scenario yet one of the two must be true.

The sergeant began to make a path toward Chelmsford and Commissioner Bartle. Henry had grown equally perplexed by events since following his General's eyes. Frederic's perception widened as if journeying across open savannah to be approached by a lion for the first time.

On reaching the stoic pair the sergeant halted to attention, "Sir, one of the natives wishes to speak with the commissioner, sir."

Somewhat taken aback Chelmsford replied, "Sergeant Bourne, I had no idea of your familiarity with the native tongue?"

"It's the native; she speaks English ... on her own!"

Chelmsford and Bartle exchanged glances, a startling revelation to both gentlemen, that this far into outback a woman might speak with a civilized tongue, "Bring her here," stated Bartle.

Lord Chelmsford transmitted a puzzled expression to which the commissioner replied, "Well, you are curious as to what this is all about?"

Lord Chelmsford inhaled, drawing in the scent of dark chestnut honey, "Alright Bourne, bring her here but keep her under close watch."

"Yes sir," Sergeant Bourne saluted to which Chelmsford replied with a nod of his head.

"What do you suppose this is all about?" muttered Bartle, a rhetorical question yet Chelmsford replied.

"You did say she was dressed as royalty," Fredric didn't like rhetorical questions while Henry had an irritating habit of putting them forth, added to which Fredric had an equally bothersome custom of answering them.

Sergeant Bourne opened the pen and led a young lady out. Under escort of two redcoats they approached the star chestnut tree beneath which a top hatted commissioner leaned against his walking stick.

The lady neared and in doing so her complexion cleared by degrees, unfolding as details of Solomon's temple might sharpen into focus on a pilgrim's approach, Sergeant Bourne marched before her, a redcoat flanking each side.

Bourne halted once more, "The prisoner sir."

"Thank you Bourne," stated Chelmsford, "That will be all."

The sergeant formed an uncomfortable expression, "Sir?"

"I said that will be all, you may return to duty."

"Yes sir," Bourne saluted before marching his redcoats away.

This was a peculiar set of circumstances, to leave the General and commissioner in the presence of an unescorted savage didn't sit well with Sergeant Bourne.

The native girl addressed the grey commissioner, "High Commissioner Bartle, I am Nkosazane, I wish to thank you for rescuing my fellow Zulu and I."

The commissioner was taken aback by her clear grasp of the English language, "You're welcome Miss Nkosazane, may I ask where you learned to speak English so well?"

She smiled, immediately Chelmsford felt something stir inside, it was faint and distant, an early morning mist observed from across Port Elizabeth's bay, the final whisps of evening dissipating in atmosphere as morning birds twitter to one another on masts of anchored sailing boats.

"I was taught your language by missionaries, before they were expelled from KwaZulu; this is why I desire an audience with you. I am requesting political asylum and the protection of Her Majesty Queen Victoria."

There was a silence, for this made little sense, first off Chelmsford was completely ignorant to political asylum. He was a military man, uneducated in such affairs. During the 19th century nearly all countries in the world possessed open borders, asylum was not a requirement if one wished to reside within the British Empire.

For in these times common criminals could be deported only if they'd committed a crime in the country requesting them, added to that their infraction must also be an offence in the British Empire.

The exception being political crimes or crimes against government and its structure, for those you could be deported and so political asylum existed. However political asylum was so rarely requested that even Commissioner Bartle felt cobwebs blow away on the young lady's appeal.

"Political asylum? May I ask on what grounds?" stated Bartle in an inquisitive tone.

"My name is Nkosazane, daughter of King Cetshwayo; I fled KwaZulu rather than be forced into an illegal union with his General."

Lord Chelmsford's eyes coursed the body of this tribeswoman, even from afar he did discern her beauty, smooth milk chocolate skin, perfect all but for a miniscule mark on her cheek and even that imperfection served only as an exception enforcing the rule.

Despite an imposing figure of a woman her face possessed a tenderness, high curved eyebrows, a long African nose that until now Lord Chelmsford failed to find allure within, although to be honest the chances he might see something he desired in any woman was slim to none for he'd been mourning his wife these past three years.

Her pillow lips beckoned his weary head to rest upon them, moving upwards deep dark eyes reminded him of Ethiopian opal's he'd witnessed in the gem markets of Cape Town and Port Elizabeth.

The opposite of Australian opals these gems were dark in colour yet despite their darkness, much like white opals, a fire did flicker within, a twinkle capturing Fredric's imagination, enticing him deeper within the dark aura of Africa.

"Excuse me but I believe an arranged marriage is a perfectly law abiding provision in KwaZulu, is it not?" stated the General, capturing the ebony Princess' attention.

"An arranged marriage in KwaZulu is lawful but not in the British Empire or so I have been led to believe, sir."

Chelmsford smiled beneath his bushy moustache, "It is illegal to enter such an arrangement against the will of a British citizen."

Bartle cut in, "I'm afraid Lord Chelmsford is correct. Although this is British territory, not every member of the British Empire has the fortune to be a British citizen. Added to that young lady, while I do commiserate with your position, neither you, your father, nor your fiancé are members of the British Empire."

Nkosazane's visage held and expression of incredulity or at least that is what Lord Chelmsford concluded for it was policy that gentlemen of his status not speak with natives, unless absolutely necessary, "Then forced marriage, if committed upon your daughter, is a crime you would refuse to prevent for want of citizenship?"

Chelmsford was surprised at her control of the language; although admittedly he'd not spoken with a native since his assignment began more than a year ago. She had a distinct Zulu accent yet her pronunciation was clear and grammar impeccable.

Bartle stopped for a moment, suspended in deep thought while lifting the brim of his hat to clear sweat gating inside, he began brewing a strategy within his devious mind, "Hmm, you're quite right Miss Nkosazane, I believe I can make an exception in your case."

Her soft lips formed a smile, two canoes stretched from one cheek to another, beautiful opal eyes sparkled with heightened intensity beneath fascinatingly arched brows, the native girl dropped to her knee, "I am in your debt High Commissioner Bartle, whatever you wish ..."

Henry Bartle was rather embarrassed at her actions as they drew the attention of every man and woman in camp, redcoats and semi-dressed natives alike, especially Soepenberg who peered from between planks of

24

hardwood forming a stockade door. The Afrikaner observed a Princess he'd travelled the length of Zululand to deliver to her father in Ulundi. This wasn't looking good for the slave trader for she was worth more than a year's profit, and a good year at that!

"Please stand young lady," stated Bartle returning the lofty tribeswoman to her feet, a few inches taller than he, "Now if you return to the pen, on reaching Port Elizabeth I'll ..."

"Come now Henry, there's room in one of my servant's tents," Lord Chelmsford cast his voice as a lion does launch its roar across savannah yanking the ears of all God's creatures to attention, "WALLAH!"

His manservant quickly exited a tent pitched alongside Frederic's, in the officer's quarter, "Yes Master?"

"Wallah we have a guest, Miss Nkosazane will be accompanying us to Port Elizabeth, please make her comfortable, understood?"

The turbaned man from the sub-continent bowed, "Yes Master."

Lord Chelmsford gestured toward his tents, "Please follow Wallah."

Before following Wallah inside, the tall native girl curtseyed, "Thank you sir."

Bartle eyed the ebony amazon as she disappeared within white canvass, "Fredric, are you sure about this?"

Lord Chelmsford raised his brow as a great beast might raise its back in challenge, "You granted her asylum, surely you don't believe her to be a threat?"

"You remember India, those sly devils sent many an assassin disguised as a servant, or have you forgotten those days?"

"Certainly not, but these natives differ to those of the sub-continent, they prefer to fight with honour, on the battlefield, rather than employ a woman to cut a man's throat in the night.

Besides, what's your business granting her asylum in the first place, are you plotting again?"

These men knew each other to such a degree it was impossible to obscure the true nature of Bartle's decision, "You're correct, if she is who she claims then her father will demand we return her ... when Her

25

Majesty's Council refuses to comply he'll cross the Buffalo River with armed men in an attempt to retrieve her ... because of honour."

Lord Chelmsford's vision moved from tent to friend, "I suspected as much."

"It's the white man's burden to bring Christianity and proper governance to these natives. Why if it weren't for us they'd still be murdering wives at funerals in India; burning them alive on the Ganges alongside their husband's corpse!"

Lord Chelmsford nodded, "I agree, although I must admit this young lady has managed to civilise herself, despite the savagery of Zululand."

They both eyed the tent she'd disappeared inside, "I do concede she speaks the language with remarkable fluency."

"I was thinking much the same old boy," noted Chelmsford in a stoic tone.

"Now what are you up to?" remarked Commissioner Bartle in a sly pitch as he peered up toward his General.

Chelmsford took a moment to gather his thoughts before he replied, "And if her presence proves to be of no advantage, what would become of her?"

"I should imagine I'd have her released into Cape Town and left to her own devices, why?"

Lord Chelmsford toyed with a ring on his left hand, his wedding band was a memento, a link to his deceased wife, "I could do with a translator and I wager this lady understands the regional dialects. She could be very useful to me, especially on campaign."

The grey commissioner's eyes narrowed as he observed his friend's thumb and forefinger spin his wedding band, its gyrations generating a tempest in Henry's gut. Anna had died in Middlesex, England, 1875, it was a tragedy since Frederic was to become a father yet that day he became a widower, Anna died in child birth, as did their child.

Henry wasn't there but it was a well-publicised event. Frederic being a hard, stiff upper lipped Englishman took the first available assignment abroad. It was all he had left, for he was a Major General in Her Majesty's Royal Army, the greatest fighting force the world had yet witnessed.

He requested a commission in Africa alongside a familiar face, no decent man could deny Fredric's petition and so he travelled by steamship sailing into port on the African continent in the year of 1876.

Whenever Lord Chelmsford spun that band of gold you could be certain the wheels of his mind were turning.

Commissioner Bartle's eyes, carved from blocks of old stone, as slits on a fort where men hold watch by the sea scanning its horizon for Napoleonic masts, observed his friend closely, "Frederic," he spoke in an abnormally soft tone, "don't get too attached."

"Attached?" His band twirled, an involuntary action by this point, he was the only person unaware of it, "Please Henry, she's a native."

"She is, yet I must admit she's the most charming native I've crossed paths with, don't you agree?"

Lord Chelmsford ceased spinning his band and replied abruptly, "I hadn't noticed."

As the day continued, Kreli, Chief of the Xhosa met with Bartle's council and signed his surrender, the final paperwork countersigned and bureaucrats satisfied, cartographers redrew the map of Africa once again. The Natal swallowed whole into the Cape Colony, the same Cape Colony recently consumed by an imperial crocodile.

Previously a democratic land yet under Bartle's eye the Cape Colony was absorbed into a new purpose, as rock cut from an African mountainside to become the anchor stone for the Queen of Africa, on this mighty dark continent.

Soepenberg's captives were released, returning to the Buffalo River where under the motherly protection of Britannia they might live their lives free of Zulu tyranny.

Soepenberg himself was to be returned to Cape Town and stand trial; the practice of slavery outlawed by Her Majesty's government since the early years of the 19th century.

Nkosazane travelled in the tent of Lord Chelmsford's servant. Upon the second day Frederic awoke to the smell of tea ... lemon tea. He recognised the brew, it was rather early for Wallah to prepare his breakfast, no, he must've overslept for his manservant was the most punctual fellow; Wallah hadn't made such an error in over a decade.

Upon rolling out of bed Chelmsford noticed today's undergarments folded neatly beside his bed on a walnut chest of drawers, a piece of furniture which had accompanied him since his days in India more than 20 years ago.

The Lieutenant-General slept naked, for in this climate it was difficult to reach a state of slumber in traditional night clothes. His long masculine legs stretched atop bed sheets to form a gentlemanly rump.

He arose to slip on a white woollen vest and underpants. Chelmsford's red sleeping suit was still folded on his chest of drawers beside them.

Next he approached a stand of wooden bars used to hang his outer garments, white shirt, black trousers and scarlet tunic, rank demarked in black and gold braid on its collar, shoulders and cuffs, campaign ribbons displayed upon chest, so all men might observe. An intimidating sight even to those well employed by Her Majesty, for he displayed honours from England to Russia to India and now South Africa.

Finishing his uniform off at one end were black boots, polished each morning by his manservant, and a bright white pith helmet at the other, its lack of tea stain denoting him not only as an officer but fearless and defiant in the face of death, something African tribesmen respected both on and off the field of battle.

The Zulu consider the greatest weapons to be courage and discipline, the tools by which they'd conquered all bordering tribes, until now, for today the British, the most disciplined and courageous fighting force to have trodden God's earth encircled their lands.

Stepping into red dawn as a farmer might survey his crop before harvest, Frederic found morning's atmosphere most agreeable in temperature. An aroma of dying embers caught Chelmsford's senses, a familiar scent which brought comfort to the General's mind. It permitted him to reminisce over campaigns of bygone years, yet the Crimea was always absent from his early morning muse for it held many bitter memories, something he mulled over on dark lonely evenings rather than a fresh cool African morning … those times were for reflection not celebration.

The camp hadn't commenced its usual hustle and bustle, a regular occurrence on preparation for another day's march. Men shifted as white rhinos bathing in mud, resting here and there, in an hour or two they might form a crash and cut across African plains to find a new watering hole.

Chelmsford moved toward his personal breakfast table, a British lion surveying his kingdom with fearless pride. Nkosazane waited on him in solitude, the hour too early for Commissioner Bartle. Colonel Wood was yet to rise. Sergeant Bourne was up, checking the camp perimeter while natives recruited for the Xhosa war to bolster British numbers slept beneath the heavens, around charcoal heaps encircled by stone.

Some were white farmers otherwise referred to as Boers, then there were African tribes with an axe to grind against Kreli's wheel stone, mostly the Fengu. A third group were the dregs and flotsam of colonial society, signing up for a free set of clothes, a shilling a month and one hot meal a day.

The ebony amazon stood up to greet her protector, "Good morning, sir."

Chelmsford smiled as she curtseyed, "Good morning." he held the back of a chair, transported in his baggage train wherever he might campaign, "please be seated."

The beaded native smiled, her bright multi-coloured dress swayed back and forth around thick thighs and pert chest … at least that's what Chelmsford imagined as she thanked him while returning to the table.

"And you may call me Fredric," stated the stoic warrior as his Indian manservant dashed over, carrying a second chair constructed using strong teak with two arm rests and cushioned back.

Nkosazane blushed; her bloom was slightly visible through milk chocolate skin. South African natives have a lighter hue compared to equatorial Africans, much as you'll find Northern Europeans possess a lighter shade than Mediterranean's.

"We must do something about those clothes," stated Fredric as Wallah squeezed, pushing tea leaves to the bottom of a French press.

"Do you disapprove of my attire, Frederic?" his name was pushed from between her thick lips, a word as foreign to her as Nkosazane to Chelmsford.

"I wouldn't say disapprove but if you're to stay with me you'll need more than a single garment, besides it wouldn't be proper," stated the Englishman as Wallah finished squeezing a slice of lemon into his morning tea.

"Proper, what is proper?"

"Appropriate," Chelmsford raised a glass to his lips and sipped, Wallah had for many years mastered the art of preparing tea at the exact temperature his master required.

"Then you do not approve, Frederic," replied Nkosazane her smile broke as she raised a glass to her lips, sipping delicately in tandem with the Lieutenant-General.

"Society would disapprove, if you're to be under my protection."

"Then I am blessed by the ancestors to have you as my guardian."

"You're under Her Majesty's protection," he attempted to distance himself from his African ward for this was the closest he'd been to a woman since his wife's death. Despite his friend's suggestion Fredric refused to find another wife, partly because no woman struck him in such a way as to match his Anna and as an officer in the Royal Army, a man of high status in English society, he no longer required company, for someone was always there. Subordinates surrounded him on campaign, while off campaign gentleman such as Commissioner Bartle and Colonel Wood were a constant fixture of what passed for high society out here in Cape Town or Port Elizabeth.

Then there were his servants, imported from India, amongst many were his Chaiwallah, serving morning and afternoon tea.

You see, base wallahs served on British military bases across the Empire, loading and packing behind the front lines, doing much of the donkey work for small pay. It was an appreciated path for a young Indian man, a valuable opportunity to elevate himself from the slums of Bombay and gutters of Delhi. Perhaps one day, through his master, bearing the redcoat of the Queen of India, Africa and the seas touching each segment of the globe, he

30

might set foot on the motherland of this great Empire and take his place amongst the highest society on the face of the Earth.

Chelmsford also possessed a Dhobiwallah for cleaning and preparing his uniform and dressing him on campaign.

On Lord Chelmsford's modest estate in Port Elizabeth he employed several wallahs in its smooth running, for Frederic was a wealthy man by any measure.

"May I ask why your Queen has come to Africa?" stated his guest in a soft whisper, a voice Lord Chelmsford found himself drawn to. Nkosazane's hue and tone was unlike that of any woman he'd engaged with previously. Her African pitch fascinated his English sensibilities as this continent does the white man on so many different levels.

For rather than a high pitched wail that did often aggravate the Lieutenant-General, at least that is how he perceived nearly every woman's voice, save his Anna, Queen Victoria and this dark lady. Rather than nails on a chalkboard she spoke with a deep yet feminine strength.

"I'm sorry, am I out of place?" stated the ebony lady, her multi-coloured beads reflecting sun as it peeped above hills rising on distant savannah.

Chelmsford, glass floating before stoic expression, considered thoughts evoked by this native, invading his life as a band of impi springing from long grass.

Crossing the river separating Zululand and the British Empire, or better known as KwaNatal to the natives, or just Natal to the British, so she may assault his British sensibilities, "Excuse me for a moment," his glass of lemon tea resumed its journey, he took a sip, then answered her question, "It's quite simple, many years ago before you or I were born in fact, the British Empire outlawed slavery, since then we've taken it upon ourselves to free the world of that abominable practice."

Nkosazane smiled and nodded, "Yes, the missionaries taught me this, is this not the white man's burden they spoke of?"

"Partly," replied Chelmsford, his demeanour changed, back straightening with pride, "it is our Christian duty to civilize the parts of the world where men continue to enslave one another and live as savages. We have taken it upon ourselves, as enlightened Christians, to do the same for the people of Africa."

Nkosazane raised her brow, a somewhat sceptical expression was mirrored in her tone, "I suppose the gold and diamonds recently discovered in this region have no gravity upon that noble quest?"

His African ward smiled, her manner remained respectful. Despite searching for insult or offense Frederic discovered neither for she spoke the truth, had a rich source of diamonds not been discovered in the Cape Colony in 1866 by a small boy on the Orange River, a pebble which turned out to be a 21.25 carat diamond, the glorious crusade to civilise this part of Africa might not have been pursued with such fervour.

The truth is, since that discovery by a fifteen year old boy this region had produced more diamonds than India had mined in the previous two thousand years, motivation enough to expand the white man's burden to the southernmost tip of Africa.

"I would say it's a fair trade, wouldn't you?" replied a stiff General.

"I'm not sure, my people still enslave one another, fight over land, commit sinful acts, all of which I abhor, however, it is their choice to do so."

Chelmsford took another sip of lemon tea; this native not only possessed a fine grasp of the language but an understanding of philosophy, "Surely they'd be better suited to life beneath the protective wing of Britain?"

Nkosazane hardened her tone a little, matching that of Lord Chelmsford, "There are always those who would trade liberty for security Lord Chelmsford yet I believe it is God who granted mankind free will, not Queen Victoria, or am I mistaken?"

The Lieutenant General realised he was up against stiff competition, this ebony woman was as studious as she was stubborn, "You're not mistaken," replied Chelmsford tentatively awaiting her next move as if engaged in a game of chess.

"Then what right do you believe you have to take that which God has granted us?"

The stoic soldier considered her words for a moment and upon discovering lack of rebuttal he replied in a wooden pitch, "Miss Nkosazane, I am a soldier in Her Majesty's Royal Army not an American statesman nor am I the Arch-Bishop of Canterbury. I am set tasks by Her Majesty and I jolly well see them through to the best of my abilities, with as little bloodshed on either side as possible.

Now when the day comes that savages stop murdering and enslaving one another in this region of the world I'm certain I shall be sent elsewhere, but until that day arrives you and your kind are my burden."

The ebony amazon took a sip of tea and smiled, "Please forgive me if I seem ungrateful, I am not. Your rescue was most timely, for had your men not appeared when they did I would have been dragged back to KwaZulu against my will."

Chelmsford released tension from his body, realising he'd gone off on a young lady who after all was only expressing curiosity, "No, forgive me for being brash. Tell me; what circumstances brought you to the Buffalo River?"

Nkosazane's nostrils flared, absorbing oxygen mixed with the odour of burnt out campfires, the Princess' mind transported cinders of her past as flakes of ash do hitchhike upon early morning breeze. Our African beauty took a moment of solitude before replying to Lord Chelmsford, "I was betrothed to Dabulamanzi KaMpande, my father's half-brother, I was to secure the family line and his kingship, that was my purpose in life, nothing more than another one of his wives, another set of hands to wash his clothes or clean his hut, for the sake of ambition.

I have no desire for such a position and so fled before anything might come of it, to the Buffalo River; where lovers have fled in years past in hope they may escape society's degeneracy."

Frederic listened intently to her story, especially the part where Nkosazane mentioned wives in the plural "Tell me, how many wives does this fellow have?"

This sable beauty, hunted across savannah for hundreds of miles as a springbok stalked by a pack of hyenas, glared down her guardian. Derision did cross her mind, for only a man could find excitement in bigamy, as an alcoholic might fantasise over owning his own distillery, yet on peering into the eyes of this hunter the springbok saw not the lust of a thirsty hyena but something else. Frederic's grey sapphire eyes contained a blue only discernible at close quarters, as if she examined a Madagascan gem. Dark at distance yet on closer inspection the stone betrays another nature, similar to the wine dark Indian Ocean testing the coastline of her native lands on a stormy day, "Forgive me, my Lord," stated the young lady ashamed of her own prejudice. Nkosazane was quick to judge men, since like a hyena they were simple creatures with but three desires in life, gratification of the stomach and genitals being the first two the last being silence or at least the silence of women which was unsurprising since in her opinion men were stubborn as a mule and disparaged any feminine counsel. Not that Nkosazane would've expressed such conviction, for she was royalty, raised to marry a prince, even her opinion was inconsequential unless it emanated from her husband's mouth.

Lord Chelmsford sighed, "I would rather you didn't call me 'my lord', I don't sit at the Old Bailey."

"What is the Old Bailey?"

"It's the central criminal court in England, where the worst criminals are tried."

"Then I was referring to you as a criminal?"

"No, no, no, my lord, pronounced 'mi lud', is how one addresses the judge."

"Yet you ARE a lord are you not?"

"I am but how might I put it, to have you constantly refer to me as lord would be improper since you're not subject to me in anyway. You're my guest; it would be poor form if I permitted you to use my title with such frequency, considering you're a lady."

African nostrils flared again as Nkosazane mulled this new information, her mind a sponge for European protocol especially English society. Since the first day she'd met those missionaries, priests of the Norwegian Lutheran Church, the white man fascinated Nkosazane.

As a little girl she learned all she could about them, for something drew her interest. She alone in her father's court could speak English and French, not only that, she did read and write in both languages.

Then on the warning of the witch doctor, a trusted advisor with whom the Zulu King would always confer before important decisions were to be made, the missionaries were expelled. Shortly afterwards Nkosazane discovered she was to be married to her father's step brother, a commander in the Zulu Royal Army, a man who might wield great power against the King should he desire it and so his loyalty was secured with marriage to the King's first and only daughter.

Therefore Nkosazane ran away, was captured and then released by the British. She knew enough to plead for political asylum yet didn't expect a native woman to receive such privilege. However, much to her surprise and no doubt her fiancé's chagrin, Nkosazane's request was quickly accepted … a little too quickly. Nevertheless, she recalled something her grandmother told her as a girl. Whenever Nkosazane questioned or over analysed good fortune her grandmother would set her straight by saying "Udla indlu yakho njengentwala!", or in English, "You eat your hair like a lice!", the meaning being not to look a gift horse in the mouth and appreciate people who are or were once beneficial to you.

Thanks to political machinations within her father's kingdom our ebony Princess was to be sacrificed to quench a man's ambition. Dabulamanzi possessed everything a woman might desire in a man, wealth, power, respect, her friends were quite envious. When Nkosazane made her displeasure clear they were bemused, for any young Zulu woman would surely be ecstatic.

Nkosazane stated her true desire … love … they laughed since without wealth a man cannot possess a woman in KwaZulu. An average man will build his wealth for years so he might meet a woman's bride price. The young man must negotiate payment in head of cattle with his bride's family. Dabulamanzi had negotiated a dowry or as it is known in these parts a lobola, of fifty head of prime cattle, a sum unheard of in living memory.

To a white man this practice was little more than cold blooded savagery, auctioning your daughter to the highest bidder, yet it was commonplace in many parts of the Empire.

After several years stationed in India Chelmsford had frequently bore witness to the practice, although their system was quite different. In India a bride's family must pay the groom a dowry in gold and other goods.

Chelmsford found it quite odd that the bride's family would essentially pay a man to take their daughter off their hands. For if employed in England he was quite sure it would result in every scoundrel in the land plundering brides from decent families ... not that within quarters of high society this didn't occur anyway. But the lower orders would be bankrupted by villains and knaves defrauding hard working families, and, like India, fathers would be distraught at the birth of a daughter for she represented a great expense with no return, a financial burden he would strive to jettison as quickly as possible, as trash from a steamship.

The Zulu struck Frederic as far more reasonable, yes the man had to pay but that wasn't something an English gentleman is averse to. In British and Zulu culture the woman was a financial expense, in return the husband receives a dutiful wife whose only desire in life is her husband's happiness, well, that's the theory.

Nkosazane smiled at her guardian over a small table set out for early morning tea, "I will do my best to remember your name, Frederic."

Chelmsford sipped tea as one of his manservants approached with a silver tray of sandwiches neatly cut into triangles, "Freddie will do, would you like to eat?"

Wallah presented a tray over his chest, "Cucumber sandwiches with cottage cheese."

"Thank you Wallah," stated the General, his manservant set the small tray on the table, sandwiches piled neatly in a pyramid the pharaoh's architects would approve of.

Lord Chelmsford motioned to this morning's breakfast, "Please try one."

Nkosazane tentatively lifted a small triangle from the top of the pyramid, carefully grasping bright white bread between sable fingers, on peering between slices her eyes lit up, "Amazi?"

Chelmsford's brow furrowed as a farmer's field, "Excuse me?"

Nkosazane took a dainty bite from the triangle, chewed and sure enough her suspicions were founded. After experiencing her first taste of a cottage cheese and cucumber sandwich she smiled at her host, "Amazi, it is a Zulu dish, we leave milk to curdle in a basket and the family all eat from the same basket until it is empty, then it is filled with milk again."

Chelmsford's furrows disappeared, "I see, we call it cottage cheese," he looked over as his tea wallah approached, "Chaiwallah, where did you purchase this cheese?"

Chaiwallah squeezed a fresh pot of hot tea and waited above Chelmsford's glass. As he poured he spoke in a thick accent unique to the sub-continent, "The merchants following our camp in Natal, Master."

"Native traders?"

"Yes Master, traders have been following since we embarked from Port Elizabeth, on nearing Zululand fresh merchants joined us."

Chelmsford nodded his head and Chaiwallah broke off from a slow pour cultivated with meticulous care in Bombay, for to be the chaiwallah of a British officer afforded greater standing and protection than all other men of lower caste in India, "The natives speak of it as amazi, Master."

"Thank you Wallah."

Chaiwallah moved over to Nkosazane, he paused until she'd finished her triangle of cucumber and amazi, "Tea my lady?"

Our sable Princess smiled, "Thank you … Chaiwallah," she stumbled over his name, "Forgive me, I'm not accustomed to Indian names."

The young man poured her tea and replied with a smile, "It is my English name, it means tea servant."

"What is your Indian name?"

"Bhagwandas Thakkar," the words rolled off his tongue in an intimidating fashion.

Nkosazane nodded her head and the young Indian slowly ceased pouring brown liquid, "Thank you Chaiwallah."

"You're welcome my lady," with that he put the tall thin pot down, "Would there be anything else you require Master?"

Chelmsford shook his head, "No thank you Wallah."

Chaiwallah nodded his head and returned to the tent. Every small event linked to British culture occurring in her vicinity fascinated Nkosazane, many cultures brought together under the flag of the British Empire, forced into compatibility by white men on a worldwide crusade to bring civilisation and Christianity from Birmingham to Bombay to Borneo stopping off at KwaZulu along the way.

"So how does breakfast take you?"

"My breakfast take me?" replied Nkosazane.

"Does its taste agree with you?"

"Yes," our sable springbok smiled while selecting another sandwich, she hadn't eaten in days, "I must say, Zulu amazi and English cucumber make a fine pairing, wouldn't you agree ... Freddie?"

Lord Chelmsford noted her almost devilish grin, yet discarded any intent which might lay behind it for he was an officer, a lord and a gentlemen, having thoughts of someone in his care would be quite improper, "They do, perhaps you'll enlighten me to more of Africa's culinary delights?"

Her ebony grin expanded, touching each cheek to form two luscious branches beckoning a man as a bee to honeycomb, "I will have to introduce you to my ikhekhe lika shokoledi."

The General took a sip of tea, his moustache hovering over cool lemon char, "I'm looking forward to that," he replied innocently much to his ward's delight.

The commissioner and his council arranged a formal surrender document, signed by Kreli, who upon return to his homeland would be subject to Queen Victoria. Maps were sketched up, Natal was split into 12 provinces each one with its own garrison of local recruits under the command of British officials. The bureaucracy moved in as an insidious vine might wrap itself around a tree, sapping its energy, throttling its trunk, regulating rainwater which would otherwise grace its roots. Preventing a once mighty Natal mahogany, a tree that grows up to sixty five feet, from spreading its branches across lands it once commanded. Today it was be-shadowed by an English oak, brought from a foreign land it supplanted the native fern, dwarfing all within its mighty shade, sustenance appropriated by the vine and deposited at the oak's roots until the heart of old England did flourish on the savannah of Africa.

Soepenberg was escorted to Cape Town where he was expected to be released for he'd broken no law. At least his crimes weren't prosecutable, for despite engaging in slavery, he did so, far outside the watchful eye of the British Empire. With no eye witnesses to his crimes it was a difficult case, he was a cruel man and few wished to cross the Afrikaner. Natives feared him for he was known to take revenge, swooping across savannah on horseback with a posse of men. Stealing women and children from their homesteads, far away in the outback where justice is rarely found and so evil doth flourish.

What man desired responsibility for the enslavement of his relatives? The demonic Dutchman had thrived on the coin of fear and misery for many years. A bitter fellow himself, he believed his countrymen the rightful heirs to Southern Africa for they'd settled here in the 17th century and traded peacefully with African tribes, European technology, mainly rifles, for African slaves who in turn worked their farms.

African rulers had no qualms concerning the slave trade for it was common practice on this continent. Everything was going well, then the Napoleonic wars ended and the British had a massive unemployment problem. Unemployed men were encouraged to travel to the Cape Colony in one of the largest movements of men from Britain to Africa. Thousands were shipped from England to Port Elizabeth in a single year.

The British, having taken the colony from Dutch rule in 1795 sent their unemployed, piling pressure into the region and then the slavery act was passed in London. In the year the British outlawed slavery shockwaves reverberated around the world ... the British Empire declared war on slavery and those slave states which profited by it. In other words the British were coming to Africa, in force. The most advanced military of the largest, richest empire witnessed in the history of mankind had engaged in a war of righteousness and Africa did tremble. For there is nothing more dangerous than an enemy who believes he fights in of the name God ... he will never surrender, never be satisfied.

While you are stained with sin any evil he doth commit upon your person or people is justified, nay it is righteous, since you are an abomination and God has granted his servants the right to extinguish the life of that abomination.

Thousands of slaves were emancipated in the Cape Colony, many from India and Malaysia. Boers, farmers descended from the original Dutch settlers, were furious for they suffered labour shortages. Without the advantage of slaves they moved north, away from the Cape, forming their own republics where they might use slaves to farm crops and raise cattle.

In the Cape Colony itself, an independently run province with its own jurisdiction yet under the protection of the British Empire, laws were passed to get around the emancipation of slaves, such as the Master and Servants act of 1841, making it a criminal offence for a worker to break a labour contract, only to be fully repealed in 1974.

It would be more than a century until all blacks were fully emancipated.

Today the Natal had been subjugated; slaves would be identified and emancipated. Boers would grumble and pay workers a wage or sell up and move to the Transvaal Republic, a separate state run by those original Dutch settlers where they could use slave labour and Soepenberg might engage in his evil trade.

Today the year was 1878, within another thirty five years the British will have annexed the last of the Boer republics, consolidating South Africa into the state you see on a map today.

Although the Dutch authority would eventually be eradicated, their influence will echo down the centuries in the form of apartheid. Without the rule of the British they'd regress to their old ways until finally accepting defeat, not to British force of arms but to reason and decency. For no man who enslaves and mistreats his fellow man may enter the gates of heaven, no matter his ancestry, Jesus doesn't do get out of Hell free cards.

Today the British had sole control of the Cape Colony, life wasn't perfect for either natives or white settlers but it was an improvement on centuries past.

Soepenberg would be released shortly after arriving in Cape Town. Despite Colonel Wood's testimony he'd keep his freedom due not only to natives' fear of an Afrikaner raid stealing family members into the Transvaal Republic where they'd be lost forever, but also his ability to pay a hefty fine, money earned from selling those same natives to Boers.

Yet where slavery was concerned justice had a strange way of following the British around; Soepenberg practiced a dying trade, in direct conflict with civilization, Christianity, righteousness and the full force of the British Empire. But rather than abandon his rotten enterprise he made hay while sun continued to shine.

The Zulu might say "Isikhuni sibuya nomkhwezeli" a direct English translation would be "The lit fire-brand has returned with one tending fire" its meaning? Well in English the proverb goes "If you play with fire, expect to be burned".

Chapter Three: Port Elizabeth

Travelling south Lord Chelmsford eventually reached Port Elizabeth, as the city neared men recruited from local African tribes in the Natal incrementally dispersed to their villages.

By degrees a British behemoth of man, horse and machine dissolved like salt in water as enemies of Kreli returned home, abandoning a victorious scarlet serpent, thinning its body. Yet a crimson head maintained constant proportions, eventually coming to rest just outside of Port Elizabeth, Elizabeth Barracks, where enlisted redcoats both work and live.

Commissioner Bartle continued to Cape Town, the capital of the Cape Colony, his seat of power. Colonel Wood's Highlanders escorted him, stationed at a barracks outside that city; along with them a shackled Soepenberg journeyed to meet charges of slavery. Unfortunately those men and women he'd captured had since scattered to the banks of the Buffalo River, none remained to bear witness of the Afrikaner's foul deeds.

However, protocol must be observed and Bartle was a stickler for such things, he'd maintain rule of law no matter what.

Henry was most familiar with colonial law since he employed it to his advantage whenever possible, sometimes to the point a savage persona shone through the light fluffy clouds of an otherwise amiable exterior. A hard mountain peak would become exposed, blackened with unyielding ice, men quaking beneath a grim scowl, berating soft savannah below.

Ruthlessness was not Henry's day to day nature by any means yet in his position as essentially a feudal ruler, a king kept in check by bureaucracy, controlled by an empress at the other end of the world, he had free rein, provided he play by a set of rules laid down in London. For should Henry gain a thirst for power his tenure would be cut short most quickly, a new commissioner dispatched and he recalled to face trial in London and inevitably stripped of all honour, left to live as a creature of pity.

Such occurrences were few and far between since men selected as commissioners had not only proven track records but were sound of character, their nature as divine as an archbishop.

To be chosen for a position as honourable as High Commissioner of South Africa, Henry had been associated with many a previous success. He served diligently as Governor of Bombay and before that he was the Commissioner of Sindh where he reformed the Indian postal system. Why, even in modern day India much of its postal system remains based upon Bartle's reforms. As the Commissioner of Sindh he helped secure the Punjab during the Indian Mutiny for which he received the KCB (Knight Commander of the Order of Bath).

His father an ironworker sent him to the East India Company College, Bartle married the daughter of Sir George Arthur, the Governor of Bombay at the time. Now I know what you're thinking, this stinks of nepotism and it's true, he was on a shortlist, however, Sir Arthur didn't allow any old scruff to marry his daughter. He saw a hardworking man serious in every task laid before him, for Henry had been Sir George's private secretary in Bombay for two years and after severe scrutiny the Governor permitted their marriage.

Two years later he became a political resident at the court of Raja Shahji Satara in the Punjab, after the Raja's death he took over as administrator until it was annexed into the British Empire.

Trained as a civil servant and employed as such for many years, slowly gaining position and yes marrying up, he finally became a commissioner then a governor and today a high commissioner. A man who came from iron and through the alchemy of hard work and determination was transformed into gold.

Henry was not going to run roughshod over a civil service which had hoisted him to these dizzying heights from the lowly son of an ironworker, no; he played the game by its rules.

Upon arrival at Elizabeth Barracks Lord Chelmsford's baggage was loaded onto a waiting "chaise and four" a four wheeled closed carriage manned by his servants. The carriage was painted black, its lanterns, handles and window frames gleamed in the sun, all crafted from brass. Drawn by four black stallions his carriage was distinct to such a degree that every man and woman in Port Elizabeth either recognised or knew of it to such proportion they might identify its owner on first sight.

Another Indian servant, tall, turbaned with large moustache, dressed in Indian attire but with a distinctly British attitude smiled at Nkosazane as she approached, her arm through Lord Chelmsford's, "Good Afternoon Master, how are you today?" he said in a polite Indian accent as he opened the door.

"Very well, thank you Atam. I'd like you to meet Nkosazane, she'll be staying with us for the foreseeable future," stated Fredric.

The middle aged Indian smiled, his scarlet turban peeking above our ebony Princess' tall frame, "Good afternoon my lady, how are you today?"

Nkosazane curtsied, "I'm very well, thank you Mr Atam."

Chelmsford held her hand, directing the sable springbok up and into the carriage, our Zulu Princess' bare feet pressed upon cold brass steps. The British Lord watched as her frame passed his eyes, outstretched arm, full bosom beneath swaying beads, a thick frame slid inwards to form a tight waist before stretching out into a pair of wide hips padded with protective layers of flesh.

As she ascended, beads shifted permitting his gaze entry behind their screen, Frederic became mesmerised by thick Africa, its form a unique method of moulding perfection from the sable void of melanin. Even in her darkness there was a radiance he couldn't explain, as if her very body were constructed of black opal, a kernel of gemmological fire pirouetting along native legs, supple in texture, satisfying in form … "I will prepare the guest bedroom for the lady," stated Atam, knocking his master out of deep hypnosis.

"Thank you Atam," replied General Chelmsford groping for words while leading his ward inside the chaise and four.

It was a delightful journey to the Chelmsford residence. Nkosazane had never left the confines of Ulundi save her escape to the Buffalo River.

For the first time she witnessed the culture she'd studied so arduously. Peering out of the window as a child on safari, eyes wide open, caught in wonder as her gaze dissects every wild beast, she would excitedly question Lord Chelmsford. Frederic smiled, answering her queries; it was a pleasure to serve as her portal to the new world of British society, delighting as Nkosazane absorbed his every word. Her tone leaping at the most inconsequential event, from women's dress to men in top hats, it was all so exotic to the young Zulu springbok, prancing here and there as her eyes jumped from one scene to the next, interrogating Lord Chelmsford as to its nature.

On reaching Chelmsford's residence Atam steadied our young Zulu lady as she exited the chaise four. Chelmsford led her into the hallway of a small mansion house he'd acquired. Passing polished oak doors Nkosazane raised her brows at the opulence within. Everything sparkled, so much so it gleamed as the African sun slipped in through windows from connecting rooms. All its interior doors lay open so as to air the house while the General was on campaign, sunbeams bounced off bright brass catching the native girl's eye, setting her in the liveliest of spirits.

Yellow brass formed a snake atop wooden struts, creating a bannister, skirting the outside of dark chestnut steps. Walls were panelled with thick wood native to her land, upon them hung paintings of old stuffy Englishmen broken up by doorways leading to who knows where?

Nkosazane ogled the scene for she'd not witnessed this European expression of opulence before. In her native land her father maintained his court yet his display was one of power more so than this white man's intricate luxury.

Her nostrils selected a distinct aroma from the environment, a light citrus, its pleasant scent brushed against her senses, causing her nose to swell open as a child's eyes on seeing snow for the first time in its life.

Until now she'd failed to notice the stench of Port Elizabeth since its odour was one of few commonalities Port Elizabeth shared with Ulundi, yet this white man's small African nook smelt of soft lemon.

Sturdy brass reflected sun, even her native wood had been restrained to the point it did this man's bidding. Cleaned and polished to a degree that even base timber did exude a sense of elite European civility in the wild of Africa.

Then the oil paintings, men in military dress appeared strident, proud, stoic, women at their side appreciative of red coated husbands, men of honour and glory, it did lift Nkosazane's soul until disturbed by a voice from behind.

"My father and my mother."

Nkosazane didn't realise but she had been transfixed in a moment of adulation. She awoke from her sleep and replied to her guardian, "He seems to be a man of great importance."

Chelmsford smiled, "He was Lord Chancellor of Great Britain and first Baron of Chelmsford, to me he was pa par."

"I have heard the term chancellor before, is he not an advisor to your Queen?"

"He filled many roles, he supervised the finances of the nation, the courts, was in charge of the Queen's Counsel and the Prime Minister's first advisor. Tell me, do the Zulu have a chancellor?"

Nkosazane scrutinized the old fellow in the painting, "My father has an advisor, a man called Xhegu, he is my father's Sangoma, he fulfils many roles in court, too many for my liking."

Chelmsford's curiosity had been piqued, "What exactly is a Sangoma?"

"He protects my father against evil spirits."

"A witch doctor?"

The native girl turned and smiled at her protector, "No, but he has powerful magic."

Chelmsford couldn't help but smirk on the mention of magic.

Nkosazane smiled, for many new to the Southern tip of Africa did react in such a manner, well, the white man did. So sceptical, yet he believes in the one God, Jesus and miracles fervently; but the witch doctor he dismissed as childish fantasy alongside fairies and unicorns, "I have seen his magic heal the sick and raise the dead for a short while."

"Nkosazane," spoke Chelmsford as a father might to his daughter when afraid of ghosts lurking beneath her bed, "these men cannot perform magic, they're deceiving you with little more than a confidence trick. Now allow Atam to lead you upstairs and you can settle in."

Atam had been instructing servants but on detecting his name he quickly moved through double doors and into the hallway, "Master?"

"Take Nkosazane to her room," he observed her traditional tribal dress, "and see what you can do about her attire will you?"

Atam's turban bobbed as he nodded his head, "As you wish Master," he stood to Nkosazane's left gesturing up a brass and chestnut stairway, "please follow me my lady."

The native girl observed Atam climb the staircase, she ascended with him. Looking back at her white lion she smiled as Chelmsford retired to the smoking room. The native Princess was closer to that which she sought and little did Chelmsford know his days as a bachelor were diminishing rapidly.

As Chelmsford was superior on the field of battle so Nkosazane did outrank him in matters of the heart. She had feelings for this Englishman and sooner or later they would bloom as a bouquet of African flowers before his eyes.

He'd found his match on the field of love, he just didn't know it … yet.

Frederic had spent the last hour or so puffing away on a cigar, it'd been sometime since he'd permitted himself the comfort of a Havana. Cigars were an indulgence this English gentleman denied himself on campaign, if his men persevered without luxury so would he. It also made him somewhat irritable and so his reputation of being a strict disciplinarian had come to be well documented … upon the slightest provocation.

The smoking room was his personal reflection space, an area where he might contemplate that which had passed. As a man might work out daily troubles via dreams so Frederic spent the latter part of his day here, considering events surrounding the previous morning and afternoon.

Furnishings were quintessentially British; oxblood leather armchairs occupied the room's focus while orbiting a small square mahogany table. Against the longest wall was a sofa upholstered in the same material, an adjoining wall wielded a fireplace built from a brown stone bordered with a dark wood.

Upon its mantelpiece rested mementoes, pieces of Africa and other faraway lands graced by this Englishman's boot.

A Russian tobacco jar purchased on campaign in the Crimea. An Ivory figure, the size of a medium vase, in the design of a Hindu Goddess with four arms, one pair held a sitar while the other pair held up a rosary and a book of Hindu scripture, she stood on a rock with a swan behind her.

Between them rested a rather ornate silver clock, a gift from the Ottoman Emperor on receiving the order of Medjidie. On his dawn rounds Atam ensured it was wound properly every morning, he'd turn it with a master key constructed for all clocks on the estate.

Occupying the wall above the fireplace a large painting from Ethiopia or as it was referred to at that time Abyssinia. Predominantly coloured blue with pastel pink and gold, it depicted four saints with golden halos behind their heads, standing in a line, they peered toward a central face. Each corner of the painting had another face, its vision locked on the central character. Concerning this piece Chelmsford was unsure of its religious significance for he'd spent more time fighting Ethiopians than delving into their culture.

His time in Abyssinia was brief, essentially a rescue mission. The Ethiopian Emperor Tewodros II had imprisoned some missionaries and members of Her Majesty's government. It was a gruesome trek over an inhospitable environment, much of it mountainous and devoid of infrastructure. Led by General Napier they captured the capital and released the prisoners. It was noted as one of the most expensive acts of honour in military history.

The men were restrained from plundering the countryside, its population spared the odious face of war … the Emperor's personal holdings didn't fall subject to such an order.

They'd trekked hundreds of miles through dry hot land and so General Napier permitted the men plunder, restricting any largesse to Tewodros II himself, it seemed only fitting.

Chelmsford rescued this painting from being tossed on a bonfire and so here it sat, beaming bright colours, igniting an otherwise stodgy room.

On the wall opposite was situated a large window casting daylight onto a writing desk/bureau. Left of the window stood a walnut table with a large music box atop.

Paintings adorned the wall; some were from India whilst others were commissioned works from England. Chelmsford listened as a beautifully inlaid music box played 'Onward Christian Soldiers'. He owned several pinned cylinders adding to his collection whenever the opportunity arose.

Resting in his armchair while Helios journeyed toward the horizon Frederic read a local newspaper, reports of the Natal's subjugation blended with articles concerning his promotion and celebrations to be held in Cape Town, a banquet and a ball.

Chelmsford groaned inside, on his mien a military grimace did take form elevating his moustache until it rubbed his nose, he didn't look forward to such occasions. Since Anna's passing social events had become rather awkward.

In fact he'd gained somewhat of a reputation for avoiding these affairs. This time he wouldn't be able to obscure his lack of presence with excuse for this celebration was to honour him.

Food, music and dance, ugh, dance, he'd have to partner with Sarah. Bartle could be rather insufferable at times, too often did he attempt to marry off to his niece. It'd become quite obscene in Frederic's opinion yet Henry was his firm friend, his only real friend, so he'd bear the trauma until honour had been satisfied.

To be fair Bartle's niece was a perfectly pleasant and polite young lady, yet Frederic wasn't going to tolerate Henry's bulldoze and oblige his niece with marriage.

As music played the smoking room's door opened, twilight graced a figure, a woman? Surely Henry hadn't sent his niece already? Encouraging Sarah to visit his home so he might invite her to the ball, forcing him to preserve her dignity.

The tight top of a rusty orange dress hugged a firm figure just above the hips. The skirt was a crinoline or a hooped skirt, an early 1870's outfit, both flat at the front and back. This change in women's fashion provided emphasis to the rear which was decorated in multiple folds and sometimes more than one bow.

This was a day dress and so it had a high neckline and long sleeves with rusty brown ruffles.

Dresses of the 1870's were much slimmer than previous decades and made of fur, lace and silk. The rear was held up high so as to accentuate a woman's behind while a bodice or corset, depending on the dress or occasion, emphasized a small waist.

It was in this decade that chokers became fashionable; women first began wearing a velvet ribbon around their neck, eventually leading to the trend.

Nkosazane wore a tea gown, a gown intended for a woman's leisure, therefore it was not so starched or tight yet she felt very restricted, like a wild animal caged for the pleasure of the male gaze.

Chelmsford rose from his seat, he recognised the gown, he'd not seen it in years, "What are you wearing?" stated the General taken aback by that which graced his senses.

"Atam said it was the only gown that would fit my frame," replied a submissive Nkosazane her movement restricted by a mobile silk, fur and lace cage, "do you like it?"

Placing his newspaper on the table and cigar in a porcelain ash tray beside it the lion stood erect. Frederic observed her gown with familiarity, "Yes, it's my wife's, was my wife's. It was too large for her but she couldn't bear to let it go, neither could I."

Nkosazane was confused for a moment; there was a short silence, quickly concluded by General Chelmsford.

"It's quite alright, I'm sure Anna would be happy to see it put to good use after all this time."

Atam entered the room holding a silver tray, two bone china cups and a sugar and milk pot, "Tea Master?"

Chelmsford pulled his sight from Nkosazane as a man might draw water from a well during drought, slowly and with caution lest its life giving essence spill and disappear into darkness ... that lonely place he'd existed for so long, "Yes, thank you Atam."

"I apologise Master, this was the only garment in the house suitable for your lady," stated Atam as he moved bone china from tray to table where Chelmsford's cigar rested, disseminating wisps of smoke.

"It's quite alright, do arrange for the dressmaker to pay a visit tomorrow will you?"

"Which time would suit you best Master?"

"Oh make it morning," Chelmsford looked down to witness Nkosazane's bare feet, "Tell Ranjit the lady will require a set of shoes."

Atam gave a slight bow, "Yes Master, anything else?"

"No, you may leave Atam."

Atam turned and exited the smoking room, closing its door behind him.

Nkosazane's ears followed the sound of music as a hawk riding thermals, she locked onto the Swiss music box and moved toward it, her eyes became bright as a child's, in a tone of delight she asked, "What is this?"

Chelmsford moved to her side and lifted its lid, opening one side while its hinge turned on the other side, forming a trap door.

Nkosazane glared within as a child peering inside her present after tearing away wrapping paper. Within, a wonder exposed itself, pins on a metal cylinder turned striking a set of small metal rods each tuned to a specific note. As the cylinder slowly turned so notes gathered as birds chirping in trees on the savannah, forming a delightful tune, its result was wondrous.

"It's a family heirloom; it was my great grandfather's."

Nkosazane smiled as the cylinder turned.

"Something amuses you?" said Chelmsford as he turned a key on the brass movement inside, halting its mechanism.

"I was thinking," said the smiling native girl, "years ago my people might have believed this to be white man's magic."

"And today?"

She turned to her right, black opal eyes meeting grey sapphire, "Today they know better but they still believe in magic."

"The witch doctor? What was his name again?"

"Xhegu, he controls my people's thoughts, something like your Archbishop of Canterbury."

Chelmsford was surprised at her knowledge of England, "I see, but the Archbishop doesn't perform magic."

"The Zulu have powerful ancestors they grant him the magic of previous generations."

Chelmsford smiled, "Young lady, when I was in India there were all sorts of witch doctors, it was a cottage industry on the sub-continent, they named themselves yogis.

Then there were those involved in black magic, the Thugee. Their super natural powers proved quite inadequate once compassed by a Martini-Henry rifle; why the Devil himself managed poor protest when the Royal Army cleaned the gutters of his scum."

Nkosazane scanned the room until her eye caught a Hindu statue; she glided gracefully to the mantel. Chelmsford noted her lady like habits, he'd not witnessed a native woman step with such grace until today, it was as much a wonder to his eye as the music box to her ears.

"Tell me about this?" stated an excited dark lady scrutinizing the four armed statue.

"An ornament from India, she's Saraswati, somewhat similar to Athene. She's the Goddess of music, art, wisdom and knowledge. She's usually depicted in white, her animal being the swan; you'll have to ask Atam if you want to know more."

"India must be a magical place."

"It's a unique land that much is certain."

"When you spoke of magic men you said it is a cottage industry in India, what do you mean by cottage industry?"

"A figure of speech, it's a practice that's usually inexpensive, so much so an individual with little or no support might take it up and make a living of it."

Nkosazane formed a wry smile, "Is this phrase derogatory?"

"Not by nature, yet it may suit that role depending on context."

"Did you intend it to be derogatory when referring to the magic men in India?"

Chelmsford ruffled his brow and gestured toward armchairs in the centre of the room, "Come take a seat before your tea grows cold."

Ever the lady Nkosazane smiled and with a nod of her head complied with her guardian's instruction. In KwaZulu a rebellious woman, yet here she was co-operative, a total reversal in demeanour.

Had her father witnessed such behaviour he'd have doubted this to be his daughter, for upon reaching the age of marriage she rebelled against his every wish, no matter its size or significance. Yet in the company of this white man she was the woman his court had spent so many years grooming to be the wife of his most dangerous rival.

Just as in the days of medieval Europe, daughters were a valuable asset, their beauty and status employed to forge alliances with foreigners and secure loyalty within the realm. Yet Nkosazane had concocted alternative plans, she'd spent much of her upbringing amongst missionaries, white men from a distant land; learning their culture, language and the way of the one God until her father lost patience, banishing them from his kingdom. Nkosazane took it personally and when she was to be married to one of her father's commanders, his fourth wife, well that was the straw that broke the camel's back, or as the Zulu might say "Impungushe kayivalelwq nezmvu." Its translation, "The Jackal is not kept on the same kraal as the sheep." This Zulu proverb warns an individual of bringing together things or people that do not mesh.

Nkosazane fled to KwaNatal, under Xhosa control, a rival kingdom to that of her father. On the Buffalo River she'd be safe amongst fellow refugees, lovers, who'd fled to be together.

However, she soon found herself unwelcome, for she reminded them of her father's tyranny. Then came Bastijn Klein Soepenberg, an Afrikaner slave trader. Rounding up lovers on the banks of the river he would sell them into Boer slavery, farmers who'd also fled tyranny, pushed out of the Cape by the British.

The British outlawed slavery some years ago, and possessed an irritating desire to enforce that law, even in lands they didn't control.

Before Soepenberg had a chance to collect on his bounty the British entered the tribal war in the Natal, crushing one of its tribes, absorbing its lands into the British Empire and releasing every slave to a man … or woman as the case may be.

The pair sat down, Chelmsford drew a seat for his dark ward before resting in his armchair. As leather squeaked beneath his frame Frederic poured his lady friend tea, "You're awfully curious for a woman."

Truth be told Nkosazane's first instinct was to take offence, had this been Zululand she would've fired barbs at the man who dared to address her so, yet she'd learnt much from missionaries concerning etiquette in European society. Instead of lashing out at Chelmsford she smiled, "Thank you my lord, are not English women curious?"

The General put down his tea pot to pick up a second lesser pot beside it, "Milk?"

"Yes please," smiled Nkosazane.

Chelmsford spoke as he poured a little milk into his guest's bone china cup, "I wouldn't say that. I should have said you're curious on subjects a lady would, more often than not, have little concern over ... sugar?"

"No thank you. I might say the same of you my Lord."

"How so?" stated Chelmsford, pouring himself a cup of tea.

"In my experience the white man has little interest beyond profit and plunder, he has scant else to discuss when engaging the people of Africa."

Chelmsford took a sip of tea before resuming his cigar, the cigar had gone out and so he picked a long match from a compartment in the wooden frame of the ash tray, struck the match upon a rough patch designed for the purpose and puffed, until a red cherry appeared on the end of his brown stick.

This room was of Lord Chelmsford in every aspect; its furniture reeked of thick leather and cigar smoke, similar to his cologne. Pleasant in many ways compared to the foulness of the city yet oddly enough, when close to Frederic, Nkosazane detected the scent of leather alone as if it shooed away any tobacco smoke attempting to rest upon the General. It was his chosen year round scent gifted to him by Anna before his first campaign.

Chelmsford restocked every year directly from his perfumers on Jermyn Street in London, top notes of bergamot and leather with a woody amber base note, his scent did distinguish him from every other man our African Princess had encountered previously.

He discarded the match in the ashtray, puffed on his Havana and replied, "That's of no great surprise considering the types who've previously settled this land. I'm sorry your people have been forced to experience the absolute dregs of Europe for so long."

"They weren't all bad, the missionaries who taught me English and proper etiquette were all good decent men, yet my father expelled them from KwaZulu, it is ironic, don't you think?"

"In my experience certain types will always congregate with one another," as he took another pull on his cigar the General realised he'd been referring to her father, "Sorry, I didn't mean to imply your father is of that sort."

Nkosazane smiled, she enjoyed his soft spoken discomfort, it tricked his demeanour so it might appear to be humble, perhaps this man wasn't the unfeeling edifice of cold rock portrayed on campaign, "There are two ways to rule in KwaZulu, through the love of your people or their fear, my father has chosen the latter and so he flocks with birds of a feather, be they black or white it is of no significance to him for they all speak one language, that of brutality and violence."

Chelmsford contemplated her words, "Every king must be prepared for war if he is to keep his throne."

"Yes, but to brutalise your own people, your own family, no king will survive long in Zululand, that is why he keeps his umthakathi close by."

"Umthakathi?"

"Xhegu is a master of magic. Many fear him for they say he is an umthakathi, what you would call a sorcerer. He looks into the future for my father. Why men have been executed for treachery on the word of Xhegu, put to death today for the crimes of tomorrow."

Holding a long thick Havana in one hand Chelmsford moved it aside allowing his other hand to bring his tea cup to his lip, he sipped. Atam always served his char at the correct temperature, double checking everything that left the kitchens.

Placing the cup back down the English gentleman smiled, "It seems there are as many methods to describe a witch doctor in KwaZulu as a politician in London, few being favourable."

55

"I am told that in England you change your ruler every five years?"

"Not quite, we have an election every five years and those who are permitted to vote may decide to elect a new government or keep the current one, but to be honest they're only deciding on whether to sack the current government or not."

Nkosazane picked her cup daintily from the table and sipped as he finished his sentence. It was evident the native girl was well trained in the basics of etiquette; protocols in which every English lady was trained before being released to her husband, "I am confused my lord, why does England have a Queen if she is not your ruler? What purpose does she serve?" inquired the native lady.

Chelmsford replied with utter certainty, "Her Majesty controls the courts, the armed forces, the prisons and the police; added to that every law and military action requires the sanction of our ruling monarch. She is the balance that keeps men who might abuse power and position from running wild as hyenas on the savannah."

Nkosazane nodded, "This is wise. An unrestrained ruler will eventually bring misery upon his own people. In KwaZulu my father only has ears for those closest to him; the people make no decisions but bear all the consequences.

Allowing all Englishmen a voice, if only once every five years, is a prudent course to take."

Chelmsford took a puff of his cigar, "Well, not everyone in England has the vote you know."

"Oh, why is that?"

"Well, there's no point in permitting the uneducated and poor a vote, it would be foolhardy."

"The poor may not vote in England?"

"To vote you must be a tax paying citizen or a land owner above the age of twenty one, this excludes most British citizens."

"Are women not permitted a voice in your land?"

"Yes they are," Frederic's voice emanated a disturbed tone, "even single women are allowed the vote provided they're registered rate payers ... but only in a local election, not a general election."

"What is the difference?"

"As the word implies, a local election pertains to the immediate region, the selection of councillors and such. A general election will ultimately decide who the ruling party will be for the next five years."

"Why can a woman not vote in a general election?"

Chelmsford drew on his cigar causing its cherry to glow, he expelled thick tobacco smoke, something Nkosazane found most unpleasant yet she maintained her demeanour, that of a grateful guest, "Allow a woman to vote in a general election?" he spoke in an incredulous tone, "If it were my decision women would have the vote taken from them altogether."

His African ward's eyebrows arched as the back of a lioness, her rebellious nature surfaced as a great beast inhabiting the largest waterfalls in South Africa. Nkosazane battled her inner monster yet a dark demon took form, manifesting itself where polite company previously existed, "Then you believe women are untrustworthy?" she snapped.

Chelmsford continued, unaware of Nkosazane's transformation from light hearted springbock into an inkanyamba, "Of course not, a woman is no less trustworthy than a man, but you see a woman's nature does not take to making important decisions, a woman will change her mind as often as the breeze; it would be pure folly to permit women the vote any more than they already have. Why you may as well hand the vote over to every Tom, Dick and Harry at that point."

The inkanyamba surfaced, a huge carnivorous eel of Zulu mythology, "Then if I were a British citizen I would have no more right to influence political decisions than a woman in KwaZulu?"

"That's not quite true, you could vote in local elections …"

The eel like monster, said by folklore to have control over the weather, opened its jaws, ready to rip asunder an unsuspecting lion watering at its lake, "Yes, I heard you, a mere platitude to pacify the foolhardy woman, yes?"

Chelmsford was rather taken aback by Nkosazane's caustic tongue; she was toeing the line of lady like etiquette. He rested a moment, waiting for the storm to subside, eyeing his Zulu Princess as she took stock of her actions, a few moments passed and the inkanyamba closed its jaws submerging beneath a bubbling basin. A familiar springbok then materialized at the lakeside as waters calmed, "Forgive me my Lord."

Chelmsford waited a few more moments, drawing his cigar before offering a reply, "Women are emotional creatures, rational decision making is a man's forte and so everything pertaining to that realm should remain with the male of the species. This kind of conversation is exactly why I never discuss politics, if a man has difficulty restraining himself concerning subjects he feels passionate over then there's little expectation a woman might remain coherent."

His words ignited fury inside Nkosazane for in KwaZulu had a man spoken to her in such a fashion she would surely have berated him publicly.

This man did cross the line, kindling her passion, yet Chelmsford's stubborn chauvinist attitude intrigued Nkosazane at the same time. It was a most confusing state she'd not experienced before in her life, "I did not intend to overstep my limitations."

Chelmsford narrowed his eyes on the dark inkanyamba transforming back into a soft submissive springbock, it was quite a feat. She'd snared her emotions, before they took flight and precipitated all sorts of mayhem. Nkosazane's feminine control did impress the English lion, "You're forgiven young lady, it's your first day in a civilized land. You can hardly be expected to understand the politics of a country on the other side of the planet."

Nkosazane went from furious to shrew, smiling she replied, "Thank you my Lord, yet it does seem odd, that your people would permit a queen to rule so many institutions rather than a king."

Chelmsford was somewhat disturbed by her logical response, uncommon when approached by the female form, "Yes, that's a matter of lineage not election, besides; Her Majesty has a plethora of male advisors."

Nkosazane smiled, "She is most fortunate to have their counsel when making important decisions."

Chelmsford did sneer but not so much as Nkosazane could detect its presence for his beard obscured irritation, "Quite," replied the English lord.

The pair carried on back and forth, taking pleasure in the other's company. Chelmsford had been starved of feminine companionship since his wife's passing and so today he indulged in the presence of his female ward.

As for Nkosazane she'd been starved of intelligent conversation since her father had expelled missionaries from Zululand. Debating the merits of Christianity, studying a foreign tongue, its culture and social do's and don'ts fascinated our Princess more so than listening to her father wittering day in day out while wringing his hands over tribal politics. Nothing bored our native Princess more so than the humdrum of who did what and when.

Naturally her father considered it the business of men, too complex for the limited female mind. Nkosazane disagreed with his assessment, she rated male tribal politics no higher than female gossip, the difference being that if you were on the wrong end of tribal politics it was likely to result in your death, female gossip wasn't nearly as detrimental to one's health!

Yet Nkosazane found female gossip as dull as thick fog after heavy rains, a viscous cloud hugging sodden jungle, obscuring the landscape to a point it would be foolish for a sane individual to enter.

Once again her individualist attitude did separate our Princess from the herd, setting her apart from that which social order defined as normal, interested in neither female nor male politics or tribal hierarchy.

Although it was easy to do so when your father is king and there were literally only a few prepared to criticise your wayward behaviour. Had the average Zulu daughter carried herself in a similar disobedient fashion she would've suffered the beating of her life from her father or husband.

If Zulu were to reign this land, like all creatures there must be a social order. The same went for men, for man must conform just as woman, and so each member kept the other in line, maintaining a cohesive group, King Cetshwayo kaMpande looking down from the top.

Yet our Zulu Princess had other plans, this life was not for her, the mediocrity of who was marrying whom, who owned which grazing land and what an opposing tribal leader was plotting. Nkosazane's desires stretched further afield, she looked to lands the Zulu had only touched on a map, for her heart lay in the land of civilization where Christian men were raised before travelling to far flung kingdoms to battle the Devil and crush slavery under imperial boot; where fair skinned women did exist, adorned in sparkling jewels and fine clothing, the very epitome of beauty and femininity.

Her father and mother scoffed at such notions, no more than a childish phase she'd grow out of before marrying Dabulamanzi to secure tribal loyalty in a game of politics. Besides, the white man could never subjugate the Zulu for King Cetshwayo had the most powerful fighting force in southern Africa, the impi, in the Zulu language the word simply means "war", formed by the legendary King Shaka a man loved and hated across southern Africa.

During the Napoleonic era while white men did battle across the continent of Europe, so Shaka waged war across southern and eastern Africa, his impi employed new tactics, crushing enemies, resulting in Zulu victory time and time again.

With such a fighting force the Zulu King was confident in his ability to repel any group of armed scoundrels who dared tread foot within his lands. The Zulu had met and defeated all its neighbours in battle, so the fact the Xhosa had fallen to the British held little sway with King Cetshwayo yet there were those in KwaZulu not so dismissive of their British neighbours.

Nkosazane's fascination with the white man and his ways would pass, Cetshwayo was sure of it, yet when her interest failed to wane the King expelled what he considered a malcontent in his kingdom, he believed missionaries had led his daughter astray. It's not as if he was unfamiliar with banishing his own people, a few missionaries made little difference.

Then one of his commanders and half-brother, Dabulamanzi kaMpande, with Zulu tradition, did request her hand in marriage.

It wasn't that he was a clear twenty years her senior, but the fact he already possessed three wives, making Nkosazane number four. It came as a shock to the Zulu Princess when her father not only accepted but did so happily, as did her mother.

She was to be used as intended, little more than an affair of state in the form of clay, employed to patch a dynastic hole in a political wall, securing the impi second in command, a possible rival to the throne. Nkosazane spoke out only to be quickly silenced, her mother wasn't concerned with Nkosazane's desires, she must comply … for the good of the tribe.

A lobola was negotiated and paid in heads of cattle. The impi commander put up a generous offer of fifty head of cattle, a price beyond any in living memory. This was surely a joyous occasion, well, for her mother and father, for Nkosazane her future horizon presented itself as a grim desert.

Our Princess had no desire to be traded as cattle. Unconcerned by an unprecedented bride price she was determined not to be a man's fourth wife. No matter his prowess as a warrior or his tribal standing, in her mind Nkosazane was destined for another, not just another man but another place, a different society where women weren't traded back and forth for coin, influence and loyalty.

And so, one night, while her mother and father were busy finalising the details of her wedding, to be no more than an ornament to finish off a barbaric display, Nkosazane slipped into the night.

Her absence went unnoticed until the next morning for the fools had been celebrating her marriage with beer, wine and spirits, drinking the night away while drums of celebration beat. Young women kicking their legs up in rapture as men, young and old, looked on, drinking from wooden bowls, animal skins and bottles … at least they'd had a good time. Yet that would be all they got since by morning the bride to be had vanished into African dusk, headed for the Buffalo River and KwaNatal where she might take refuge amongst the Xhosa.

Nkosazane discovered scant refuge amidst those her father had oppressed in the past. She was an unwelcome guest, wedged between tyranny and animosity, a ship caught in the leading edge of two storms. In exile Nkosazane was unable to acquire that which her father's former subjects obtained, for they would not permit the springbok to forget King Cetshwayo's crimes against their liberty.

When informed he'd captured Princess Nkosazane kaMpande Soepenberg was ecstatic, a bounty existed to bring her in, in fact Zulu warriors had been scouring the river, her intended husband having sent small bands of impi whenever circumstances permitted.

Nkosazane awoke surrounded by Soepenberg's men, betrayed by other refugees in the vain hope they'd receive freedom in return. The springbok realised the chase had ended, she'd been run down and captured, her father wouldn't permit her another chance to escape.

Then, while travelling the road northwest toward the Transvaal, Soepenberg met a detachment of British troops. The slave trader was restrained until their commanding officer arrived, when Lieutenant-Colonel Wood came upon Soepenberg he had his entire party and cargo detained. Soepenberg would be brought to justice in Cape Town and his slaves released, yet Colonel Wood was a man of caution and it was not his place to decide the fate of civilians, that was his superior's burden.

Released into the protection of Lord Chelmsford Nkosazane was dressed in the, albeit ill-fitting, clothes of an English lady, sipping tea and discussing politics, much to the dismay of Soepenberg.

Somehow the fates had brought her to Chelmsford. By a series of follies she sat in the care of an English lord, a very single English lord, a fact which hadn't escaped our native Princess.

Chelmsford was totally ignorant to the thoughts passing through Nkosazane's mind. While they made chit chat she plotted the Englishman's immediate future, well his future for that evening.

Had Lord Chelmsford been aware he would've done something to prevent it, but being a typically ignorant male he was oblivious to the scheming of the fairer sex.

Nkosazane understood that making her way into the bed of not just a white man but a baron and a General in the British Royal Army was no small task, for between her and her goal lay prejudice and perhaps a natural aversion to African women?

This would be a risky venture but Nkosazane noticed Chelmsford snatch sly glimpses of her frame. She wasn't so innocent to dismiss English eyes scrutinising Zulu garments as his mind considered what lay beneath, the question was, if given the opportunity would the Englishman act upon those considerations?

She would have to be patient, as a sable springbok enticing a ravenous white lion into chase. Nkosazane would test not just her abilities but the desire of her pursuer.

Then there was another consideration, was HE playing a game? Getting set for the right moment to pounce upon the helpless fawn? Waiting until Atam retired for the evening, no longer at his master's beck and call? Surging as a lion tearing apart a helpless springbok? The thought warmed our African Princess, her face, despite its melanin pitch glowed with the heat of desire.

"Are you feeling well?" inquired Chelmsford on observing ruddy cheeks.

"Quite well thank you, may I retire my Lord?"

Chapter Four: The Bed Chamber

Ra, the African sun god, dipped beneath Cimmerian dusk into dark underworld leaving humanity for another twelve hours. As twilight reigned, Port Elizabeth slowed; aside from drinking taverns here and there, man and beast, along with Ra, retired to their abyss.

Chelmsford withdrew to the master bedroom while Nkosazane took refuge in an adjoining bedroom; its architect intended this bedchamber to be that of the lady of the house.

It contained a generous brass bed, large wardrobe and beautiful dressing table with stacked drawers and a jewellery box, the native girl was drawn by its presence. She placed herself on an ottoman before it, her opal eyes twinkled with fire for this dressing table was fit for a Baroness.

She went through its many drawers pulling them out and viewing the weapons by which an English lady might seduce her prey, its many powders confused our young lady for Zulu women had little regard considering such items.

In her culture a woman didn't require facial pigment or perfume, a natural Zulu woman sufficed to arouse a Zulu man. Nkosazane wondered as to whether the white man was even attracted to white women, why, if a white woman required pigment and coloured powder in order to seduce her own kind surely the white man must find her repugnant in her natural state ... what other explanation could there be?

Nkosazane had learned much concerning European society, its language, protocol and a woman's place in the world but missionaries could only teach so much, the rest she must experience for herself.

Lamps attached to walls consumed whale oil. As flames flickered shadows danced the tango upon an embroidered melanin tapestry that is our Princess' face, a beautiful creation even by Western standards, not that any decent gentleman would openly say so.

Atam closed the door and left Nkosazane to her own devices, she was faced with undoing her garments by herself for there were no female servants in the household, and undressing for bed was something ladies kept between them.

She successfully removed her skirt and the slim cage it sat on before removing her underskirt and a decency skirt, a piece of cloth that protected the most sensitive parts should the skirt somehow be blown about by wind.

The outer layers Nkosazane removed instinctively yet her corset presented a puzzle of a more complex nature. A combination of cloth over bone, it was difficult to put on and remove without feminine assistance, it seemed there were some things a woman could do better than a man.

Atam had engaged female kitchen staff in the job of cladding our Princess in her silk and lace corral. Unfortunately, those women serving on Lord Chelmsford's estate had returned to their homes in Port Elizabeth. Only Atam and his wallahs remained until daybreak.

Dressed in nothing but corset and knickers Nkosazane picked up her lamp and moved toward doors connecting her room and that of Lord Chelmsford.

While an oil lamp flickering in one hand the other twisted a brass knob and the door creaked open, inside Lord Chelmsford stood at a dressing table preparing his beard for a night's rest.

As the door creaked, the lord, while examining himself in the mirror, spoke out, "Atam?"

Nkosazane stood quietly, timid as a springbok on savannah when it detects the roar of a lion.

"Don't just stand there man," Chelmsford turned around, he fell silent, "oh ..."

Dressed in a freshly pressed red sleeping suit, the forbearer of modern day pyjamas, the lion froze at the sight of a young impala. He'd not been this close to a woman since his wife's passing and Frederic felt somewhat ambushed by the sable Zulu.

"I was wondering if you could help me, Master?"

"With what exactly," replied Chelmsford in a direct fashion.

Nkosazane approached, put down her oil lamp and faced the door by which she'd just entered his bedchamber, "My corset, would you be so kind as to remove it for me?"

Chelmsford stepped back, "Don't you think Atam …"

"Would you have Atam and Wallah ogle my nakedness?"

"Why of course not," he began unlacing the whale bone corset from behind, "I'll employ a maid in the morning, this is quite intolerable."

Nkosazane smiled, "You dislike my form?"

The room diminished in its gathering darkness, his vision firmly set on his ward as Frederic unlaced her garments, observing an orange light frolic on Nkosazane's back, at this moment he had the look of a man setting out on an adventure into the darkest corners of wild Africa.

"Certainly not … what I mean to say is that this is intolerable for you."

"Why?" asked the smiling springbok.

"A lady requires a maid to dress and undress, I'm afraid I've lived alone so long as to overlook your needs," the final lace was undone and the corset came away. Chelmsford expected the native Princess to hold it in place, removing the whale bone corset from her body upon returning to her room.

When she let it fall to the ground his heart jumped a little, the African beauty turned and his eyes could not resist the sight of her naked breasts.

With a smile reticent of the Devil before he engages in high mischief Nkosazane spoke softly, "Perhaps you've neglected your needs … my Lord?" and before Chelmsford might reply she crouched down to retrieve the corset.

Looking upwards at her tall English lord Nkosazane's heart took its turn in a leap, as a Zulu springbok on the savannah facing down a British lion, she wasn't sure what would happen next, terrified yet excited the sable springbok cast her eyes upon her quest.

The Englishman had never taken advantage of a woman and certainly wasn't going to make a habit of it now, yet before he might help this young lady to her feet and escort her back, she placed her hands on his body, an area of the male anatomy where, quite frankly, a lady you've only recently met shouldn't venture to engage. If the English lion had difficulty in compassing his ward's previous intentions it was no longer so.

Nkosazane's eyes became as fire, her hands tingled with excitement, she felt Chelmsford grow as if filling a bucket at a well; powerful waters did swell to spill from the brim of her hand.

Chelmsford didn't know what to say, he was stumped and while he could not find words to match the situation in which he found himself, Nkosazane made good use of opportunity afforded by this African evening.

She popped open the front of Frederic's woollen sleeping suit until his form manifested as a mountain lion appearing at the entrance to its cave, its power developing before her eyes, she caressed as a lady might her favourite minx coat.

Contrary to her mother's opinion, Nkosazane had confirmed this white man was not averse to African femininity. Chelmsford couldn't control himself in the presence of this sable Princess.

Knelt before her white lord the native beauty, the original beauty from which all female merit is born, did entice the lion, transforming faint doubt into wicked wonder via black magic.

Were Lord Chelmsford aware of the many surprises Africa had in store for him the British General wouldn't have taken this commission yet it was too late, for he was trapped by a native huntress seventeen years his junior … almost half his age, yet twice as cunning in the dark art of love.

He was both young and old in the same moment, advanced in years, yes, yet abound in newfound vigor.

She massaged his manhood raising his spirit from the pit within which it had dwelt since Anna's passing. The ghost of his former wife shooed away by Zulu voodoo. Nkosazane felt the draw of this man ever since meeting in the Natal, she was uncertain of his attraction aside from stolen glimpses of her body through native dress.

Our dark Princess wouldn't normally have approached a man in such a direct manner but there's an old Zulu proverb, "Iso liwela umfula ugcwele," which in English translates as "The eye crosses the full river," which in plain English means, "One who has a strong desire to do something, cannot be stopped by anything."

As for Chelmsford he was stuck between two minds, withdraw this native Princess from his room by force lest he be accused of taking advantage of a young lady in his protection or … permit Nkosazane to continue her dark artistry.

While he mulled over his situation this African woman performed an intricate ebony enchantment upon a General in Her Majesty's Royal Army, who despite campaigns in Russia, India and Africa was now grasping for a decisive answer to his predicament.

For never had this man been between two minds, he was from a family who taught ridged discipline, socially and militarily. Lord Chelmsford was never without a battle plan until today, until this magical woman put him under her African spell.

Luscious pigmented lips rode pink flesh, pulsating with passion, passion penned up inside his heart for three years now. All of that time he'd kept a stiff upper lip for he saw no need to engage with another woman despite many offers. Friends and comrades alike had all attempted to pair him with young eligible ladies, usually family members, especially since his ascension to the title of 2nd Baron of Chelmsford.

Yet Frederic, 2nd Baron of Chelmsford, refused to yield, for the memory of his wife did haunt his mind as a spectre might inhabit an old house, frightening away prospective patrons.

Nkosazane was not so impeded by societal protocol; she sprang upon opportunity as a crocodile might leap from a muddy river while antelope drink during a hot day. At Frederic's moment of greatest vulnerability the young lady struck, her large jaws swallowing tip to base as a crocodile would a young wildebeest's head.

She sensed restraint slowly release from his psyche, it was exciting to kneel before a gate as it opens and wild lions are let slip from years of captivity. She felt his hands clutch the sides of her head, Nkosazane was hesitant, for she was unclear as to her guardian's intentions, would he pull her away and bring his first night of pleasure, in three years, to an end?

Our sable springbok's heart moved toward her throat in anticipation until she felt him grasp African hair in two fists. Firmly holding his Princess in place he reassuringly chaperoned the beauty in his protection. He'd decided which side of the fence to come down on and it was that of pleasure.

Strong hands guided Nkosazane onto her feet until she stood before Lord Chelmsford, smiling as an innocent African girl on her first night with her husband, but he did not smile back, restrained emotion emanated from grey blue eyes, the eyes of a crazy man. Had she met such a man in public Nkosazane would've crossed the road to find refuge on the other side. For he resembled a shabby genteel, a fiend, yet his addiction, his desire, was neither opium nor cocaine but directed at the Zulu woman before him.

At 5ft 11 inch, Nkosazane was only three inches shorter than Chelmsford and so they glared into one another's eyes as hawks in combat.

He removed his hands from Nkosazane's head sweeping her off her feet, carrying his ward to the bedside, quite a feat considering the size of this African lady.

All the time their perception remained fastened in a powerful brace of passion on one another, her innocent African visage opposing his noble English mien, yet they spoke not a single word, for verbal language was needless. Nkosazane read his soul moment by moment, each second transmitting an array of emotion Lord Chelmsford was unable to express in words, for as an English gentleman he made a point of remaining detached, it had served him well in all walks of life.

Chelmsford carried our sable springbok to his bed and softly lay Nkosazane down. Lord Chelmsford slowly undressed, his manhood stood to attention as a young redcoat, its pulsating pith helmet saluting African beauty.

Nkosazane eyed his soldier; now that her guardian had taken control fear entered her heart for she'd never permitted a man to have dominion over her. Our African beauty's rebellious nature baulked against masculinity yet tonight she lowered her shield for this white nobleman.

On hearing an orchestra of love inside her heart Nkosazane did dance to its passionate tune for the first time in her life, while Lord Chelmsford conducted its melody.

Frederic removed his night clothes, she her cotton knickers exposing warm ebony flesh. Chelmsford's eyes set afire as the remaining pieces of a treasure map did fall into place before his eyes, he'd not seen such a glorious sight in his life. He'd conquered armies in India, sacked cities in Russia, captured Kings in Africa, yet the glossy flesh before him did be-shadow those achievements.

Some might ask "how could a naked African woman compare to defeating the Russian Tsar in the Crimea?" One is a picture of beauty and magnificence the other of pain and sorrow; it was a simple selection.

Nkosazane monitored his eyes and felt fear touch her breast from within, for Frederic appeared as a fiend yet she made not a sound. He moved upon her as a lion might fall upon a springbok to consume its flesh, she remained still, compliant and co-operative, for should she resist Nkosazane was certain her keeper would have none of it. His redcoat moved into an attack position, astride our helpless African girl, Lord Chelmsford's hand grasped her throat. Nkosazane's heart beat hard, was this normal? Perhaps he was going to murder her?

Nkosazane contemplated her predicament while his powerful grip squeeze her throat, was this love, lust or hatred or perhaps a strange combination of the three? She was too young and naïve to understand the nature of the beast she'd unleashed, fear and passion met one another, battling for supremacy in our ebony woman's heart until Frederic kissed her lips, dispatching calm through her body as ripples in a lake.

The noble gentleman pressed upon her, black and white, ying and yang, two opposites coming together, parts of a puzzle, one piece inside the other forming a whole, symmetry from two broken souls. A pair of shattered spirits did discover safe harbour in the other, forming a complete entity.

Our young melanin girl felt truly helpless for the first time in her life, at the mercy of a man, yet this man did not detract from her spirit, quite the opposite. Frederic fulfilled Nkosazane, pressing so deep as to saturate not only her body but touch her soul with his. Spiritually Nkosazane detected completion beneath a white beast holding her throat with one hand; the other pushing the soles of her feet to the ceiling. This passionate consummation was a place our sable springbok had not realised until now, a place she'd not even seen on a map as a distant land to be conquered.

Nkosazane's breath synchronised with her custodian as he pressed longer and harder until her lungs did gasp at cool night air, then they locked eyes, for humans are the only creatures to make love staring into one another's eyes, it is one of God's blessings.

She peered through dark blue, deep into his soul, while he plumbed the depths of her African opals, afire with passion. Our young woman's beautiful Zulu features lay somewhere between pleasure and terror as Frederic pushed harder and with each stroke Lord Chelmsford's beautiful native Princess neared a summit, forcing whimpers from deep within her soul. Nkosazane's voice sounded more like the cry of wild Africa than that of a civilized human being.

Their shadows melded on the bedroom wall, cast by a flickering lamp consuming whale oil plundered in the oceans off Africa, a Zulu flame cavorting on the end of a long thick English wick. Bouncing back and forth with vigor, energy is expended to illuminate the room with fire, casting lovers' hot shadows onto a cold wall, their melded image morphing at a growing pace into weird and wonderful designs of passion.

Nkosazane was until now a virgin, earmarked for her father's favourite commander, yet tonight she understood true love … threefold … what it is to be a woman, a lover and what it means to have a man who loves you.

Yet did this man love her? His hand squeezing her throat, his rod pushing inside her body, if he did not love her surely he wouldn't be doing this? Her father had warned Nkosazane about men and their desires, was this the terrible act he'd warned her against? For it wasn't as awful as the Zulu King depicted. Nkosazane did not believe she was being taken advantage of, since for the first time in her life she experienced true love and this must be Frederic's expression of the love he held for her.

Our dark springbok, gazelle eyes wide open, mouth panting for breath, whimpered at the crown of each stroke as steam condensed in cool crisp night air; this was by far the greatest intensity she'd experienced with another human being. It was no wonder girls weren't taught of this before they married; now she fully comprehended why men and women fled KwaZulu to the Buffalo River. It was for this feeling, this fabulous high that only a man could ignite within a woman, a spark of love transforming what was no more than transparent vapour into a violent eruption. Lord Chelmsford a noble and proper gentleman pierced her body, filling it to total satisfaction, igniting a previously inert atmosphere surrounding her heart, causing Nkosazane's soul to burst into flame.

The bed creaked under muscular bulk as Lord Chelmsford pushed and pulled at speeds Nkosazane could only sense within. A new feeling crept upon our dark springbok, as a demon hidden beneath cover of night is exposed in increments by a flickering lamp, had it been there before? Only Nkosazane had failed to notice it? Our native Princess was unsure, her eyes moved side to side in confusion. On noticing her gazelle like action he squeezed harder pressing black calves against broad white shoulders, locking Nkosazane's legs in place, permitting no method of flight from a taught aristocratic frame. As Nkosazane's sable body jerked with instinctive resistance, her nobleman pushed in proportion, maintaining control of his African Princess.

Zulu girls, along with all women of this era, were granted little to no sexual education, they were expected to learn from their husbands who unless significantly older possessed scant insight themselves.

This sensation building inside her, causing her heart to beat harder and faster, it was somehow influenced by the thick rod coursing her love canal, was this some kind of white man magic? She was unsure ... her heart began to beat uncontrollably.

"Stop! Stop!" shrieked Nkosazane.

Chelmsford, halted for a moment, his manhood pulsed inside Nkosazane's tenderness so that when together the pair did connect perfectly, as if God had designed them to be one, nothing seemed more natural to the Englishman at this moment, "Do you want me to stop?" he said in between heavy breaths.

Nkosazane took this moment of calm to scientifically scrutinize the shape of her emotions, her feelings and her body's responses. Different sensations gathered as winds fashion a furore on the high seas, a tempest of euphoria such as which she'd never experienced before, it was astounding yet it began to recede.

The native girl sensed her rapture slipping away despite desperate efforts to claw it back. Nkosazane had forgotten about the hand squeezing her throat, in fact nothing passed through her mind at all save that of a receding tide of pure ecstasy. She wanted that tide to come in and drench her beach … forever … yet it stubbornly retired within dense fog hanging over a sea from whence it emerged unannounced, "NO!" cried Nkosazane as she grasped the Englishman and pushed his taught backside, returning her redcoat to his former duties.

Frederic established a foot hold, advancing hard and fast, bayonet fixed he marched at pace on his ward. Lord Chelmsford pressed his native girl with greater intensity than before and so resurrected euphoria from the fog it'd pitched tent beneath.

Nkosazane relaxed as ecstasy splashed across her body, giant waves of pleasure she never knew existed. With each stroke, each grunt, each bead of sweat which clung to the end of his moustache like a pearl before splashing onto her body, intensity increased exponentially. Nkosazane's entire being became more sensitive to the world around her, it were as if she could feel every throbbing vein on her lover, carrying Nkosazane to loftier heights with each movement.

Frederic did touch Nkosazane's soul in every manner imaginable, he brought jubilation to her body, an emotion not only of delight but danger for she was skeptical as to whether she'd live to see the next day, yet her gratification was so intense, so raw, so real that in that moment Nkosazane no longer cared, for if she were to die in this man's arms, so be it. Nkosazane would be satisfied if this were the last night of her life for she could imagine no greater elation.

Our sable springbok's fantasy of Zulu native and English lord did triplicate in a moment, nearing a frenzy until Frederic's master key unlocked a music box hidden within her soul, releasing deep rhythmic beats of all-encompassing love. Chelmsford's penetrative seal were as if he forced a wedding ring upon Nkosazane's body, locking them as one for eternity, and just when our native girl felt that the wonder of her new life could not become any more intense, her English Lord lifted another velvet veil, permitting her access into a new universe. Nkosazane's entire body went into convulsions, she was in the grasp of God, being tossed back and forth as a rag doll, all negativity shook from her psyche … only thrilling euphoria remained, it were as if in that moment she had been anointed by the Almighty. Nkosazane's African bowl overran with enthralling love, our sable springbok closed her eyes as they rolled back inside her head, she cried out, "UHHHH, AWU NKOSIYAMI!"

She was helpless, secured into place and pressed deep into the mattress by taught aristocratic muscle. Nkosazane had no idea what she'd let herself in for, her body leaping to and fro as an animal desperately attempting to gain freedom from its captor's jaws.

Chelmsford pressed, pulled and pushed with long fast power strokes, our native Princess was certain she was experiencing a heart attack, an overload of joy. A sable springbok, clasped firmly in the jaws of a noble white lion, she was soon to die, yet Nkosazane had never felt so intense. Conflicting messages befuddled the young woman and so our sable springbok allowed her lover to decide her fate, for she trusted this nobleman who grasped her by the throat. Lord Chelmsford did possess Nkosazane's body and now her soul … she was his … his soul mate.

Our native Princess lurched involuntarily, up and down and from side to side. A bullet shaken in a glass could not produce more rapid movement nor sharper noise as a great wail emanated from our Princess, awaking every wallah from his slumber.

Eventually Nkosazane sensed euphoria slowly ebb as if a tide exited Algoa bay, a fascinating action of mother nature unexplained for many years though integral to those who live by its shore.

Atam stood guard outside his master's bedchamber, for he was familiar with the world of the feminine and masculine, and how their spheres did collide as two opposing armies in certain fields of operation, at certain times of the day.

In the locality of his lord's bedchamber at the witching hour he took lookout duty as a sailor in a crow's nest, preventing trespassers from disturbing his master's engagements with the black magic woman of Zululand, shooing curious wallahs back to their slumber.

Chelmsford continued, his rod pushing principled British vitality, yet Nkosazane's euphoric Zulu detonations diminished. Our native Princess realised she was not having a heart attack yet remained unsure of what had actually occurred. Nkosazane was convinced the white man had documented this sensation, for the white man does document and analyse everything, but why had she not been informed of this function before today?

She moved up and locked lips with the English nobleman, holding the back of his head she felt an all-encompassing love, something Nkosazane could not have imagined to be of the masculine before this evening, "Thank you, Master," she whispered.

Chelmsford didn't reply but maintained regular strokes until he evacuated inside her. For the first time in many years, desire had clouded Chelmsford's judgement. This African Princess was not only beautiful but enjoyed the act of love. She didn't profess to be above or uninterested in sexual desire. Nkosazane embraced his passion with hers, blending together to form the eye of a hurricane.

"What took place my Master?" inquired Nkosazane as Chelmsford rested by her side having poured his soup, somewhat recklessly, inside his African ward's brown bowl.

The tall Englishman kissed tender African lips and in his deep commanding tone he replied, "We became one."

Our doe eyed springbok smiled both deep and wide, her visage as innocent as a new-born lamb, for she'd discovered a treasure named passion, the wonder that is orgasm and unbeknownst to Chelmsford this young Zulu Princess stumbled upon the wealth that is love, for she now experienced that which every man and woman seek in their lives.

A segment of her master rested within not just her body but within her soul, a born again soul, a spirit emerged from the fog of ignorance, from the misery of being hunted across Africa, it discovered refuge in an English lion's love.

What this naïve springbok grasped, as a man might pick berries from the chestnut tree, the lion failed to divine with similar clarity. The passion, the touching of souls deep down, ying and yang, black and white, man and woman, two opposites yet a piece of one residing within the other, this Chelmsford did sense as he grasped her throat and the pair touched lips again and again, each time with greater passion; yet unknown to Chelmsford this man and woman did complete a masterpiece, a work of love, fate and destiny which combined to form a single, unique bond.

Nkosazane understood, for her heart, via the enigma of a woman's intuition, did quickly harmonized with love's sonnet; for as each stroke hit a note it did form a symphony in her body, building into a wonderful crescendo striking hidden cords deep inside her African soul, notes only this English aristocrat could reach, leaving her impossibly devoted to him.

Had Chelmsford been aware of Nkosazane's feelings toward him he'd have arranged their connecting doors locked, yet, as all men, Chelmsford was blissfully unaware, only the passage of time would expose the revelation of true love. For now he kissed the beautiful Zulu woman, a wondrous sight. Her smooth ebony body, tanned African features, very different from standards of beauty he was accustomed to, yet she created a spark, igniting his passion, a sentiment dormant for over three years. Only this native girl was capable of rousing Chelmsford's spirit in such a manner.

Many women had attempted this feat in the past, he was the 2nd Baron of Chelmsford, a lord and to marry him would bring great honour and financial security. A General in Her Majesty's Royal Army, a conqueror, honoured on three different continents by African Kings, Asian Emperors and the Queen of Africa herself, Queen Victoria, the Empress of the greatest Empire in human history.

Yet until this moment no woman had managed to snag General Chelmsford, and they'd tried. Every occasion in the Cape Colony from Port Elizabeth in the east to its capital Cape Town in the west, along with the scheming of his friend, High Commissioner Henry Bartle, constantly of the mind Chelmsford ought to marry his niece, Frederic found himself under feminine siege.

The British lion remained disinterested in the female form until the day his vision graced our Zulu Princess, recovered from a slave trader in the Natal.

76

Yet even as he lay beside Nkosazane, Chelmsford's hand leaving her throat to stroke thick sable thigh, he was unaware of the changes taking place within him. The English Lord believed this was but a single night of passion, thick juicy Africa and stiff upper lipped England locking tongues, indulging in one another's essence. Unbeknownst to this Englishman she tasted his soul, and he hers, for despite the act of love being behind him, Chelmsford's desire did not wane, nay it grew in size, entrenching itself in his soul, ready to take any onslaught launched by the cold beast that is male logic.

The pair were soul mates, a concept our native springbok understood perfectly for her soul was open and transparent, yet the lion's passion still operated from within a cloud of male coherence. It is rare for a female to have such perfect clarity over a man for in most situations it is the male who works under crystal clear logic, stubbornly unwavering in his cold rationale, where a woman will change her mind as often as the savannah breeze.

For this reason it is men who build empires, decide the path of nations and head the family. However, on matters of love a woman is supreme, for love is her domain where she rules the jungle and man doth stumble from one crisis to the next, unable to forge a clear path without feminine providence.

In the kingdom of emotion the queen doth rule the king, not because she has his consent but because the king is little more than a cripple, lurching through an emotional dusk which swallows the light of sanity. In this tangled labyrinth, where man will grope and fumble in a vain attempt to navigate love, he requires the female of the species, since in this terrifying realm her light alone may allow him to discover the correct path, cut out by God, to salvation.

All of this was far above the English lion's thick head. He'd strolled headlong into an African Jungle of love, unaware of its pitfalls. Chelmsford would only become cognisant of his pitiful state, as most men do, after the torch of femininity had been withdrawn.

Yet for now he took pleasure in a beautiful oasis within the thick foliage of Nkosazane's forest. After three years suffering an unforgiving desert of single life Frederic took refuge under the shade of beautiful African herbs, drawing deep on their honeyed essence and revitalizing his shrivelled lungs, plunging his entire body within a Zulu haven that is Nkosazane's soul. He absorbed her spirit as a desert flower drinks the sky, Zulu clouds falling in to feed an arid English wilderness that has suffered three years without the grace of femininity.

Nkosazane sensed love yet spoke not a word of it for in this arena men are fickle creatures, fear of commitment might cause this mighty lion to flee, so she indulged in the pleasure of the moment. Each time her master placed his hand on her throat her heart did leap into it, she knew not why. In the past Nkosazane would never have permitted a man such liberty, yet when this nobleman grasped her flesh Nkosazane sensed naught but affection, both in her and he, each time he squeezed she pushed and their lips met.

In her past Nkosazane refused all men access to her heart, any man who wished to dominate this African Princess left in regret. This is why despite having reached the age of twenty five she'd not married. Had she been a proper Zulu woman, feminine, co-operative, submissive to masculinity she would've wed many years ago.

But which man is prepared to pay a fortune in cattle to marry a rebellious woman? Her father had to negotiate with Dabulamanzi since he was unwilling to part with his herd without a political pledge. In truth had it not been for her father's position as king, Nkosazane's lobola would've remained unmet.

Yet tonight this man breached the walls to a Zulu fortress that is her heart. Nkosazane felt love, her rebellious streak disintegrated as a once impenetrable mud brick wall is transformed into useless rubble by a powerful storm. Nkosazane had no greater desire than to submit to this lion, the sable springbok didn't know why yet it was a powerful feeling, like the flow of a spring river. As ice surrounding her cold heart melted so torrents of passion and desire gathered, the more she submitted to his dominance the greater its flow … she was being dragged out into an ocean of love and Nkosazane wished nought but to drift away and drown in its masculinity.

The following morning Nkosazane awoke in her lover's arms. Chelmsford was a starving sailor who'd indulged himself in Nkosazane's African oyster, tasting a woman for the first time in years. A firm dark shell obscuring soft pink flesh within.

The pair did partake in breakfast, Nkosazane dressed in her ill-fitting gown, before a local Indian dressmaker arrived to fit our African Princess into fresh attire. After spending the afternoon measuring her from head to toe she was fitted with several new gowns befitting a Victorian lady.

Choosing from a selection of bonnets and shoes, our native girl was ready to meet her European counterparts; the tailor would take some days before her wardrobe was available. Until then Nkosazane remained with her protector, the lovers spent every day together and soon became the talk of the town, not only in Port Elizabeth, for word quickly discovered ears in Cape Town.

Commissioner Bartle became concerned, he intended Chelmsford to marry his niece, yet rumours emanating from Port Elizabeth were rather disquieting. It seemed scandalous that a British General, a lord of the realm might engage in intimate relations with an African woman.

Perhaps it was merely rumour? He would clear the issue with Chelmsford. The commissioner was holding a ball in Cape Town, in celebration of Chelmsford's victory in the Natal and Bartle's niece would be there, naturally.

Another evening passed, Chelmsford and Nkosazane indulged in one another, stroking her hair the British General smiled, "Henry is organising a ball in Cape Town, would you be my guest?"

The innocent girl smiled, her lips forming a luscious African canoe, "You are not ashamed?"

"What have I to be ashamed of?"

"Making love to a black woman?"

"Don't you mean of others knowing?"

Nkosazane's smiled widened, "That also."

Chelmsford ran a hand down his lover's silky cheek, "People can think as they please, I've brought glory to the Empire on three different continents, I do believe I'm entitled to a little happiness, what do you say Nkosazane?"

Our African Princess moved her hand below the sheets running her fingers across his manhood, with an abrupt jerk it came to life. Massaging him slowly she clutched its base and smiled. Frederic may be her master but she did control his desire as a queen controls a slave. In truth, through dark African artistry, she had a lock on his aristocratic libido, invoking it whenever our sable springbok felt a proclivity to do so.

Frederic caressed rough native hair, watching as she pleasured her Lord with intent, never before had Chelmsford experience such bliss even from his former wife.

Many ladies considered themselves above such bedroom activities, yet this doe eyed springbok did take gratification in satisfying her white master. He was tall, over six feet, straight jawed, an air of nobility accompanied him wherever he travelled and Nkosazane felt safe beneath his roof, what more could she ask for in a man?

Nkosazane was more than willing to provide Frederic every delight a dutiful, obedient wife could possibly offer.

While tasting his soldier our springbok planned her conquest of Chelmsford for she was unwilling to let go of her white man, no woman was going to take advantage, not while she shared his bedchamber.

Chelmsford relaxed in his bed as Nkosazane worked her African magic, coaxing a once dormant volcano into violent eruption. As lava splashed from its top our dark skinned Princess captured its explosion, supping magma spilling over her lover's peak.

Once Vulcan's passion had been indulged the British lion grasped his sable springbok's throat, manoeuvring her head atop feathered pillows. Without saying a word, for soul mates communicate to one another via instinct, he moved down her body until he reached her moist oyster, indulging himself in its divine cuisine.

He did find her to be a wonder, firm chocolate outside and soft pink within. Nkosazane's contrast was as beautiful as her taste was exciting. Chelmsford took his time consuming his ward for he understood how a woman is most likely to climax and his pleasure was inextricably linked to hers, unless his Princess touched the crest of elation her master could not fully enjoy their time together.

Nkosazane's breathing became heavy as Frederic intensified, running his tongue up and down, ringing what men of this age referred to as the Devil's doorbell, until it brought her heart to a furious beat once again.

Our African Princess had become accustomed to a man's task when making love and Chelmsford did accomplish that with utter competence. Her legs raised in the air, knees pressing on her breasts and soles of her feet to the ceiling, a position she understood to offer him best access.

The springbok's breath quickened, a groan here and there, she experienced climax yet possessed greater control, the sweet honeyed nectar of love flowed from her firmness onto her lover's tongue.

These opposites engaged in one another for several days, a few excursions around Port Elizabeth raised eyebrows and word spread everywhere of the white lord and black Princess.

Nkosazane set her task, could she persuade this English lord to commit to her? A relationship greater than sexual intercourse? Not that their relationship wasn't the most intense connection she'd ever had with another human being, white or black, but she wanted more, she desired a pledge but was it too early to push? For if she pressed her lord he might demonstrate an adverse reaction.

Women are the weaker sex until relationships and commitment become a factor, in which case a man is likely to fall apart at the seems like an old coat in stormy weather, forcing its occupant to flee for cover.

Nkosazane wasn't seeking a long term relationship as we understand it in the modern age, not that people had "relationships" in Victorian high society, not any more than Zululand. In these times should a man and woman engage in intimacy the onus fell upon the man to propose, that is, providing a financial transaction had not taken place.

In KwaZulu a woman had little say in her husband.

The father of the bride held veto, essentially similar to a British general election, he would decide on whether to sack the current selection or not before starting lobola negotiations with potential parents in law.

Events of the last few days concerned our native Princess for white men had been known to take African wives but never a nobleman nor had an African noblewoman taken a white man; this was a precarious situation if more was to be made of it than two ships passing in the night.

Nkosazane played her part, always the compliant Christian woman, that is to say never quarrelsome with her guardian; she always brought a smile to his face.

And so the pair became inseparable, whenever one was seen in town the other was sure to be by their side. Gossip spread far and wide, not that Henry Bartle paid much attention to it, he remembered soldiers taking wives in India but an officer such as Chelmsford would never lower himself to the level of a native woman.

Bartle's thoughts were based in cold male logic and a prejudice which high society held against the natives of the Empire, besides, at every given opportunity Henry pushed hard to place Lord Chelmsford with Sarah. The commissioner's niece was a beautiful blonde girl in her late twenties and her uncle had promised Sarah a satisfactory husband for some time, however, a suitor was yet to materialize.

Chelmsford strolled along the pavement, his African ward's arm threaded through his, a dark strand of wool through the eye of a white needle.

Scarlet blazer beaming out as sunlight bounced off gold braids, our African Princess delightful in expression, her smile always present for she treasured each moment spent with her lord. Nkosazane was attired in a fine Victorian bodice and skirt; both were navy blue, the same shade as her bonnet.

A young Indian lad followed them through the streets, carrying an umbrella and a large wicker basket. After a short stroll they emerged from the hustle and bustle of town, the scent of sea salt intensified as they passed the dock and onto a sandy beach.

It was a sunny day and many soldiers of Her Majesty's Royal Army took time out from the barracks to spend with their families who'd followed them from all corners of the realm, mostly Britain, India and Canada.

Upon witnessing Lord Chelmsford enter into view the men immediately moved from beneath their umbrellas and stood to attention. Their families remained seated on blankets, one for each family, surrounded by provisions to enjoy Port Elizabeth's cool weather.

Nkosazane stopped in her tracks unsure as to what had occurred, her lord put her at rest with a reassuring smile, "As you were gentlemen," stated the Englishman in his deep morning tone.

The men returned to their families, relaxing on individual sections of beach. Our sable springbok's ears pricked up for there was an undertone to conversation across the waterfront. Women did chatter to one another concerning the native woman escorted by Lord Chelmsford.

Chelmsford's men, despite being widely dispersed across yellow sand, were rather embarrassed. Their wives spoke above the lapping of waves, a noise which usually created momentary lulls in gossip as cannons reloading on the battlefield. Frederic feigned ignorance and carried on with the day as intended.

"What do you think?" asked Chelmsford.

"I think gossip is not a Christian virtue," replied Nkosazane with a broad smile.

Chelmsford chuckled in reply, "Yes on that there can be no argument. However I was inquiring as to placement of our beach blanket."

Our African beauty blushed a little, though not detectable to the average white man Chelmsford was accustomed to nuances in his ward's behaviour, "Perhaps that space will suit us?" she pointed with her eyes for her left arm was firmly threaded in his right while her right hand clutched a parasol … besides, pointing in public was unladylike.

The British General followed her eyes before turning to his left, "Wallah, pitch your umbrella per the lady's request."

The beach went silent for our General had referred to his ward as a lady. Chelmsford halted, scanning salty sand broken by men and women enjoying cool morning breeze as it travels over sea, "Is there a quandary gentlemen?"

The beach quickly returned to its former business, our African springbok and British lion glanced at one another and grinned before approaching their destination.

Wallah lay down a large woollen blanket ahead of placing a wicker basket, a wicker table with two matching chairs and angling an umbrella, deflecting direct sunlight from the pair of beachcombers.

The couple were familiar to odd looks, long pauses and gossip; it amounted to little more than amusement.

During the day, other picnickers grew accustomed to their presence and so continued their morning rest along calm coastline. After an hour or two an open carriage, pulled by two horses, halted at a road just off the street which led onto the waterfront.

A child soldier leapt out, his tartan trousers informed Frederic he was of the 91st Argyllshire Highlanders, Colonel Wood's regiment based in Cape Town. The young lad ran up to Chelmsford and saluted, "SIR!"

The General sat up in his chair, "What brings you here boy?"

"A message from the commissioner, sir!"

"Yes?"

The young cadet in scarlet tunic and tartan trousers spoke with a Scottish accent, travelling on a wave of fear. He blurted out a reply, "The commissioner invites all officers and their wives to a ball next Saturday," the young cadet outstretched his hand, a piece of paper awaited Chelmsford's grasp.

The British lion took the card, unfolded it and quickly read its contents, "I see, let the commissioner know I'll be bringing a guest."

"A guest?" the boy's eyes strayed onto our African lady, seated across the table from his Lieutenant General, a most curious sight.

"What's your name lad?" growled Chelmsford.

"Grant sir."

"Rank?" stated Chelmsford in a frustrated tone.

"Drummer, sir."

"Listen here Drummer Grant, I want you to return to Cape Town and inform the commissioner I'm inviting a guest, is that understood?"

"May I ask who your guest is, sir?"

"NO YOU MAY NOT! NOW GET OUT OF MY SIGHT BEFORE I SEE TO IT YOU'RE BLOODY WELL FLOGGED FOR INSOLENCE!" roared the lion, furious that the lowest rank in the army had spoken to his superior in such a manner.

A terrified Grant saluted and ran off down the beach kicking plumes of sand onto soldiers as he sped through blankets and umbrellas pock marking yellow coast.

Nkosazane passed her drink to Wallah before she comforted Chelmsford, "Why did you speak with such a sharp tongue to the boy?"

The lion calmed at the touch of the woman he'd spent these past weeks with, "I'm a Lieutenant General and he's a drummer, in my day if I'd spoken with as much brass neck as that boy I'd have had the skin lashed off my back."

Our springbok smiled as she grasped his arm tighter, leaning into her nobleman, "Yet you permitted him leave with but a warning?"

"Demoralizing your own men is a foolish strategy. Nobody gains satisfaction in a boy taking twenty strokes of the lash."

Nkosazane pecked his cheek with her lips, proud of her lion, for mercy is one of many Christian virtues he demonstrated in her company.

Other attendants relaxing on yellow sand did raise their brows in a most uncivilized fashion, at least for a public setting. Men, women and children ogled in wonder at our dark Princess placing her lips on the white baron's cheek. Their brows raised a further distance, furrowing foreheads, when the Lieutenant General's attitude shifted from tempest to tranquillity, two events equally shocking and unique in the experience of every person populating the coastline that day.

As the lion and springbok enjoyed one another's company ... a sinister form concealed itself off the seafront. A blonde haired figure peeked out from the shade of an alley between local stores, its eyes twinkled as an evil spirit poised to strike at the first moment of weakness, a shabby genteel shrouded in wickedness, nursing a vengeful heart ... it was the Afrikaner, Soepenberg.

Chapter Five: The Ball

A carriage swayed side to side as dirt remodelled itself into cobblestone; Chelmsford grasped Nkosazane's gloved hand, her apprehensive expression transformed to one of calm on meeting her guardian's gaze.

Our African Princess was adorned in powder blue, covered with ruffles, a lady's evening attire hidden beneath a white overcoat. After a visit from a pioneering American lady and her team of three tribeswomen, Nkosazane's hair no longer displayed texture typical to an African woman.

An American named Annie, her services purchased by Frederic for the purpose of making over his Zulu ward, presented an intriguing offer.

The American had recently discovered a method to chemically straighten textured hair without damaging the scalp or hair follicles.

Nkosazane found wigs to be very uncomfortable and so opted to undergo a test run of Annie's prototype product.

And so Nkosazane possessed a full head of luscious black hair indistinguishable from the locks of European ladies, with whom she was to mingle.

After a successful straightening, by method of Annie's invention, destined to become one of the most lucrative products in the hair care industry, smooth African fibre was sculpted into a pompadour style, a trend gaining popularity amongst the fashionable of late 1870's Britain.

The sable springbok's new hair was collected and lifted upwards at the upper rear of her head, either just offset or on the crown, leaving curls to fall down at the side.

The native girl remained somewhat apprehensive, unsure as to whether she might carry a foreign fashion, despite Chelmsford's reassurances.

Shunting from side to side the sun set behind the city of Cape Town, militia patrolled its streets as their carriage rolled past. Native reserves were unaware of its contents or destination and so carried on with that which occupied their minds ... women and drink for the most part.

Peering from within Chelmsford noted tardiness, tardiness irritated the British lion, he'd seen men flogged for less in the Crimea; Frederic would make a point of it with Colonel Wood.

His native ward leaned over in curiosity. On witnessing drunkards who ought be sober as a judge, she whispered into her lover's ear, "Uchakide uhlolile imamba yalukile."

Chelmsford, attired in dress uniform of scarlet, black and gold, medals gleaming as they rocked back and forth, turned to the beautiful young lady, "Please explain."

She smiled, "The weasel is at ease because the mamba has gone out."

Chelmsford felt tension distance from temperament. Nkosazane had that effect on him. He leaned back into leather upholstery, "We have a similar proverb, when the cat's away the mice will play. However, I must say I prefer your Zulu weasel, it's most apt."

She held onto his arm and moved closer, "When the lion is going to the ball the hyena shall indulge itself."

He looked her up and down, "If it weren't for the fact I'm escorting you, I'd have given those layabouts a ruddy good thrashing. Nevertheless, I'll make certain Evelyn gives them what for tomorrow."

Nkosazane noticed fellow tribesmen amongst the militia, men who'd fled her father's tyrannical rule for safety under the British flag. The springbok squeezed her lover's arm, "Show them leniency, Master."

Chelmsford's brow ruffled to form waves of incredulity, "Why on earth would I do that?"

"These men have no ball to attend, permit them their celebrations, the Zulu say Ingwe ikhontha amabala ayo amlhlope namnyama."

Chelmsford sighed for this woman had control of his heart and resisting her request would be a foolish endeavour, "Pray tell its meaning?"

"It means the leopard licks both its black and white spots."

"In plain English?"

"In plain English, those in authority ought to employ equal justice, so allow them their ball while we enjoy ours."

The lion grumbled beneath his breath for it was against his nature to show leniency, rather he would dispute every bush, rock and patch of long grass on the African plain, yet during these past weeks Nkosazane had caused much deviation in his routine, "We'll see," growled her English lion stroking his lover's hand.

On reaching the Governor's mansion their hack chaise (hired carriage) waited in line, fountain to the left and a marbled reception area to the right. The reception area was populated by footmen assisting guests from taxis while announcing their presence to those within.

This building was constructed in 1679 by the Dutch East India Company, its former purpose being that of a slave lodge (by which it's known today). The building was expanded over the centuries into the large construction it is today; a great central archway cut from white stone led inwards with five large windows each side and a second storey.

Thick and tall white columns flanked the doorway within and the first two windows, stretching upwards to support a semi-circular stone of white and yellow atop.

The Lodge was three times as deep as it was wide, its walls a pastel yellow hue.

The fortunes of evil that men do to one another modelled this testament in Cape Town yet today it had been refigured into a beacon of civilisation. An example to the wicked of the world that Christian men prevail in the face of villainy, for upon the abolition of slavery it was purchased by the British.

Nkosazane was fascinated by the hustle and bustle of British high society, its pomp and ceremony, ladies dressed in stunning gowns, young men scurrying around attending to their every wish, it was all so exciting.

Soon their chaise moved into place, positioned at the point of disembarkation, its door agape. While a young man held its door wide open, another stood beside its exit as Frederic descended onto the carpet.

"LORD CHELMSFORD!" cried out the young lad.

Chelmsford gave him a rather stern look yet the footman, dressed in uniform with a top hat, didn't flinch. The British lion outstretched his hand, which Nkosazane took in hers, her other hand lifting the front of a thick ruffled skirt so as not to trip on the route down.

Everything stopped, the footman's jaw dropped as Nkosazane exited the chaise dressed in powder blue, a firm bodice and skirt hovering a couple of inches from the floor. Since this was a ball gown there was neither bustle nor ribbon at her rear.

Nkosazane descended as an angel from the heavens, sent by the almighty in an act of kindness toward the white man, passing through breaking white clouds to the awe of humbled boys below. Silence stretched into awkwardness as men and women in carriages, waiting to disembark, peered from within to witness God's Zulu messenger. Eventually chatter reasserted its presence, intensifying as a great noise rising and falling on the air, so much so it reminded Nkosazane of the Buffalo River.

"Well? Aren't you going to announce us lad?" stated Chelmsford with a gritty stare.

"Erm, yeh alright," replied the footman in a cockney accent.

"You'll address me as Lord Chelmsford you little pip squeak!"

Chelmsford drew his stick from within the carriage, a martial mind issuing orders to muscular limbs that he might thrash insolence from the man, yet Nkosazane settled her angelic hand on his fiery arm, "He is only a boy."

The footman glared at the stick, half in and half out the carriage, the lad began to sweat for Lord Chelmsford was known as something of a tyrant; Frederic had seen men whipped to death before now for the crime of stealing a loaf of bread from locals. The Lieutenant General often let himself go in the current of fury, as men do voyage in their dreams. The boy had no doubt Chelmsford was in the mood to give him a taste of frontier justice.

Fortunately his ebony escort dammed the flow of a tempestuous river about to burst its banks and flood this lad's meagre frame. Frederic took his walking cane out of the carriage and fixed it by his side much to the delight of Nkosazane and relief of the footman.

The young man pulled out a piece of paper and announced the pair, "Lord Chelmsford and Princess Nkosazane kaMpande," the boy peered up at the tall dark lady.

Our springbok smiled, "That will do, thank you."

The pair strolled along a short welcoming carpet and through a wide doorway guarded by another young man, entering a marble atrium. Here servants took hats and cloaks before leading them through, into the main reception area, and then directly on to the ballroom, an area employed for the purpose of a billiard hall when not pressed into service for occasions such as this evening.

Bartle fluttered to and fro as a hawk moth between flames; two inches long this unique creature is able to sustain its flight for long periods, even during rain. He hovered over guests, accepting warm congratulations on the latest effort to confederate the Southern Cape of Africa.

As soon as Chelmsford caught his eye the old civil servant trundled over, drink in hand and smug visage, he had more than one reason to invite his old friend. Congratulations on a job well done being the first, his niece being the other cartridge loaded into this evening's social shotgun.

The old bear was to ambush the lion again and hope his weapon didn't misfire, that is until he noted a sable springbok by Frederic's side, dressed up as an English lady, it was quite an oddity, "Good evening old boy," he turned to Nkosazane and raised a glass, "and to you young lady, I must say, you look rather fetching."

The dark lady in powder blue curtsied, "Thank you Mr Commissioner."

The old man smiled, "Henry, please. So how has the General been treating you?"

Nkosazane grinned, catching a glimpse of her guardian's smile before returning her eyes to the commissioner.

Henry Bartle, dressed in black tie for this evening's pleasantries, took a moment to consider expressions traded between his commanding officer in the Cape Colony and its most important refugee, a refugee that would hopefully lead to the confederation of the Zulu Empire, under the British flag.

Henry didn't know this African Princess at all, yet Frederic he knew inside and out. The lion wasn't one for expressing himself unless obliged to remedy the lower orders, as a farmer might restrain wayward cattle. In fact Henry hadn't witnessed a smile pass Chelmsford's lips since, well, since Anna was alive.

This was a bad sign for the commissioner. He'd often pressed his niece upon the old lion, yet consistently Chelmsford refused to take the fresh meat on offer. Henry felt as if Chelmsford were a lion and he the hunter, the commissioner considered if perhaps his bait were lacking yet his niece was a beautiful young lady in her twenties. Full locks of golden hair, a fine complexion, many officers had expressed an interest but Henry had rejected them all, he waited for Frederic to bite. Yet Henry's forte lay in confederating real estate more so than pairing human beings.

"Why don't you join the ladies Miss Nkosazane?" Henry gestured to the other side of the room, "I have important business to discuss with Frederic."

Nkosazane looked to her guardian for confirmation, for this environment was completely foreign to the Zulu lady.

Frederic smiled and nodded, "I'll join you shortly, I'm sure the ladies are fascinated by your presence in the colony."

Nkosazane nodded her head and replied, "Yes my Master," before gliding elegantly toward on looking wives of officers and officials.

Henry made a suspicious visage as grimness filled his being, "Master? What on earth's going on there old chap?"

A waiter interrupted the pair with a tray of drinks, "Aperitif Commissioner?"

Henry placed his old glass down to lift a fresh one of white soup from the silver tray. Now don't be fooled by its moniker for white soup is merely the name given to eggnog commonly served during balls of this era.

"Aperitif General?"

"Thank you," stated Frederic as he selected a glass before the young man returned to orbiting the room, maintaining attendees in a refreshed state.

Henry loaded tonight's shotgun with a pair of polished shells, grace and gregariousness, raised its barrels and began to take aim while sipping his drink, "Well?"

Frederic sampled his eggnog and replied, "The vanilla is rather agreeable."

"I wasn't referring to the drink old boy."

Frederic chuckled.

Henry was doubly alarmed for his old friend was developing a sense of humour, something he was devoid of even when married. This was not a good sign … well … for his niece.

"Is there something going on between you two? Now don't hold back on me!"

Henry expected the General to deny any interest in the Zulu girl so when he didn't, in fact he did the opposite, the commissioner was stunned, "I've been enjoying Nkosazane's company this past fortnight, I must say, I hadn't noticed an absence of female company before her arrival."

Henry pulled the trigger on both barrels only to hear the click of a misfire; he broke opened the barrel, discarded the dud cartridges and placed a fresh pair inside. Civility and cordiality were popped into the chambers before both barrels were snapped shut again, "What of Sarah? She's looking for a husband you know."

Chelmsford sighed, took another sip, swallowed and replied, "I'm flattered but she's not my type."

Bartle took aim as the lion rose from long grass, focused, pulled back both hammers, "Not your type? Why on earth's that? Look at her," Henry pointed in a rather brash manner toward his niece chatting amongst a group of ladies, the gentlemen caught her eye, she smiled and curtsied from across the room, "she's perfect for you."

Chelmsford scanned Sarah, dressed in a wonderful blush ball gown, it were as if Goldilocks had grown to womanhood, "I'm sure she'll find a suitable husband. However, I'm afraid you'll have to exclude me from her list of suitors."

CLICK Damn! Another double misfire! This ruddy beast had the luck of the Devil! "Well you're going to have to marry soon old boy you can't remain a bachelor forever, people will start to talk," remarked Bartle in a concise undertone while nursing his glass of soup.

Chelmsford cast his eye as a fisherman's net in an attempt to capture beauty, it inevitably snagged Nkosazane, he smiled, "Yes I've been considering that old boy."

Nkosazane returned his smile, quickly picked up by the commissioner then his niece, Sarah.

He went to load two more cartridges, high grain with a hard shell, shame and responsibility, enough to take down any beast walking God's earth ... bloody hell! His servant had forgotten to bring extra ammunition! "I say old chap what are you considering?" stated Bartle in a rather exasperated tone for if he'd read the room right something disastrous was brewing that evening.

Chelmsford returned his vision to Henry Bartle, "Nothing obscene."

"You're not considering a savage?"

"Nkosazane is not a savage, I've spent a lot of time with her and she's very pleasant company I'll have you know."

"I'm sure but you do believe Darwinism don't you?"

Chelmsford raised an eyebrow, "And you do believe the bible, don't you?"

"What bit?"

"Here there is no Gentile or Jew, circumcised or uncircumcised, barbarian, Scythian, slave or free, but Christ is all, and is in all."

Bartle grimaced at the substance of Frederic's retort while throwing away his empty shells and riding back to base camp ... this safari was a definite no show, "I suppose so."

"Suppose? Its scripture, if at any time you feel the need to look it up, Colossians ..."

Henry cut him off, "Yes alright, I'm here to enjoy myself not to engage in a theological debate."

"Then less talk about Darwin?"

"Very well," Henry gestured to our beautiful native Princess stood across the room, "I've had word Cetshwayo has placed a bounty for her retrieval, she might not be with us for much longer."

"Oh? How so?"

"I was banking on a declaration of war or at the very least a threat that's actionable."

"I doubt it," stated the General as he monitored the ballroom floor focusing on his lover.

"What brings you to that conclusion?" replied Bartle.

"From what Nkosazane has told me her father isn't a reckless man, you don't become King of the Zulu without some guile."

"I see," Henry quaffed his custardy aperitif, "She's offered insight into his mind?"

"He has an advisor, an umthakathi, a sorcerer. I do believe the key to any conquest depends on defeating him."

"A witch doctor?" stated Bartle in an incredulous tone, "What on earth might a magic man do to prevent the Royal Army old boy?"

"That I cannot answer, however I do know the entire tribe has faith or fear in him. If that were to be undermined I believe anyone might march into Ulundi and take control."

"Are you suggesting bribery?"

"Honestly I don't know but he'll advise the King on what to do next and I'm quite sure the King will follow that advice."

Henry was delighted with Frederic's new information, "Excellent, tell me, have you managed to pump your Princess any further?"

Chelmsford gave Bartle a stern glare, "Excuse me old chap?"

Bartle retrieved his former statement, "I meant to say, has Nkosazane divulged any further intelligence pertinent to the consolidation of the Cape?"

Chelmsford relaxed, sipped white soup and replied, "No ... oh she was to be married to an impi commander, a cousin of hers. He may be prone to reckless behaviour what with the humiliation and all."

"Humiliation?"

"Yes, his bride to be running away rather than marry him."

Bartle looked up at Chelmsford and spoke in a devious tone, "Of course, if you could find someone for her to marry here it might well provoke the savage into something actionable."

"Yes, I was thinking much the same, if he brought his impi over the Buffalo River you'd be forced to defend the realm, wouldn't you?"

Bartle grinned, "Excellent."

On the other side of the room women gathered, chattering to one another as a gaggle of geese. The conversation lowered to a silence as Nkosazane approached, women of high society were stunned to see an African woman in the form of a Victorian lady.

"Bonsoir, Quel est votre nom?" inquired a middle aged lady in a thick golden wig with matching gold ballroom gown, obviously the leader of the pack.

"Bonsoir Madame, Je'mappelle Nkosazane," replied our native Princess without missing a beat, bewildering those in ear shot for the golden lady's intention was to humiliate our African Princess yet she achieved the opposite.

"You speak French?" replied a flabbergasted lady fanning herself furiously.

"Yes, the missionaries who taught me English insisted upon it."

The golden lady's fan moved as a hummingbird's wing, "How quaint, I'm Catherine, Catherine Fere."

The native girl curtsied, "I'm pleased to make your acquaintance Miss Fere."

The gaggle laughed and Catherine smiled, "Oh no, Mrs Fere, I'm Henry's wife," she halted her fanning movement to employ it in a polite gesture picking out her husband from across the room.

"Forgive me my lady."

"Never mind, now tell me, how on earth did you find your way into that dress and this event?"

"I'm Lord Chelmsford's guest."

"Oh really?" stated the lady.

Women close by began to gossip, then as a conductor might direct an orchestra, with a twirl of her fan they ceased. Scrutinizing our twenty five year old springbok from head to toe Lady Fere inquired with a smile on her face, "You must be the young Princess staying with Frederic?"

"That's correct my lady."

"You've made quite the impression upon Freddie, why he hasn't been seen with a woman since his wife passed; to be truthful rumours were beginning to do the rounds."

The officers' and officials' wives snickered much to the confusion of Nkosazane, "Rumours?"

"Yes, when a man in Frederic's position fails to show interest in the opposite sex, well, rumours are bound to emerge."

Nkosazane peered toward the gaggle of wives, narrowed her eyes into arrow slits and stated, "I wonder what type of ill-natured person would spread such slander?"

The ladies went silent, Catherine smiled, "Indeed, you've chased away that terrible talk."

"I'm sure Frederic will be relieved when I tell him," replied Nkosazane in a sardonic tone.

"Touché my dear," Catherine paused for a moment before continuing, "my apologies for any insinuations, life can be rather dull for us women."

Nkosazane looked around the ballroom and up at chandeliers hanging from its high vaulted ceiling, "Dull?"

"I imagine this is very different to Ulundi yet one will grow familiar even with the most fantastic surroundings," stated Catherine following the native woman's eyes across the room.

"I would say it's wondrous beyond anything I've witnessed before now. It is truly amazing. Your people are so wealthy you decorate your halls with diamonds."

Catherine chuckled, "Oh no, those are chandeliers, they're made from crystal glass."

Our Zulu Princess ogled radiant ornaments hanging from the ceiling, "Oh, forgive me."

"Think nothing of it; it's an easily made mistake. Tell me, do they host similar occasions in Ulundi?"

The women gathered around focusing on the young lady, "They do yet our celebrations are, how might I say? Less refined?"

"In what manner?" inquired Catherine.

"Zulu use the inungu drum in all our celebrations, along with dancing it marks important events in life. From the beginning of femininity to the year's harvest to a great victory in battle, men and women will dance in celebration and drink umqombothi."

"Umqombothi?"

"It is a traditional Zulu beer, the women brew it in a special hut for such occasions, we also drink from clay pots or from a gourd."

"What's a gourd?" came a voice from the gaggle.

"It is a hollowed plant which we use as a communal vessel to drink umqombothi, the women always drink first."

Catherine sipped white soup, "How civilized."

Nkosazane quickly interjected, "In order to prove to the men that the umqombothi is safe to drink."

"How ghastly!" asserted the golden lady.

"In Zulu society the man is of greater value than the woman, is it not so in English society?"

Catherine glanced at her husband, catching his eye, he smiled across the room, "They are but please don't permit them to hear those words."

"Why not?" inquired our native Princess.

"It would go to their heads, take Frederic for example, he's only recently defeated the Xhosa and been promoted to Lieutenant General, his ego doesn't require further inflation."

Nkosazane was confused by such an attitude for in a Zulu woman it would have been dishonourable, to view an accomplished warrior with such, well, disdain, "Yet he has earned the respect and honour of your Queen has he not?"

"What do you mean?"

Nkosazane considered her own words before replying, "I think I understand your criticism of Lord Chelmsford. Your society is not a patriarchal one."

Catherine furrowed her finely crafted brow, "What makes you say that?"

"Well, you have a queen but no king; she is an unwed mother, yes?"

The gaggle broke out in chatter for to speak ill of your husband was one thing but to suggest Queen Victoria might be an unwed mother was quite scandalous.

Catherine quickly brought our Zulu Princess' train of thought to a conclusion, "Certainly not, her husband died almost twenty years ago. You would do well to take my advice young lady and not suggest that our Queen, the Queen offering you safe harbour, is a lady of ill repute!"

Nkosazane curtsied, "Forgive my ignorance."

With a flit of her fan Catherine discarded all scorn, "Never mind, it's to be expected."

"May I ask why she has not married again?"

"She remains in mourning. However to rule the British Empire a man is not required."

Nkosazane nodded her head, "In Zululand a woman cannot rule over the thirteen tribes, only a man can lead, only a man can fight other men and rule them."

Catherine rounded on Nkosazane, "Tell me why did you flee Zululand?"

Nkosazane sipped her advocaat, an odd aperitif, it was no wonder they named it white soup, "I was to be married to my father's half-brother."

There was a gasp from the gaggle, Catherine examined the Zulu lady in powder blue, shock graced her eyes, "How frightful! Why would your father do such an awful thing to his daughter?"

"Tribal politics, his half-brother is the second highest impi in rank. In order to secure his loyalty my father arranged our marriage but I was not prepared to be his fourth wife."

Another gasp went up, "Fourth wife?" said Catherine fanning herself furiously as the hummingbird took flight once more, "what sort of ghastly practice do Zulu men engage in that they require four wives?"

"It is a mark of his power and position in the tribe, most men can only afford a single wife."

The fan hummed as Catherine's pert powdered nose offered honeysuckle to the atmosphere, "Don't tell me that women are bought and sold in Zululand!"

Swallowing a little soup Nkosazane quickly replied, "No, yet every woman has her lobola. I was to be wed for fifty head of cattle, a remarkable price."

The wives of officers and bureaucrats had never heard anything so scandalous, women bartered in exchange for cattle, why it was positively savage. Catherine's forehead folded, "Lobola?"

"Lobola is a woman's bride price; surely you have something similar in your culture?"

"Certainly not!" yelped Catherine, alarmed to hear of the depravity Zulu men forced their women to endure.

Nkosazane eyed Catherine's gold and diamond engagement ring, "What of your ring? Is this not a lobola of sorts?"

Catherine's frown became a grin, "I wouldn't go so far as to call it a bride price."

"Yet without it would your father have accepted your husband's proposal?"

Catherine stopped fanning herself, the Zulu girl was correct, without a satisfactory ring to demonstrate commitment her father would certainly have rejected Henry's proposal of marriage, "Touché my dear."

A moment later trumpets sounded from the orchestra and a fellow approached the ladies with an armful of programs for the evening. He read out a name at the top before passing the program to its corresponding lady, halting before our native springbok he struggled, "Nik, niko, erm ..."

Our native girl put the young man at ease, "Nkosazane kaMpande."

The gaggle laughed.

Catherine noted her guest's confusion and quickly moved over, plucking Nkosazane's paper program from a well-dressed man's hands, "Thank you."

The fellow made a bow and exited their presence, Catherine handed a blank program with Nkosazane's name written atop, "There you go."

"What is its purpose?" enquired our native girl, one hand clutching a small glass of eggnog, tonight's program in the other.

"Shortly, a gentleman will approach and introduce us to his friends. They shall place their names on our programs for the purpose of a dance."

Nkosazane peered up from her blank sheet to witness men strolling across the ballroom floor, her lover's vision fixed upon his Princess. Chelmsford approached with calm dignity, tall and magnificent in a scarlet and black officer's uniform, he whipped out a pencil and placed his name atop her list. As he wrote the Englishman whispered, "You look wondrous this evening."

Nkosazane smiled, curtsied and spoke so the gaggle might catch her words, "Thank you my Master."

Men and women previously engaged in sorting dance partners stopped, the gaggle was taken aback, traumatised would be the best description. Gentlemen equally so, yet the source of their aghast was yearning, for envy did pass within their ranks.

Frederic was rather embarrassed, for men thought as men think yet it was the judgement of Bartle's wife and her gaggle of geese which caused the old General discomfort.

"Call me Frederic, please," stated the British Lord in a warm tone.

Nkosazane curtsied and replied with equal warmth, "As you wish Frederic."

Men coveted Nkosazane's sensibility while women found it repellent, though you'd never know for during such occasions Victorian society was on its best behaviour.

Floor managers made certain that guests acted suitably, the Master of the House co-ordinated affairs often taking cues from Bartle or his wife Catherine.

At this stage of the evening a gentleman introduced his lady guest to his male counterparts. Those men would request a dance by pencilling their name onto her program. A Victorian lady could not refuse the request of a gentleman to dance during a ball, unless she had a previous request, otherwise she might be accused of uncivilised behaviour.

Those popular women with too many requests would recommend less fortunate ladies as a polite method of rejection.

Chelmsford escorted his lover around the room introducing her to fellow officers, gentlemen were polite yet none of them etched their name on her sheet. Having noticed this Bartle leapt into action and made his way to the couple as they sought out another officer.

"Has no one requested a dance yet?" said the grumpy old bear glaring at her program.

"Frederic will dance with me," smiled our dark Princess, no longer carrying her glass of white soup but her right arm threaded inside Chelmsford's left while in her left hand her program betrayed but a solitary name upon it.

"May I have the honour of a dance?" requested Henry.

"Of course you may Commissioner."

The grey fellow took her program as she passed it to him. Henry pencilled in his name while Catherine watched from afar.

Chelmsford was suspicious of Henry's motivations for his niece was at the ball, Sarah, dressed in a light blush muslin lace over a silk petticoat and silk gloves. A tight bodice demonstrated her hourglass frame, lusciously curled hair with a single pink carnation in it for decoration.

Henry had been trying to offload her for the last three years. Frederic successfully avoided the commissioner's niece without bruising any egos, why? Well it wasn't that Sarah lacked in looks or youth, quite the opposite. Sarah possessed everything an English gentleman might desire, good looks, good breeding, good manners, there was nothing to critique.

Yet Frederic was a contrarian by nature, if he caught wind you were trying to press something upon him the fellow picked up on it quickly and would resist by instinct, it was his character. How Nkosazane had managed to corner the lion and grasp his heart was a question existing in the minds of all men and women at tonight's ball ... perhaps she was the exception proving the rule? This African woman was certainly exceptional in Frederic's mind whereas the white women perusing him seemed to meld into one another, even Sarah. To reject one was to reject them all for they seemed indistinguishable, as a great shoal of fish following a military transport, feeding on trash dumped overboard, how could even the most experienced sailor separate one from another day to day?

"Sarah!" Henry called his niece over and Chelmsford grimaced inside for he understood the old man's intent ... draw Nkosazane away so his niece might dance with the Lieutenant General.

The lady in blush glided over thick hard wood floor as the orchestra played a little music, "Yes uncle?"

Her strawberry blonde hair and perfect nose did strike Nkosazane deep inside, for she immediately understood Henry's intentions and those of his niece, more so our Zulu Princess could not fathom how Fredric might prefer her to this woman.

It is a great failing of both men and women that they often refuse to attribute to the opposite sex character traits they possess themselves. For instance, women consider all men to be undisciplined and obsessed with little more than their next meal or sexual encounter.

Now granted this isn't a totally false assumption, however, when your lover is a man of Lord Chelmsford's stature, a woman ought to give him the benefit of the doubt for Frederic was the most disciplined of men on the battlefield, in society and in the company of women.

Also it's well known that a man is unable to separate love and sex, the two melding into one another before, like oil and water, they separate, the woman he once embraced becoming repugnant as former lovers fall out.

All these weaknesses Nkosazane did attribute to her lover for he is man, and man, despite his great strengths, physical power and mental fortitude superior to that of a woman, is woefully deficient in one area, an area God had decided to make woman his superior.

Yet Lord Chelmsford was not visibly moved by this European beauty, as the magnificent warrior his uniform portrayed him to be, he held his ground, ridged as an edifice of dry rock jutting out from the savannah, stubborn as a monkey yet glorious as a lion. Nkosazane smiled as she peered up to him for she recognised that stalwart stiff upper lip, equally it did cause Bartle and his wife Catherine sorrow, for they'd long conspired his marriage to Sarah, with little to no progress.

Frederic was stubborn as a mule, a contrarian attitude which kept him single until the day Kreli surrendered, for the moment he met Nkosazane his heart betrayed his bachelor lifestyle, the dark skinned springbok's allure so great, it broke the lion's resistance.

"Frederic, would you do my niece the honour of a dance?" requested the commissioner.

To refuse would be the height of incivility and Lord Chelmsford was a man obsessed with maintaining the decency of Her Majesty's Royal Army abroad, "It would be an honour," stated the English General removing a pencil from his top pocket to scrawl his name, adding it to a list of suitors at tonight's ball. Many of this evening's suitors were young officers climbing the ranks, hoping to make a good impression on the commissioner's niece and perhaps gain an opportunity to request her hand?

The chances of that were somewhere between slim and none provided Chelmsford was a gay bachelor ... closer to none!

Trumpets sounded again and as tradition dictates, a lady escorted by her gentleman to the ball would permit him the first dance of the evening.

And so the orchestra played as gentlemen and ladies formed squares of two to four couples, this style of dance was known as the quadrille. Couples formed a square to dance with one another, pairs of dancers forming different geometric shapes such as circles, squares, rectangles and diamonds. Moving through one another sometimes at a light trot, others a slow waltz.

"I do not know your dance," stated Nkosazane in a hurried pitch as Lord Chelmsford led her to the floor.

The old warrior spoke softly in a deep tone from beneath his beard, "Concern yourself not, it's quite simple just follow my movements and those close by as best you can."

Couples lined up, women on one side, men the other, forming groups on the dance floor of four couples. Music began, men and women joined hands forming a circle consisting of a man and woman alternating.

Dancers stopped as a single pair stepped inside, they twirled around for a short time before breaking off and re-joining those who formed the edge of the circle.

The dance was very simplistic since men and women both stood upright, men didn't hold onto women other than touching hands for this was how high society in Victorian England did court.

The music was more a military march than anything else, women with their long silk gloves held the hem of their light coloured gowns a few inches above the floor while using the left hand to touch that of their partner.

Men stood erect, backs straight and heads held high, leading ladies in the dance.

The shapes and movements were very simple; Nkosazane had no problem picking them up however it was their number and how often they changed from one to another she found difficult to keep up with.

Chelmsford recognised her struggle and moved extra slow in his dance, his slow pace regulated the other three couples in their square, for no man was foolish enough to go against Lord Chelmsford, even in a dance.

The Lieutenant General was notorious for his temper, a strict disciplinarian he'd seen his own men swing for looting, something many leaders might turn a blind eye to, certainly on campaign. Yet Frederic presided over men who were tried and executed for stealing from locals, both on manoeuvres and at war.

Therefore when Lord Chelmsford slowed his step so did men in his square and by extension their ladies followed, permitting Nkosazane time to catch up on steps she might have otherwise dropped.

Our native Princess recognised her lover's magnanimous attitude. The springbok appreciated how he put her before every man and woman in the room … perhaps even Sarah?

Nkosazane's eyes stole glances across the room searching out the strawberry blonde beauty, after a few seconds she caught her … glaring back at Nkosazane and her lover … Nkosazane's heart jumped before she stumbled. Chelmsford took her hand tightly preventing our Princess from tripping over.

Dancers changed direction and Chelmsford lowered his head to whisper into Nkosazane's ear, "Don't concern yourself Nkosazane, follow your partner and I will see you never fall."

Our African girl looked away from Sarah and into the smiling eyes of Lord Chelmsford, causing hers to betray emotion in the form of tiny pearls gathering at the edge of sable opals.

Sarah's visage was locked onto the pair as a hawk might follow a hare; strawberry flushed her cheeks while dancing robotically with a young officer who attempted to catch her attention.

The young man failed to distract his partner for Sarah was consumed by Lord Chelmsford and that African woman he dragged around with him, even on the dance floor!

After fifteen minutes the orchestra ceased, the Master of the House saw to it that while they prepared for the next dance as many of the young ladies present did have young men to dance with. For on these occasions young men would come alone to court a lady, while single ladies attended such events in the hopes of snagging a young man on his way up in Victorian society.

Music began as the new set started, Bartle approached Nkosazane, stood at a proper distance he bowed with hand stretched out before him, "Will you favour me with your hand for this next dance?"

She looked up at her guardian for approval; Chelmsford offered a smile and a nod. Nkosazane returned her vision to Henry, smiled and placed her gloved hand upon his, "With pleasure sir."

Henry escorted our African Princess to the floor. After Frederic's tutelage Nkosazane was fairly proficient in the quadrille.

At that moment Sarah approached Lord Chelmsford despite it being unbecoming of a lady and outside the bounds of Victorian etiquette. On such occasions she could not request a dance of him. Yet she stood before Frederic and curtsied, "Lord Chelmsford."

He bowed, "Sarah I ..."

"YES!" she grabbed his hand leading him onto the dance floor before he might finish his sentence.

Chelmsford was taken aback for he was not prepared to dance, there were plenty of young officers, single and most suitable. All eager to meet Sarah on the ballroom floor, for that evening, officers' signatures upon her program were prolific as fish at market; she possessed her pick of the piscine more so than any other lady.

However, there was but a single man Sarah was interested in, she wanted the greatest prize in the ballroom that evening, Lieutenant General Frederic Augustus Thesiger, 2nd Baron of Chelmsford.

Unfortunately for her so did every other single lady, yet Sarah was widely accepted as holding the best chance due to her outstanding beauty and her uncle's position, Henry Bartle the High Commissioner for the Cape Colony, Frederic's best friend of many years.

As the pair danced our African lady peered over Henry's shoulder and scrutinized them. Sarah stole a glimpse and returned a smug grin to Nkosazane before reasserting her attention on Lord Chelmsford, "How do you find the savage?"

"I'm sorry?" replied Frederic.

"I said how do you find the savage girl, the one you've been protecting?"

Her tone, as well as her choice of words, displeased Frederic for they both reflected Sarah's stuck up and entitled attitude. A young lady who'd experienced nothing but privilege her entire life, access to the best schooling, finest clothes and attention from every man. Then there was the advantage her looks brought, her fair complexion alone would've provided entry into high society minus the other benefits life bestowed upon her.

Of course she'd never displayed the trait of gratitude, no, she seemed to expect these things and the license they provide to run roughshod over others feelings. Frederic found it quite detestable though he took pains to never betray such emotion, for the sake of his friend, Henry.

"Nkosazane has been most pleasant company these past weeks, I was unaware how much I've missed feminine companionship," replied Frederic as they turned in a circle to the orchestra, arms joined in the centre as hands on a clock face.

Chelmsford had managed to pique Sarah's petulance. She felt as if it were a slight against her femininity, for to find any woman other than the fabulous Sarah interesting was, well, how dare a man do such a thing?

"Really? My father always thought you should purchase a pet dog to keep you company. I fear what will become of you when you have to return it to its native kennels," sniped the blonde locked girl.

"Nkosazane will not be leaving my company Sarah. I intend for her to remain at my estate for some time," replied the old lion in a cool calm growl, further irritating the young girl.

"Oh, how awful, if you're understaffed you only need speak with Uncle Henry; he has servants of fine character he might recommend."

They made a rectangle with the other dancers in their group, each man chatting with his partner, entertaining his lady with pleasant conversation as is tradition. The conversation Sarah experienced met a fork in the road only to take a terrible turn for the worse.

Frederic, unwavering on the ballroom floor as on the battlefield, watched her smug grin disappear, shooed away by fear, it gave him satisfaction. His tiny grin lay invisible beneath a thick mutton chop moustache yet it was there, "Oh no dear Sarah, I intend for her to stay on with me, as my companion."

Sarah was shocked, as were the other dancers. Upon hearing Chelmsford's statement their group of eight dancers fell silent after eavesdropping on the preposterous proclamation as it skirted the edge of decency. Dumb as a herd of mutes, if only for the purpose to clarify that their own ears weren't deceiving them, the other dancers listened with intent.

"Companion?" a weak visage, somewhere between humour and horror took a grip of Sarah, "I don't understand?"

"Feminine company so that I might have someone to talk with on dark August nights at this end of the world. Nkosazane is a fascinating young woman you know?"

"I'm sure," stated the strawberry blonde with indignation, incensed that Chelmsford, rather than chat about her, preferred to discuss that native woman. Sarah was set on preventing this savage becoming a permanent fixture, "but uncle Henry says she will have to go home once peace has been negotiated."

Frederic peered over the floor to examine Henry Bartle dancing and chatting with Nkosazane then in a sly tone the English lion growled, "We'll see about that."

Chapter Six: The Proposal

Stars shifted across night's sky while Frederic danced to the orchestra, young women all competing for the company of Lord Chelmsford, the most eligible bachelor in Cape Town and some might argue the African continent.

As to Nkosazane, she was occupied by Henry for the purposes of his niece, Sarah, a woman who took every available opportunity to snare the English Lord's attention and perhaps his heart. Yet Sarah's likelihood of success was pitiful, for the old lion's vision was clearly fixed upon his African springbok.

The orchestra stopped and his sable gazelle, somewhat out of breath, took a moment with the ladies while Chelmsford broke away and approached the Master of the House.

The Master of the House made it his business that every lady should have a dance, paying particular attention to wall flowers, yet he'd do this unperceived by the ladies, moving through guests as a panther slipping in and out of a mad mass of human beings, so as not to wound feminine self-esteem.

The springbok watched on as her domineering lion whispered in the panther's ear, background music faded as a stream, receding from full flow to a trickle before suspending as a moment in time. Guests slowly ceased their chatter, forming an ebb in conversation's progress, halting those within proximity until all attention was cast within the English General's orbit. Nkosazane looked toward her lover, proud and forthright, awaiting the crowd's attention.

When only a mumble did remain Chelmsford spoke in his deep, almost growling tone, "Ladies and Gentlemen, I'd like to make an announcement if you don't mind?" his vision shifted across the ballroom floor, fixing on our dark skinned lady poised centre and forward.

Henry's attention followed Frederic's eyes, locking onto the subject matter of his attention.

Sarah's thoughts adjourned as a distracted jury mulling over scant evidence strewn before it, she listened intently, perhaps the moment was coming? Finally the object of Sarah's desire was to proclaim his love ... and not a moment too soon! The ivory dove's heart did lift alongside her aunt's yet her uncle wasn't so optimistic, for he knew his friend and this was not common to Frederic's habit.

"As you may or may not be aware I have missed my dear departed Anna for some years now, three to be precise."

Sarah fanned herself, hot blood coursing her body as tributaries feed the Nile before its delta does flood, so much so she felt the need to cool her face lest her makeup smear. Catherine's lips widened for finally the lion was to cede. Henry permitted the slightest grimace to grace his visage.

Catherine turned to her husband offering a congratulatory grin only to be met with a cold stone edifice akin to an old fort, grey stone in the depths of a bitter Crimean winter about to take the hard furore of British cannon.

Henry was transfixed on Frederic, Catherine considered the scene for a moment only to realise the lion's intent may not align with her wishes. She glanced at Sarah, her niece was transfixed, the blonde belle's youthful expectation reflected by fellow spectators, a proposal to Sarah ... for whom other than Sarah might be the subject of Lord Chelmsford's affections?

Then out of the corner of Catherine's eye bitter darkness snatched her attention as a vile Crimean winter gaining momentum upon icy black sea, yet this menacing winter's origin was of Zululand. Our sable springbok observed the scene as her white lion prepared to make an announcement; for Nkosazane had no inkling as to the nature of Frederic's revelation. This Zulu girl was ignorant to many customs of Victorian high society and so observed with naïve curiosity.

Catherine and Henry were not so impaired and a sense of apocalyptic foreboding filled Catherine. Lord Chelmsford had ignored her niece for years, a beautiful young lady who by Victorian standards had thrown herself at him, or at least, Henry had thrown her at him.

The chances that tonight Chelmsford did plot a course for her lands quickly reduced in Catherine's mind, the sweet taste of victory transformed into unpalatably sharp defeat. Henry's wife considered the fact Frederic had been spending his time with Nkosazane, yet she was a native, a mere African, a feeble shade of European femininity, it would be preposterous for Frederic, an English Lord, to propose to a savage. Nkosazane was a delightful Zulu princess but unless the Zulu could be separated from the princess it was an outrageous suggestion ... wasn't it?

Frederic continued as party goers listened with glee, expecting a proposal to Sarah, for whom else had the General spent his time with? "Tonight I would like to take this opportunity to remedy that situation."

Murmurs of approval emanated from men in red tunics, a contented Lord Chelmsford could only be a positive and besides, after his victory against the Xhosa surely he was entitled to a little happiness?

Chelmsford dipped his hand inside his jacket pulling a small velvet octagonal box from his inner pocket, "This is it!" thought Sarah ... Henry filled with dread on a biblical scale, Jesus was punishing him for this evening's blasphemy in the most ironic and cruel fashion. Henry should've known no good could come of Darwinism! Why, the old grey bear was renouncing his former stance with the adroitness of a saint as he begged the Lord to intervene for the good of his overindulged niece.

Nkosazane had no idea as to the box's purpose or what lay within, for in Zulu culture engagements are not a custom as Europeans understand it, and so Nkosazane remained quite ignorant to the velvet package's part in tonight's function.

The room went silent as the tall General moved from orchestra to ballroom floor, where attendees observed in silence. Sarah's heart leapt in excitement as Chelmsford approached, everyone watched on, expecting him to drop to one knee before the blonde locked lady. Murmurs increased while Sarah's heart sunk in exactly the same measure when the lion strode past the ivory dove, ignoring her presence as the elephant would the ant.

Ladies and gentlemen chattered, discussing who the lucky "Lady Chelmsford" was going to be, since no unmarried woman would be so foolhardy as to refuse one of the most sought after positions in British high society.

Henry's gut wrenched harder on observing Frederic pass his niece as if she were a bowl of stale bread at the dining table, for dread lay not only in the fact he'd discounted Sarah but the possibility of an even more scandalous outcome. Bartle was hypnotised as Chelmsford reached Nkosazane and dropped to his knee, that knot in the commissioner's stomach did wring as if twenty washer women twisted his innards dry, draining his body of balance, mind of moderation and soul of serenity, blood depleted from his visage as water from a burst fish tank.

Our sable springbok was befuddled, not only with the fact Frederic dropped to one knee, for she had no idea as to the purpose of his gesture, but the sudden rise in chitter chatter accompanying it as a stiff wind filling the sails of a tea clipper. Our Zulu Princess sensed talk sailing upon a tone of shock and scandal, as a transport might be tossed about while rounding Cape Horn.

Lord Chelmsford opened his blue velvet box to reveal a gold ring, its centre stone a sapphire of 5 carats surrounded by smaller diamonds; it twinkled as a star beneath the light of chandeliers.

Henry and Catherine recognised it as the engagement ring of Frederic's now deceased wife, Anna.

Surely this was a practical joke? That thought passed through many a confused mind but not Commissioner Bartle's for he was familiar with Lord Chelmsford ... Frederic Augustus Thesiger did not jest over such matters.

"Would you, Nkosazane kaMpande, do me the honour of being my wife?" stated the British lion in a deep growl.

Our African gazelle peered into the velvet jaws of his small box eyeing its innards. An old European cut sapphire mined from Ceylon, modern day Sri Lanka, gleamed and sparkled. This small piece of jewellery caused so many gasps you'd have thought they'd never witnessed a gem in their lives, yet it was not the engagement ring but its recipient who would invoke so much scandal in the Cape Colony.

For a white man to marry an African, out here, in the Cape Colony, it was certainly not unheard of nor was it a common event. However, for a

British officer of note to marry an African woman, princess or otherwise, onlookers took rude remark.

Added to that a British General of Lord Chelmsford's stature? Perhaps he'd lost his mind? Perhaps during the recent conflict with the Xhosa Frederic had been overexposed to the African sun? Why before now men who forgot to drink regularly and wear their pith helmet did find themselves suffering a terrible delirium!

Henry considered having Lord Chelmsford committed to the local army hospital, so he might gather his wits and see sense, yet the commissioner quickly discarded his plot for there was no-one in the Cape Colony, even its high commissioner, capable of coercing Lord Chelmsford to do his bidding save our African Princess.

Henry was desperate to cut this short and he would have but for the fact they were surrounded by Chelmsford's officers, fighting men of honourable character, all prepared to sign off on his proposal.

Nkosazane, poised elegantly in her powder blue dress, scrutinised her guardian with a curious visage alongside the ornamental offering in her midst ... why did he prostrate himself in such an odd fashion?

A whisper emanated from behind accompanied by a slight nudge, "Say yes," stated an excited young lady much to the ire of Sarah.

"To what would I consent?" replied Nkosazane.

"Lord Chelmsford, he's asking you to marry him!" squeaked a young wall flower.

Before our African Princess might utter a word Sarah stormed forth as a violent hurricane does blast cold air; ruffles upon her blush dress bounced up and down in defiance, "Lord Chelmsford, this is outrageous, why, you can't marry a fuzzy wuzzy!"

From the crowd a tall man intervened to decry her statement, "I say that's a bit uncalled for!" It was Lieutenant-Colonel Evelyn Wood, Lord Chelmsford's most loyal officer, a man who'd die to preserve his General's dignity.

The commissioner quickly stepped in and took his niece by the hand, "My apologies, it's been a long night for Sarah," he turned to his niece, "come now, I'll call you a carriage."

Sarah yanked her hand back, "I'm quite well uncle, it is Lord Chelmsford who requires a physician!"

Henry called for a footman, "Please take my niece home she's become quite hysterical."

"Yes sir," stated the footman escorting a most unhappy and undignified Sarah home.

Once the squawking bird had exited the room Colonel Wood cried out, "Come on!"

Within Nkosazane's mind events reduced in pace, after analysing her lion's previous deeds she returned to Lord Chelmsford's proposal, ah, a marriage proposal?

This was most uncustomary in her part of the world for amongst the Zulu a man was required to send a letter to the bride's parents, requesting her hand, if the answer was yes then a negotiation would commence concerning her bride price.

This set of circumstances was quite foreign and since her parents were in Ulundi there would be no letter, not that her father would ever accept such a proposal.

Nor would there be a negotiation, for Frederic would offer an engagement ring, a family heirloom, once owned by his wife Anna, soon to be the possession of his new fiancé, Nkosazane; a bride price her father would've immediately rejected.

Our African springbock began to feel her body shake, perhaps it was an earthquake? Yet she alone seemed to be afflicted by this subterranean thunder, her voice restricted becoming somewhat timid in tone when she replied, "I accept?"

Chelmsford took her hand and at that point Nkosazane witnessed tremors not of earth but heart, forcing her hand to quiver like a leaf on a chestnut tree in high wind.

The British lion steadied his springbok, plucking the ring from its box he removed her silk glove and slid the engagement ring onto her ring finger.

The beautiful starburst of Indian gems twinkled as men clapped. Nkosazane inspected the ring moving it up and down her ring finger with some difficulty. Colonel Wood bellowed across the room, "BY JOVE! IT FITS!"

Chelmsford rose to his feet, grasping both her hands tightly for fear she might vanish, an apparition of African beauty sent by the spirit world to taunt his heart. Frederic kissed his bride, the orchestra began to play and merriment ensued as officers of Her Majesty's Royal Army did congratulate the pair in a large huddle.

Catherine watched on as a vulture might scrutinize a dying animal on the savannah, she moved close to her husband and remarked in a hushed tone, "Sarah will not be pleased."

Henry grimaced, "Sarah will have to like it or lump it!"

"HENRY!" Catherine elbowed the commissioner while extending her fan, denying the lady's words passage from her mouth to another's ears, "Don't be so cruel."

"Cruel? That little princess has had an easy life compared to the rest of us, her greatest labour is selecting between jam and marmalade on a morning!"

"Really Henry, I never knew you could be so heartless!"

"Oh please, spare me your righteous indignation woman. I've far greater tasks on this continent than searching out a husband for that spoilt brat!"

Catherine's eyes widened as the swirling pools of Charybdis, ready to swallow any poor sailor who might wander within her draw. Henry felt little regard for his wife's exasperation as he peered across the room to witness Lord Chelmsford standing on both feet and leading his fiancé into a dance. While the orchestra tuned instruments in anticipation of a merry waltz to honour the occasion, Commissioner Bartle realised he was between Charybdis and Scylla, an ancient Homeric tale concerning a choice, namely the lesser of two evils.

Should he sail too close to Charybdis his entire vessel would be consumed by its mighty whirlpool, too close to Scylla and the sea monster would rip men off his ship's deck consuming them whole.

I suppose if this were the Homeric epic then Catherine is in truth a poor substitute for Charybdis since punishing her husband for his cruelty was an exercise in futility.

Henry could not challenge his friend, not here, not now. The grey bear would attempt to shake some sense into Chelmsford at a later date, without causing any embarrassment. His wife had little understanding in the matters of men just as his comprehension of the affairs of women remained scarce.

The difference being that he wasn't poking his nose into feminine matters, nor did he require a woman's influence to elevate him up the ladder of high society.

Well that wasn't completely true for when Henry married Catherine he did inherit some of her father's status. Catherine's father was the Governor of Bombay at the time and Henry his private secretary, yet Henry worked diligently to progress through the ranks of State … and that he did.

Bartle considered the situation, perhaps he'd turn this to his advantage, if word were to reach Ulundi of Nkosazane's engagement it may well provoke King Cetshwayo into crossing the Buffalo River? If so, Henry would have the perfect justification to mobilise his troops and declare war on the Zulu, a swift battle, defeat the savages and consolidate KwaZulu into the British Empire.

As the orchestra tuned for a waltz Henry strolled up to the couple, bureaucrats and British officers made way as the high commissioner approached, his hand poking past a stout belly, "Congratulations to the happy couple," proclaimed Bartle, "Well this is quite a turn up for the books old chap, I remember soldiers taking Indian wives in the Punjab but an African lady? Never! I suppose that makes you a prince?"

The men laughed yet women weren't so merry, Chelmsford's happiness was of slight regard if that joy lay with a woman other than themselves. It would've been one thing had he proposed to Sarah, as expected, why, she had the General set aside as a farmer might keep back a bull for slaughter.

Yet tonight the bull was being slaughtered for the sole consumption of an African princess, it brought every woman together, against Nkosazane, for if an African beauty could waltz in and take the prize of the herd, what of them?

Married women squeezed their husband's arms a little tighter in the Cape Colony from now on. Single women wrung their hands at the very sight of a native girl, since after this ball these African beauties carried a smile when passing an Englishman in uniform. Why, it was bad enough in India, as rare as it might have been for a soldier to marry a native girl, but Africa? In Africa they believed themselves secure, each and every white bull set aside for the slaughterhouse of an English swan. These dark skinned savages weren't considered marriage material, not while perfectly attractive white women remained available.

Yet Chelmsford had fallen in love with his native ward to the point of proposal, and who was going to step between them? For with the abolition of slavery and the Church's declaration that God created all men equal, a man was free to marry into whichever race his heart did incline and Frederic's heart guided him to Africa.

Chelmsford shook Commissioner Bartle's hand and stated, "Have no fear Henry you can forgo 'Your Highness' ... for now!"

Men laughed as did Bartle for Henry observed a silver lining to this cloud, yet single ladies sensed but a dark smog of depression cast its miserable shadow over the room. This example could be detrimental to their ambitions here in the Cape Colony. There was already a shortage of dashing noblemen in the colony including young officers and if they started taking African brides, well, that would be the entire journey, from one end of the Earth to the other, wasted!

Henry took Nkosazane's hand to observe her engagement ring, a sparkling sapphire and diamond ring. Miraculously the native Princess' slender hand accommodated the band perfectly, what were the chances?

"Isn't it beautiful? I remember when Frederic had it made, that Ceylon sapphire was owned by a Maharaja, a gem of royalty young lady," stated Henry.

"What is a Maharaja?" inquired Nkosazane in a timid tone; so much attention cajoled her shyness into raising its protective shield around her.

"It's Sanskrit, it means a Great King in India. He was forced to sell it off, to fund a war he was having with a nearby Maharaja. Frederic here snapped it up and fashioned Anna's engagement ring, excuse me, your engagement ring.

You're a very fortunate young lady, there are women who came to this colony with but one aspiration … to snag themselves a British officer, old Chelmsford being the main prize," Henry grinned "then you come along and take him down, something like big game hunting wouldn't you say?"

Before Nkosazane might reply Catherine made her presence known, "Really Henry, there's no need to be so gauche! Permit the happy couple a dance."

Henry was somewhat surprised by his wife, he let Nkosazane's hand go and nodded, "Yes of course, let's have a waltz for the happy couple shall we?"

Gentlemen clapped while single ladies brightened their faces, for Chelmsford was but one of the herd, there was plenty more game on the ballroom floor tonight.

Music played as men and women danced in pairs to the waltz, Lord Chelmsford moved at a reduced pace for Nkosazane's benefit. Our sable springbok had never waltzed in her life and it took time to follow her fiancé's lead without tripping. Frederic guided her around the ballroom, chatting to his native beauty, "I'm sorry if I ambushed you tonight."

Our sable springbok smiled, still somewhat timid, "You're forgiven my Master. Tell me, will Sarah be looked after?"

"I'm sure she'll be alright, I believe she had a touch of woman's hysteria."

Every time Nkosazane referred to Chelmsford as "Master" it gave him an ego boost, lifting his spirits to a higher plain. Frederic wondered, was this a devious stratagem, a feminine tactic? If so it was working.

In fact it was a term of affection, Nkosazane's method of displaying love toward her lion, for never in her life had she submitted to a man. Rather she'd be at loggerheads butting into any man that might wish to impose dominance upon her. However, in Lord Chelmsford she discovered that which had eluded the springbok her entire life, in fact, Nkosazane had snagged THE man every woman in the Cape Colony desperately desired.

Sarah had taken quite a nasty turn, having spent years dangled as bait yet not once did the Englishman bite, it was no wonder that on sight of

Chelmsford dropping to one knee before a native girl, he'd been acquainted with for only a matter of weeks, she took a turn for the worse.

Commissioner Bartle had already recovered, even as the pair waltzed to the orchestra he watched on, plotting how he might use this unfortunate set of events to his advantage. For Bartle was here not to marry his miserable niece, no, he was here to confederate Southern Africa under the British flag and this Princess might be exactly what he required to justify a declaration of war against the Zulu.

Merriment filled the room ignited by fresh news of marriage mixing with carefree twirls of the waltz in a swirling brew stirred by Mbaba Mwana Waresa, or "Lady Rainbow" to the Zulu.

The goddess of the rainbow is especially loved by the Zulu for bringing them the gift of beer. Despite living in splendour amongst the gods, residing in a palace constructed of rainbows, she was unable to find a husband amongst them, due to their martial obsessions. So she searched the land of mortal men until discovering a cattle herder named Thandlwe.

Gentlemen lined up taking turns to partner with our dark goddess and with each waltz she picked up steps becoming accustomed to the white man's method of dance, very different from traditional Zulu dance yet no less pleasant.

For she would waltz and men would make conversation, congratulating her in person, complimenting her engagement ring. Single ladies smouldered as coals in the night, fury and envy twisted and turned as partners in a vitriolic waltz across feminine faces. These ladies attended tonight's function for the exact purpose of catching Lord Chelmsford's eye yet this native girl, bordering on six feet tall and dressed in powder blue silk, had become not only the belle of the ball but she'd taken down Chelmsford in less than a month!

Single ladies waiting on a partner did mutter amongst themselves, scrutinizing the springbok's features, they considered what Lord Chelmsford had seen in her?

The initial conclusion was that if you can't find a swan then a crow will have to suffice yet that declaration did suggest they were not swans but inferior to a crow.

119

Well, women will talk … talk mutating into gossip, gossip transformed into innuendo until before the waltz had finished rumour encompassed the ballroom. It became alleged amongst wallflowers that this African Princess was involved in the dark arts, why, how else could she have snagged a British lord? Especially over them!

Just as Nkosazane had mastered the waltz, a step, slide and step in ¾ time, the orchestra stopped for a break and to be honest our African Princess required it. For despite the waltz being of slower pace than anything Zulu girls performed, it was a marathon compared to a sprint and she was panting, ever so slightly.

Single ladies seethed, they could only pray to be so tired at a ball whereas this woman strolled in bold as brass from the plains of Africa and snatched the attention of every male. Why, even junior officers leading them in a waltz made conversation concerning their General and his African fiancé. It was quite frustrating yet a polite English lady would never permit such ill feeling to surface, that would be the height of bad manners.

Lord Chelmsford approached his fiancé as she glided daintily across the floor, she'd witnessed how other ladies moved so elegantly and did replicate their step, "You're flustered," stated her uniformed lion.

Nkosazane waited a few moments, catching her breath in a ladylike fashion, "Only you and Commissioner Bartle would dance with me yet now I'm flooded with gentlemen as a steamship before setting out on a great voyage."

A young officer approached the pair, standing at a proper distance he bowed and stated, "Excuse me my lady, but would you do me the pleasure of joining me in the next dance?"

The orchestra was tuning up and the next waltz would begin shortly, Nkosazane was exhausted, however an English lady was not to refuse a gentleman when asked to dance at a ball, it was the height of bad manners. Nkosazane was aware of this protocol and so, despite her weariness, after having danced with most of the men in the ballroom, she was about to gracefully accept until Lord Chelmsford cut in, "Look here Parsons, Nkosazane is rather fatigued would you mind if she caught her breath?"

The young officer, an artillery Captain at twenty five years of age gracefully accepted rejection. To be rejected by a young single lady would be quite the humiliation yet when it was your commanding officer, a Lieutenant-General with more silverware on his chest than Henry VIII's dining table, you take your loss as magnanimously as possible. No man was so foolish as to disagree with Lord Chelmsford's judgment.

Captain Parsons, a young officer with good prospects, looking for a lady to court, nodded to his superior, "Of course sir, my apologies." He turned to Nkosazane, bowed again, "another time my lady."

Our African Princess smiled, "It will be my pleasure Mr Parsons."

The Captain's honour somewhat rescued he smiled and walked away, searching out one of the wall flowers upon who's card he'd etched his name earlier that evening.

"It seems you're the belle of the ball," stated Lord Chelmsford monitoring the room.

"What is the belle of the ball?" inquired Nkosazane.

"I thought you spoke French?"

"I do, however I wouldn't want to be presumptuous."

"Well have a guess, what do you believe it to mean?"

Nkosazane considered for a moment and replied in a deliberate tone, "I presume it to be a marriage of French and English, the fairest of the ball?"

Lord Chelmsford gave a smile of approval, "Well done, it also implies you're the most successful lady at the ball."

"Successful? I don't understand?"

"A lady attends events such as these for the purpose of catching a gentleman's eye."

Nkosazane pulled a face of incredulity, "Catch a gentleman's eye?"

"It's a figure of speech," he looked at her unmoved visage, "a metaphor?"

Nkosazane's expression unwrinkled, ripples on her forehead returned to smooth chocolate, "I see, they are attempting to gain a gentleman's attention for the purpose of courting?"

"Exactly and the lady with greatest success in doing so is declared the belle of the ball."

The African gazelle blushed, "You flatter me, my Master."

Dance and conversation consumed the evening; some repartee was of an eloquent nature while a good chunk consisted of gossip spread amongst wall flowers. The single subject of all intercourse orbited Chelmsford's proposal, Nkosazane, and his deceased wife's engagement ring. The fact Anna's ring perfectly fit this African enchantress manufactured debate concerning fate, as if ordained by God that these two lost souls had found one another, two great lovers separated by time and distance. By the grace of the Almighty they'd come together, soon to be bound before the Lord in matrimony.

Chelmsford didn't believe in fate himself yet fate was a strong belief amongst the Zulu and as Nkosazane waltzed the evening away in the capable and protective arms of her fiancé she did sense destiny had intervened in her life, expelling chaos.

For until now she'd wandered, searching place to place for refuge only to find turmoil. The people she met along the way often held bitterness in their hearts, for they fled KwaZulu due to her father and his tyrannical rule. Ironically, her father's tyranny being the same rationale behind her flight, yet it mattered not to them, there was no sympathy to be unearthed along the banks of the Buffalo River only the rotten roots of resentment, and so she drifted as a piece of dead wood.

It was upon being released into the hands of Chelmsford her life improved, the ancestors of the Zulu did smile upon our springbok that day.

Yet Nkosazane held no grudge against her father, since to be King of the Zulu a strongman was required and if he were not a tyrant on some level his rule would be brief. Cetshwayo's brutish nature was not a fault of his own but of breeding and necessity, she still loved the old brute yet Nkosazane refused to be some fool's fourth wife.

Tonight, dancing in the arms of an English General, her life bordered on a dream, something she could only have considered in fantasy. The yearnings of a foolish young girl as her father would say ... on many an occasion.

Yet here she was, waltzing with a man who for a start was taller than her, not a simple achievement when you're a five foot eleven inch lady. Why that fool her father arranged Nkosazane to wed ... she could see the sky above his head! There are women who would've overlooked such a difference, no pun intended, but Nkosazane was a princess not some maiden that carried water in a clay pot on her head all day.

Nkosazane was also fascinated by the culture of the white man, specifically the English. She learned as much as possible while missionaries were permitted in Ulundi, absorbing knowledge as a dry sponge plunged into water.

The more this African gazelle learned the greater her fascination became and soon she discovered an interest not only in the culture but its men and tonight she danced a waltz with the most dignified, the most respected, the most accomplished white man in the Cape Colony, and perhaps Africa. He'd actually proposed to her, a Zulu woman, despite the social mores of European culture.

Not that it was illegal for white to marry black, British and French soldiers married into native populations wherever stationed in numbers for long periods. However, for a lord to marry an African woman, even a princess, it just wasn't the done thing.

Nevertheless our dark gazelle danced with a care free spring in her step, twirling in the arms of her lover. Nkosazane cared little for the thoughts of others, she grasped that which she'd pined for, and to be honest, she had that which Sarah and many young ladies sought out; having travelled thousands of miles across the equator in the hopes of snatching a gentleman for themselves.

Chelmsford had his pick of the litter, should he desire any one of the beautiful, young, single ladies inhabiting that ballroom tonight he could've taken her hand in marriage, should he so desire.

But only one woman piqued the General's interest, every other woman existed in such a fashion as to meld into one being. As many leaves forming a shrub they are indistinguishable from one another, nothing to entice the focus of his sensibilities ... until the day he met Nkosazane. Even in her traditional Zulu attire she played on his senses, luring his masculine nature to the surface, dormant for three years until this African lady ignited a passion in the lame lion. He witnessed a sable springbok on the other side of the river, her form reinvigorating his heart with the keenness of a freshly issued cavalry sabre, his body with fervour and muscles with prowess so he may skim above the depths in one mighty leap from bank to bank and take the springbok between his jaws.

Waltzing in one another's arms as if other guests didn't exist, merely a backdrop to our beautiful African enchantress, her smiling eyes enough to bring empires to war and capture his soul.

Nkosazane's vision was locked with that of her dance partner; grey blue eyes hypnotized the sable lady, a man obsessed, she appreciated an electricity between the pair. Onlookers observed with awe, for in Victorian society the gaze which cemented these lovers in soulful synchrony was almost pornographic!

As the evening wound down Nkosazane whispered into her fiancé's ear, "My legs are tired."

Chelmsford took her right hand and threaded it through his left arm, "Then it's time to leave."

She smiled and he led her over to Henry who'd been listening to his wife's lamentations all night, "Thank you for an excellent evening Henry, I and my fiancé will be retiring to our hotel," Chelmsford shook the hand of a glum Henry, next the lion turned to Catherine and gave a bow, "it has been a pleasure my lady."

Catherine was somewhat less sparky toward the evening's end, not from a pair of tiresome legs as was Nkosazane's issue but a set of fatigued lungs; for she did scorn Henry, holding him responsible for this disastrous turn of events. Henry, as all good husbands, is supposed to be clairvoyant; he should've employed that prophetic foresight and taken the African girl with him, to Cape Town.

"The pleasure has been all mine," stated Catherine as sincerely as possible, which wasn't very sincere at all, nevertheless she was polite. Catherine turned to our powder blue princess, "Please let me know when you're organising your wedding, we'll make it a day to go down in history."

Nkosazane performed a deep curtsey to which Catherine scoffed, "There's no need to curtsey anymore my dear, you're to become a baroness, you must remain upright as your title requires."

While Catherine gave our African Princess a rundown on social etiquette for an English baroness, Commissioner Bartle took his friend aside and spoke in an exasperated tone, "I say old boy, what in the blue blazes do you think you're up to?"

"I take it you're referring to my proposal?" replied the tall lion in a deep growl.

"Of course I'm referring to your bloody proposal, why didn't you inform me of your plans beforehand?"

Frederic made a curious expression, "I had no idea it was necessary."

"You know what I mean!"

"I'm afraid not."

"It's an excellent plan and all; I'd only appreciate a little notification beforehand."

Chelmsford remained befuddled as to what Henry was trying to get at, "I don't understand."

"Well, this proposal, it's all a scheme to draw out the Zulu, isn't it?"

There was silence for a moment, the sound of orchestral strings tuning up were carried upon waves of gossiping individuals discussing tonight's proceedings.

Chelmsford maintained the visage of a redcoat preparing for tribal assault, a natural severity transmitted Frederic's footing to all those who dared peer in his direction, "I'm afraid you've missed my intent, I'm going to marry Nkosazane as soon as it might be arranged, as for the Zulu, they can go hang for all I care."

Bartle was taken aback, "Really, you can't be serious? I assumed this was a plot but you really intend to marry a savage?"

Chelmsford glanced over toward Nkosazane, "Does she strike you as a savage Henry?"

The commissioner's eye coursed the young lady, dressed in powder blue linen and silk she was a Victorian lady in every sense, until you considered her dark complexion and African features, those large lips and squat nose.

To your average Englishman she was too alien to ignite desire, for they'd recently arrived from the shores of England. Although there were those from India and Egypt, men who'd served the Empire for long enough they no longer harboured an aversion toward foreign women. Many ended up marrying since the women of those regions did not strike one as so drastically alien after a while.

Sub-Saharan Africa was another matter as the features of their women were of a different grade. Also it was rather elementary to consider them savages, for when women are walking around in broad daylight with breasts on display, well, what else is a Victorian gentleman to think?

Zulu men wore less clothing in daily activity than Chelmsford wore to bed! It was difficult for a civilised white man to open his mind and consider the possibility that these people weren't mentally deficient, a supposition that would be the undoing of both Chelmsford and Bartle.

But for now Bartle maintained his air of superiority, justified or not, she may be dressed in the cloth of civilization yet Nkosazane's features did betray savage threads running so deep that if removed her entire tapestry would become undone, "Frederic, if this were anyone else I'd have him committed."

Chelmsford replied in his signature growl, "Men married locals in the Punjab; you brought no protest toward those unions."

"Those men weren't ranking officers; they were the dregs of British society."

Chelmsford took offence to his words, "The dregs? Those men put their lives between you and certain death. I'll have you know they deserve better."

"In the name of Christ won't you reconsider this proposal? If it lures the Zulu out I can call it all off."

Once again Chelmsford was taken aback, the insinuation that he'd act in so cowardly a manner or that his friend believed him so craven, angered our lord, "Listen here Henry ..."

Before Frederic might finish the angry lion felt a set of soft hands touch his arm, he looked over to witness his springbok's dark brown eyes. Nkosazane observed their heated discussion and decided to rescue Lord

Chelmsford from himself, "Master? I'm feeling most weary, might we retire?"

Nkosazane monitored his visage, anger melted away, lifting her heart while transforming his mien to a smile, for she sensed his love, their souls touching one another when close. As two electric probes, when charged, current does leap through atmosphere intoxicating one another. Her femininity and his masculinity, positive and negative, their souls a flux so bright every man and woman in the ballroom did witness its passion, as two great lovers separated by history and distance, were by the grace of God brought together on the Southern Cape of Africa.

Separated by race, culture and language, no two could be more different on the face of the Earth, yet commonality existed. Nkosazane for reasons unknown to her was stimulated by Frederic, his masculinity superseded that of any man she'd encountered in the past, even her father. Added to that he was tall, a requirement to be met before she'd even register a man's existence.

His dominant personality did ignite femininity in her soul, strong and confident enough that he disciplined her rebellious nature, a fascinatingly erotic sensation. The masculine lion dominating a feminine springbok, he was the only man capable of controlling her because she took joy in his discipline.

As for Chelmsford, Nkosazane was the first woman since Anna's death he was capable of making love to. Other women, for whatever reason, failed to pique his curiosity. Somehow Nkosazane manipulated her lion's heart at will, not that he was averse to her behaviour for unlike other women she wasn't interested in Chelmsford's wealth or titles, they held little meaning to a girl who'd grown up in Ulundi.

On leaving the ballroom Nkosazane witnessed a congratulatory multitude consisting of Chelmsford's officers. The remainder of the guests, civil servants, bankers and merchants were somewhat sheepish in the face of her fiancé. For he did radiate an aura of confidence intimidating your average man so much so he might seek solace in a corner, rather than stand before one of the greatest warriors to step foot on African soil.

Nkosazane considered that he and Shaka Zulu might be equals, two men at the head of mighty armies, fighting the odds to consolidate a region wrought with rebellion and bloodshed.

A footman opened a door exiting the ballroom, while another brought Nkosazane's coat. The fellow held her garment and our gazelle slipped inside. Chelmsford led his beau outside their feet moving from clean, well lit marble to dank and dirty stone, a carriage drawn by two horses pulled up, a footman hanging on the outside dropped down and opened the door for our African lady.

Chelmsford held onto her hand and with a slight push assisted her ascent. Nkosazane relaxed on leather interior while her fiancé called for the coachman to make haste.

The English lion's hand grasped his springbok's as their carriage bounced up and down, on its way to their hotel. Nkosazane observed her engagement ring; she couldn't tear her attention away from its twinkle.

In such a short space of time her dreams had manifested to fruition. Her lion peered over and in the privacy of their carriage, engaging his lips with those of Nkosazane, those unique pieces of art did raise his spirit as if he were a great white whale and she his air. He had little option but to surface, drawing her spirit, the spirit of life, raising him from the pitiful depths he'd wallowed these past three years. Now, thanks to Nkosazane this old beast was reinvigorated, much to the chagrin of Sarah and her aunt.

As for Nkosazane, she'd been transformed into a new woman, from an African princess to an English baroness. Her father would be livid, even worse her intended husband in Ulundi would be ranting and raving. Dabulamanzi required Nkosazane's hand to secure the throne, or at least that was his scheme. Our sable springbok released a smug grin at the thought of him going absolutely bananas on receiving news his intended wife was engaged to a white man, a Lieutenant General no less.

Chelmsford noticed her grin, "Did you enjoy yourself tonight?"

"Yes," stated our African beauty, "I was considering what my family might say on hearing news of our engagement."

"How do you think they'll take it?"

"Not well."

"And that's amusing?"

"Both Dabulamanzi and my father shall be furious."

Chelmsford betrayed a tone of concern in his voice, "Are they likely to do anything about it?"

Nkosazane smiled comforting her fiancé with softness in her speech, "I doubt that very much, my father will not cross the Buffalo River under any circumstances."

"Even for his daughter?"

"Even for his daughter, we have nothing to fear from him."

Their carriage moved off into the night, transporting our loving soul mates to their hotel for the evening.

Chapter Seven: Sarah's Revenge

It was a fine day in Port Elizabeth, during spells such as these Frederic took his beau for walks in a local park, arm in arm they'd feed the ducks or venture a stroll around Fort Frederick, named after the Duke of York. That is, Prince Frederick, the second son of George III.

There were many pleasant beaches and a local catholic church Nkosazane visited on Sundays, reacquainting herself with missionaries formerly expelled by her father. All together our young African Princess found life rather agreeable yet there was one person dead set on bringing her new world down.

On a warm Cape Town night in a local public house, a grizzly figure huddled around a tankard of ale. Music played, bringing life to low hanging dense smoke inhibiting the senses of common men. A blonde haired fellow nursed his drink while drawing on a pipe. His boots were smeared in a streaky henna hue mimicking his shag stained teeth. Attired in grimy trousers, thick coat; his shirt, yellowed with age and dirt did resemble post mortem chicken flesh. He was none other than Bastijn Klein Soepenberg, a forty three year old slave trader previously convicted (thanks to the testimony of Colonel Wood) and fined for acts of slavery.

Down on luck and short on coin, his outline indistinguishable by reason of murky tobacco broth hanging about his frame as sulphur cloud might obfuscate the Devil.

He'd decided to meet with a business prospect, there was little to lose at this point. Soepenberg had invested a fair amount in rounding up those slaves, hiring men, purchasing supplies and pack animals, only to be thwarted by the British.

Then after his arrest Soepenberg was made to choose between two ominous options, Charybdis and Scylla ... pay a princely sum or wallow in a dank British prison ... leaving him but a destitute demon.

The pub door opened, a lady entered dressed in hat and cloak, chatter died down as did a slightly mistuned violin, she was too refined to frequent this dingy establishment.

A young woman dressed in chocolate brown, so as to blend in with the crowd, scanned many tables until her eyes met with those of a sinister outline, obscured by dim light. Whisps ascended from pipe and cheap cigar as trunks of trees, forming a smoky jungle canopy. She glided towards Soepenberg; it was obvious to patrons that this young lady was of a better sort.

Upon arriving at her destination music surged, taking her by surprise as a rebellious wave might break the shore and splash bathers. Men chuckled beneath corrupted breath before returning to discuss whatever foulness engaged their putrid minds that evening.

The lady lifted her veil and peered down through her nose at the Afrikaner. She spoke in an accent as carefully cultivated as an English rose, "Mr Soepenberg I presume?"

"Aye, that's me," he held out his hand to which Sarah's lips scrunched up like a piece of paper, prior to being dispensed into a waste basket.

His hand was dirty, filthy in fact, reflecting his line of work. Sarah wasn't about to touch this vile character. She considered her gloves too refined to make contact with his spoilt skin, "Good evening Mr Soepenberg," Sarah took a seat opposite the slaver.

"Would you like a drink?" asked her Afrikaner opposite, much to Sarah's horror.

"Certainly not Mr Soepenberg, I'm here to discuss business not soak myself amongst sots. Now, I hear you're somewhat bereft of finances, am I correct?"

"Aye, you could say that," he took a swig of ale before puffing on his pipe.

"I take it you're aware of Lord Chelmsford's intent to marry the savage?"

Soepenberg chewed the stem of his pipe, "Aye, I heard."

"Well, her father is offering a bounty upon her return, one hundred sovereigns."

Soepenberg made a grumpy noise, "Humph, what good's that to me? She's under Chelmsford's protection; I'd be skinned alive before snatching her."

Sarah grinned, "Lord Chelmsford will be inspecting the barracks next week, he is to run his men through efficiency drills. The savage will be alone."

"She's never alone, there's always someone watching her."

Sarah took a breath through her nose as her lips expanded into a smile, "So you've been observing them?"

"Aye and there's no way to get me hands on her."

Sarah leaned forward, "On a Sunday morning, after church, she likes to take a stroll on this beach here ... alone."

Sarah placed a folded map on the table; Soepenberg opened it and noted an area pencilled out with a time and date attached. He closed the parchment and looked over at Sarah, "What do you want?"

"If you're successful Mr Soepenberg I shall obtain that which I came for ... to be rid of that damn savage forever!"

The dusty Dutchman shook his head, "Hell hath no fury like a woman scorned, aye?"

Sarah became somewhat upset, "Mr Soepenberg, do you want the map or not?" she moved as to retrieve her plans yet the Afrikaner drew her parchment closer to his chest as a man reeling in a fish.

"I'm going to need funds."

"What on earth for Mr Soepenberg?"

"I'll need horses and a carriage, I mean, I can't take the train to Ulundi!"

Sarah huffed and reached inside her purse producing a small bag of coin, "Here take this Mr Soepenberg, only make certain you fulfil your task or I'll be after you too!"

She placed a small leather purse on the table, the auburn Afrikaner took it, a cursory glance informed him sufficient coin dwelled within to subsidize his villainy. Pulling its drawstrings he smiled at the young lady, "You think of everything don't you?"

"You have five days Mr Soepenberg. I suggest you board the first available train to Port Elizabeth."

The petit purse and accompanying parchment were carefully placed inside his grimy coat, "Aye, if it's possible I'll get her back to KwaZulu, but you better make sure Chelmsford doesn't find out about our business arrangement."

"How will he? You shall be living in the Transvaal with one hundred sovereigns and I shall be accepting Lord Chelmsford's proposal."

Soepenberg laughed, "Hah, hah, hah, you've got some imagination there girl."

"Imagination?"

"Aye, you think he's gonna forget about his Zulu that quick?"

"Why of course," Sarah's forehead folded to form the Egyptian hieroglyph denoting water, at the same time her voice exuded an incredulous tone, "why wouldn't he?"

Soepenberg laughed again, "Hah, hah, hah, listen girl, I've seen men get attached to these Zulu women before, they reckon it's some kind of spell, you know from the umthakathi."

"I'm sorry, what's an umthakathi?"

"A witch doctor, they get a piece of hair or something from their target and the witch doctor casts a love spell."

"Really Mr Soepenberg, surely you don't believe in such poppycock?"

"Then how do you explain Chelmsford's proposal? Are you saying it's true love?"

Sarah considered her options, he was right, it was either true love or a witch doctor's spell, a separate rationale failed to make its presence clear. After a few moments of deep thought Sarah pulled herself from deliberation and back to the villain before her, "Love or not it is no concern of yours Mr Soepenberg, you shall be reimbursed nevertheless, do we understand one another?"

The demonic Dutchman grinned, "Aye, this time next week I'll have her in Ulundi and you'll have Lord Chelmsford pining for his Zulu girl."

Sarah stood up and fixed her veil so it once again dangled before her face, "Lord Chelmsford shall be my concern Mr Soepenberg. Good day to you and I genuinely petition our paths never cross again," the young lady hovered out of the drinking establishment with a smile on her face, having set the wheels in motion of Nkosazane's downfall and presumably her return to Lord Chelmsford's good graces.

That Sunday, after church service, Nkosazane strolled along her favourite stretch of beach while Atam, sitting atop a horse and carriage, watched from afar.

As our African Princess finished her daily constitutional of sea air and exercise she returned to the carriage but before she might step inside another chaise and four appeared from the corner of her eye as a crash of rhino charging from the forest to crush all that lay in its path. Dragged furiously by four stallions the carriage closed distance in seconds, granting Nkosazane no time to take action.

A scruffily dressed African youth grasped the reins, barely maintaining control of its beasts, seemingly on loan from the Devil's own stable.

Before she or Atam might speak a word to one another the carriage came to a halt, four satanic steeds neighed tossing their heads wildly. Two burly Xhosa tribesmen appeared from inside brandishing shotguns, their stench enough to subdue any civilized human being. Then a familiar face, the blonde haired brute materialized from within, a spectre from her past. Nkosazane was sure she'd seen the last of this demon some months ago but nay, he was back with a vengeance and brandishing the most offensive blunderbuss in the colony.

A vile villain, foul in dress, demeanour and bouquet. A sniff of his aroma and our sable springbok recalled the toad plant, native to her homeland. It disseminates the scent of rotting flesh from its large star shaped flowers, one of God's largest blooms. Its flower growing to more than a foot in diameter and coloured in a tobacco stain yellow, it was no wonder the thought appeared in her mind. The rotten villain pounced directly toward Nkosazane as his fellow beasts held Atam at gunpoint.

"What is the meaning of this?" demanded Nkosazane as Soepenberg grabbed our lady's arm.

"You're coming with me Princess," he tugged on her Sunday church clothes, a simple silver bodice tailored to fit her frame with a lace blouse peaking from beneath its collar and cuffs while displaying intricate patterns, her skirt a faded brown.

"I am certainly not!" rebutted our Princess.

Soepenberg let go and slapped her face with the back of his hand, Nkosazane recoiled at the crack, her silver bonnet flying onto the pavement. The loathsome Afrikaner reaffirmed his grip. Tugging our young lady he dragged her to his carriage, for the evil of gold coin had endowed this mortal man with the will of a hellion, "Now get in and shut up!"

He bundled the poor girl inside as his accomplices maintained their attention on Atam, their wide gaze primed with a charge of violence, ready to fire the ammunition of certain death as they slowly retreated to their carriage.

Soepenberg and Nkosazane sat inside along with one of the Xhosa tribesmen. Her captors' overpowering odour, as immoral as it was nauseating, assaulted Nkosazane's senses. Two tribesmen were perched atop, one grasped the reins while his partner in crime rode shotgun. Soepenberg tapped his trumpeted barrel on the ceiling, beneath the driver's seat.

The youth thrashed his whip wildly, horses jeered and the carriage moved swiftly as the blow of a demonic axe, bound for Ulundi. It would take a night's rest before reaching their destination.

By the time Chelmsford was informed it was too late to change the course of this devilish river, his fiancé was long gone.

Chelmsford came as quickly as possible yet all he could do was clutch her bonnet and stare stoically out to sea … its breeze passed over him, long grass twisted to gusts and so Chelmsford bent to the forces of evil that'd kidnapped his twin flame, his soul mate. Frederic could still smell her hair, a sublime coconut scent which followed his Zulu woman wherever she travelled. The more her perfume filled his nostrils the greater his rage grew until eventually all men cowered at the beast love had created, a beast that refused obstruction whether by bloodshed or by battle.

It was a Monday morning when Soepenberg's carriage arrived at the gates of Ulundi, the seat of Zulu power. Impi warriors guarded every entrance of the city. On recognising Xhosa tribesmen their carriage was brought to an immediate halt, for Xhosa are long-time rivals of the Zulu. After all, show me a European nation that has not squared off with its neighbour, exactly, it is the rule of nations to clash with those adjacent.

Refused entry due to their tribal origin, a voice emanated from within the carriage, "Lapha!"

An impi drew closer, armed with iklwa, a short stabbing spear, and ishilangu, a large cowhide shield. The warrior wore a kilt of genet tails and an isicoco, a head ring denoting his marital status.

Peering within the warrior immediately recognised the King's daughter; he'd been on hand at many royal celebrations of which Nkosazane attended.

The city guard stepped down and waved the carriage on. His commander had been kicking up a stink night and day ever since our Princess fled KwaZulu.

The carriage trundled through dirt streets, an impi hanging to its side directing the Xhosa youth toward the royal palace, past many communal indus huts, all skilfully constructed in the form of a large mud and straw dome.

A European might consider this form of building to be somewhat barbaric yet for this climate it was quite excellent. Zululand could be hot and unforgiving country and these huts did offer welcome relief. When the rains came they would absorb its downfall, if they were washed away new domes were quickly constructed.

The carriage pulled to a halt before a gateway, the impi hanging on its side spoke to guards, naturally one of the guards checked its contents, he peered within then stated, "Nginike izikhali zakho."

The Xhosa froze waiting on Soepenberg. Nkosazane stated, "He wants your weapons."

"I know that!" snapped Soepenberg while considering his options.

"Well?" responded Nkosazane, "What are you going to do?"

Soepenberg turned to Nkosazane and sneered while raising his hand as if to strike, that is, until the impi howled brandishing his short spear in reply, "MISA!"

He wasn't going to allow this man to strike the Princess Royal, not on his watch.

Soepenberg lowered his hand, a defiant Nkosazane refused to flinch; her rebellious nature had re-emerged as the Inkanyamba that lives in a lake near Pietermaritzburg. This beast has the head of a zebra and appears amidst rains, a terrifying creature known as far back as man painted on cave walls.

On entering the gates of Ulundi the Inkanyamba within her soul would rather take a blow than shrink in fear of a man's hand.

As her Inkanyamba appeared Soepenberg's Devil did shrink, surrendering his blunderbuss, his Xhosa henchmen did likewise before their carriage was permitted access into the palace courtyard.

A hustle and bustle arose as game might stampede upon the plains, kicking up a cloud of dust in the distance. On entering the royal kraal word of Nkosazane's return had reached court before the carriage pulled up.

Outside her mother and father waited in disbelief, for they were certain their only daughter was lost forever.

The impi swung open a carriage door and from it emerged a Xhosa, Soepenberg and then, to royal gasps, our African Princess materialized, her silver Victorian bodice gleamed beneath African sun. Women of the court began to gossip much to the ire of King Cetshwayo kaMpande.

The King, a fifty two year old tribal chief dressed in leopard skin kilt and throw stood six and a half feet tall. His large protruding belly formed an imposing figure to all those who fell within its proximity, "Nkosazane, welcome home."

Behind him her Zulu husband to be, the second in command of her father's army, Dabulamanzi kaMpande, dressed in cheetah kilt, his body toned and ready for battle, anxious to take possession of his bride.

"Is this how the Zulu welcome their own? By stealing a woman from her husband?" stated our dark skinned springbok so that all gathered, courtiers and servants alike, might listen in.

Chitter chatter broke out amongst those present, much to the disdain of her father, for King Cetshwayo did despise court gossip, "Your husband is HERE waiting for you, my springbok."

Dabulamanzi stepped out from the King's shadow and into light so all could witness his fine masculine frame. Dabulamanzi's visage was one of extreme displeasure, his attitude impassable as the Drakensburg Mountain range, for this woman had humiliated him before the entire tribe.

Nkosazane sneered in a most un-lady like fashion, no doubt a reply to his miserable face, "This … man … is NOT my husband! My husband is waiting for me in Port Elizabeth," she held her left hand up so all present might examine diamond and sapphire twinkle in the sun, "and he will come for me!"

King Cetshwayo stepped forward his bare feet forging a path through dusty courtyard, he grasped his daughter's left hand and examined the engagement ring.

Now, in Zulu culture an engagement is initiated by sending a letter to the young lady's father, an engagement ring was a totally foreign object.

"What is the purpose of this ornament?" stated the King while scanning a beautiful Indian sapphire surrounded by diamonds set in 18 karat rose gold.

"It is my engagement ring," replied Nkosazane proudly.

The King peered at Soepenberg, the appalling abductor grinned like a devil while igniting a pipe of fresh African shag, the slave trader turned bounty hunter answered the King's inquisitive mien, "Aye, she's engaged to an Englishman!"

Gasps rang out as Dabulamanzi marched forth, unable to contain his anger. He grabbed her wrist and yanked the ring off her finger. Our African Princess did protest but to no avail, this impi commander was uncontrollable in his rage. The evil we call jealousy, conceived as the rejection of a man by a beautiful woman, growing into humiliation, found vent in Dabulamanzi, his eyes fixed on Nkosazane's engagement ring. Had her father not been present this raging bull would surely have beaten our sable springbok into submission.

After scrutinizing the springbok's sparkling band he handed it to Soepenberg, "Here, return this, tell him Nkosazane rests with her rightful owner!" and with that he placed the ring in the abductor's palm.

For a moment Soepenberg considered keeping it but that was far too dangerous, were Chelmsford to discover such a deception he'd see him swing. No, he was going to get one hundred sovereigns in exchange for returning our Princess and he wanted to be alive to spend it.

Of course the Zulu had no idea they were playing with fire, any other man and they might have got away with it but when at odds with Lord Chelmsford, commander of all British forces in the Cape Colony, this was likely to end poorly for them.

Nkosazane flashed her eyes at Soepenberg, "You tell him where I am and I'll put in a good word for you … when your time comes Mr Soepenberg."

The demonic Dutchman glanced between her and the engagement ring, that devilish grin disappeared from his mien for he'd planned to disappear into the Transvaal, but now the slaver was wedged between a rock and a hard place, Charybdis and Scylla … a raging Zulu bull and a ferocious British lion.

Chelmsford, a man of honour, was undoubtedly going to use his position to take his fiancé back, by force if necessary, and Bartle would certainly support that. Not that Soepenberg cared, however, if he was left holding this ring when the dust settled then he'd be next on the lion's menu, and he didn't like the thought of that.

A hesitant Afrikaner stretched his hand out offering the ring back to Dabulamanzi, "You keep it, I'm sure it's worth a pretty penny."

The impi commander, fiancé in hand, sneered at the slave trader, "I am not a thief …"

"Yet you'll steal another man's bride!" cried Nkosazane.

The impi commander's fury was drawn to a greater stratum of existence, as a ferocious flock of vultures rising on thermals of vehemence to nest in the dark forests of Table Mountain. He'd suffered enough due to this rebellious woman and he wasn't going to tolerate it anymore. Dabulamanzi raised his hand to strike our African Princess, as his hand came down Cetshwayo thrust his swagger stick between his daughter's face and would be son in law's hand, "ENOUGH!"

Dabulamanzi retracted his fist yet his fury remained.

"Do as you wish with her when you're married, not before," stated the King as he turned his attention to Soepenberg, "and you; return this ornament to its owner, the Zulu do not steal from others."

Soepenberg placed the ring inside his grimy coat as he followed the King and his entourage into the palace, his Xhosa henchmen remained outside under the close scrutiny of impi guards.

Inside the main kraal it was cool and the ground moist yet hard, made from cow dung and ant heap soil. Traditionally Zulu homes look like beehives and though seemingly primitive from outside they in fact require great skill to construct.

They walked inside a large assembly chamber; a throne inhabited one end allowing the Zulu King to hold audience and banquets, serving similar functions to that of a Viking long house yet circular in construction. Soepenberg gazed upwards to witness intricate ribbing of wood and rope with straw thatch. The Dutchman was somewhat in awe that a building this size built of mud brick, wood and rope, managed to hang together. Yet it remained steadfast serving King Cetshwayo as his main audience chamber.

The giant hippo sat on his throne, his treasurer appeared from an adjoining chamber to the rear, clutching a small leather purse. He spoke again in Zulu and the fellow approached Soepenberg, "Ngicela uvule isandla sakho," he said politely.

Soepenberg understood well enough to open his hand, he'd traded with tribes in this region for many years, being a white man granted him a form of neutrality, permitting him license to conduct his sordid vocation.

The white rat accepted his blood money, "You won't mind if I count it?"

King Cetshwayo's face cracked disdain, despite conducting commerce with Soepenberg in the past he despised this man, "Leave this place Soepenberg, your presence is no longer required nor desired!"

The white rat wasn't going to argue with the Zulu King for he'd received his thirty pieces of silver and the King hadn't short changed him in past transactions, he was a man of honour.

Soepenberg climbed up onto the driver's seat alongside one of his Xhosa henchmen, placed his bounty inside his coat and cracked the whip.

Nkosazane watched on as her last hope of escaping this nightmare trotted through the kraal's main gates, leaving her to suffer in purgatory for a rebellious character.

The palace was a large circular enclosure, two mud brick walls curved into a large gate with circular dome huts of mud rope and straw in between, some for storing palace food others for King Cetshwayo's wives and separate huts for sons and retainers.

It was a large complex with a massive central courtyard and dominating palatial structure. At every entrance, where brick wall broke permitting men and cattle passage, stood tall pillars of stone with massive elephant tusks jutting out at right angles in all directions.

Women could be seen going about their duties often engaged in beadwork, something the Zulu tribe is noted for to this day. Zulu women amongst the most beautiful and hardest working in Africa, a fact advertised in their handicraft.

Many European traders visited this area. After examining these kraals, constructed with mud brick, stones, wood, elephant grass, water proof thatched roof, thick hinged doors ... it often astonished those civilised men that these sturdy constructions could be put together by Zulu women.

On initial observation it doesn't seem possible that a woman would be capable of such advanced architecture, but it's just one of many capabilities at a Zulu woman's disposal, from beadwork to architecture these beauties are the supporting pillar of the Zulu tribe, permitting its men to go forth and conquer every other tribe in the region.

In fact they can be compared to Norse women, remaining home, maintaining structures, herding livestock, weaving clothes, doing every job expected of a man and a woman while their husbands fight to the death in glorious battles at the edge of the known world.

The most beautiful, capable and intelligent women in Africa, it was no wonder Zulu men fought so hard to protect this valuable resource and Chelmsford had fallen in love with one such beauty, a sparkling Zulu diamond amongst a heap of English coals.

King Cetshwayo waved his swagger stick in the air, "Bring her!"

The direct royal family, its servants and impi commanders moved inside leaving the rest of court to retreat to their business and gossip on today's events.

One man watched the whole incident from the shadows, indistinct, the reflection of a horror in a terrifying nightmare.

During this tempestuous vision we call nightmare, a man's attention is drawn to the horror itself not its dark brother, who observes the captive man's terror with glee.

Shifting through a small side entrance the shadow followed the royal party inside. His appearance was starkly different, a horrifying old face painted sheet white, a dreadful visage whether its onlooker be man or woman, African, European or Asian.

He wore a shabby headdress of animal feathers, his upper body covered by a hair shirt with horse hair plumes at the elbows and wrists, a skirt reached to his knees, covering the lower body and made of what looked like brown sack.

He walked bare foot, in one hand he brandished a tall stick with what seemed to be a large honeycomb carved in its top. In his other hand he carried a witch doctor's wand, constructed from a foot long lion's mane, bound with leather at one end to serve as its handle.

The old man seemed to be in his 70's, though no-one in the tribe knew his true age for he'd always been there, older than the oldest member of the tribe, so much so their parents had not known a time when the African sun rose without Xhegu to meet its dawn, added to that no-one had witnessed what lay behind his chalked complexion.

This magic man stalked the party through shadows as an ethereal demon, mirroring the royal family from afar, now orbiting Nkosazane. They chided our springbok not only for her rebellious behaviour but also her locks of chemically straightened hair.

"Look at you!" snapped Cetshwayo, "You are Zulu, not umlungu! Get out of those ridiculous clothes and cut that hair!"

Our springbok matched his veracity of tone, "I will not!"

"You have not lost your rebellious ways but I swear, after taste of much correction, you shall change your mind child!" roared the hippo.

The Queen, King Cetshwayo's first wife and Nkosazane's mother touched her husband with affection, "My love, she is young and foolish but she should not be punished too harshly, not with her wedding close at hand."

Upon meeting the soft tone of his wife, the King's anger subsided. Royal beadwork covered her regal frame in many fantastic colours, something traders as far as Japan and England exchanged for silver.

"She will not taste correction from my hand but her husband's … once she is married. The sooner this wedding takes place the better. This troublesome child has cost me enough in sleepless nights and gold coin," grumbled the Zulu King

Cetshwayo was a man in his early fifties, tall, dressed in leopard skins, a fearsome individual yet at the same time a skilful negotiator, a requirement if he were to be a successful ruler. His daughter, unfortunately for him, was cut from a similar cloth, skilful, cunning, tall and almost impossible to control or at least force into a course of action opposing her will.

The only man with the ability to exert his will on our beautiful springbok was her English lion in Port Elizabeth. For he was the only man to whom she found submission not only agreeable but desirable, other men she did oppose with every ounce of Zulu spirit in her body.

"My husband will come for me and he will punish you and your thugs, before you bribe this worthless woman beater with my flesh!" snapped our rebellious springbok.

The old man with white face waved his wand, "The dark springbok must return to the white lion."

The court fell silent as they turned to observe the horror behind them. Dabulamanzi grimaced at the old aberration and in a moment of madness he lashed out at the demonic hallucination, "Someone silence this crazy old fool! Before I do it myself!"

No-one replied, for Xhegu, seemingly odd, at least to a European, was King Cetshwayo's magic man, something like a sorcerer, healer and a spiritual protector all rolled into one. It's not easy to define to those unfamiliar with the Zulu culture; nevertheless, despite Dabulamanzi's words Xhegu was a respected nay feared man in the court of King Cetshwayo.

Xhegu was also the King's most trusted advisor for over the years Cetshwayo had profited thanks to the old man's counsel, the King wouldn't dismiss Xhegu's words quickly.

"Speak your mind," stated the King.

"The sable springbok and the white lion must be together," he stated with an omnipresence as appalling as it was fearful. A mysterious tone Xhegu often employed which caused men and women to strain in order they capture his abominable words.

Like a sailor exerting his senses to detect the rumblings of a distant storm, he desires only to divine its terrible nature in order he might gain intelligence enough he avoid the tempest.

"And if they are not?" demanded the King.

"Then the white ox shall fall."

There were concerned mumbles, for the Zulu are a symbolic people as much as any inhabiting God's earth and the white ox held particular significance. In Zulu culture a man's material wealth was defined by cattle held in his kraal, a corral would be its closest relative in Anglo culture.

If a white calf was born that calf was given to the King, also, the colour white was the colour of the ancestors. To a Zulu, Xhegu's meaning was quite clear.

The white lion defined Chelmsford as the leader of the British for the lion is their symbolic creature. A white ox is not just the creature of the Zulu King but it also represents their ancestors, their history, all that would be brought down.

The springbok represents a joy that cannot be found through material wealth. To every member of the court the meaning was as definitive as it was hard for Cetshwayo swallow.

Nkosazane smiled for she'd gained an advocate in the royal court, she looked at her father, her silver bodice standing out amongst men in leopard furs and women in beads.

"That is unacceptable!" barked Cetshwayo.

Dabulamanzi sighed with satisfaction yet others remained ill at ease for this old man had been proven right more than once in the past.

"Perhaps," rasped a bent old man, one hand on walking stick the other waving his lion's mane wand, "yet it is, for the buffalo shall bleed this year until the princely cockerel is killed, then thunder and lightning, from clouds of chalk, shall rock Ulundi until the lion and springbok are joined."

The impi commander became irate once more, raging at the old man he stood directly before him and bellowed, "Speak once more old fool and I shall see you never speak again!"

Xhegu snapped at Dabulamanzi, "You doubt my magic?"

The court fell silent, even the King had no desire to confront his magic man ... in fact he was curious to see what might become of this confrontation. For the hippo was more diplomat than warrior and if Xhegu were to, let's say, dispose of Dabulamanzi, he'd have one less problem to deal with.

Dabulamanzi bellowed in the old man's white face using his size and power to intimidate, not that it worked, "When was the last time your magic won the Zulu a battle?"

Xhegu's eyes widened, his lion's mane wand raised, the old man's black eyes glimmered as horrifying reflections in the darkness, he chanted unfamiliar words, immediately Dabulamanzi clutched his chest, a pain lashed his innards as if an electric charge struck his heart, it ripped apart the impi commander's body as cracked earth is split by shifting tectonic plates.

Dabulamanzi, holding his chest, began to groan in pain, something stabbed his heart, crippling his body, and there was nothing to be done. An English doctor would have diagnosed a stroke.

The impi crumpled to the floor as an abandoned hut in furious rains, Cetshwayo quietly observed from his throne. Nkosazane looked down upon her African suitor wondering if the old witch doctor was about to decide her husband. Dabulamanzi croaked in pain grabbing desperately at dirt, in the hope something or someone might rescue him from the magic man's spell.

Then, as if it were nothing, the white faced Xhegu waved his wand above the impi commander's head releasing the fellow from his terrible fate.

Court members were confused as Dabulamanzi gasped for air, still clutching his chest, spit dribbled from his lips forming a muddy pool in the dirt; for they did not understand why the old man had released him from the jaws of death.

Nkosazane was quite aware, if Dabulamanzi doubted the sorcerer's magic he did not now. Brought to the edge of the abyss and forced to stare fate in its eye, exchanging looks with death's dark reflection, he'd not abuse the witch doctor again, not if the impi warrior had any sense. As Caligula once said, "who cares if they hate us, as long as they fear us."

Unfortunately for Nkosazane her Zulu fiancé was spared, clamouring to his feet as a concussed boxer he retreated to his African Princess, leaving intimidation and acrimony in a damp patch on the floor.

Xhegu turned to the King, "Heed my words King for the white lion and the sable springbok will be together."

Dabulamanzi remained silent, nursing his throat, everyone's eyes turned to King Cetshwayo; what was he to do? If he permitted his daughter to return to Chelmsford it would be seen as weakness and surely a challenge for his crown would ensue, possibly civil war. Yet were he to keep her, according to his magic man the British might invade … well might … for Xhegu spoke in riddles, and men often decipher prophetic mystery to suit their own purpose.

However the future does not change to suit a man's desires, in fact it is the opposite. Cetshwayo sensed his own abyss, destiny pulled him in two separate directions, if he gave way to the wrong one he would surely be torn to pieces, Charybdis and Scylla beckoned his vessel to pass their straights. The easy way out at that moment was to keep his impi commander happy since the alternative had more than one translation, and of course he sided with political expediency in the moment, rather than a more cautious approach for the long term.

Nkosazane would remain with her people and marry Dabulamanzi; it was the least troublesome path out of this quagmire. Cetshwayo had been in similar situations in the past but never against an enemy as brutal as the British Empire, this time his tribe and his leadership would be tested to the full.

Xhegu witnessed fear on his King's gruesome visage, "You must make a sacrifice to the ancestors if the Zulu are to survive."

"Enough!" barked the stout King, "this discussion is over, my daughter shall remain with her people and marry Dabulamanzi."

"I WILL NOT!" announced Nkosazane at the top of her lungs, antagonising a clearly irritated father.

Cetshwayo was furious, he'd had enough, "Child, you shall do as your father declares or suffer much correction."

It made little difference to our dark skinned springbok for her heart was set on her white lion in Port Elizabeth. She knew he was coming to rescue her, love and honour demanded no less, of this Nkosazane was aware long before the witch doctor's revelations.

"And for the love of the ancestors get her out of those clothes, she looks ridiculous!" roared the mighty hippo.

The Queen, standing by her King all this time walked over and placed her hands on Nkosazane's arm, fixed her gaze upon Dabulamanzi and stated, "You may release my daughter."

The bull permitted Queen kaMpande to take possession of his bride to be, the Queen turned to her King, "May we be excused?"

A gruesome warrior King snorted beneath his hippo breath, "Very well."

And so the party did exit the great hall from a side door into a hallway, circumnavigating the circular edge of this massive royal kraal until they reached the women's royal huts.

Once inside and having shut the door the Queen placed her hands upon her hips, "My, my! What in the name of the ancestors do we have here?"

Queen kaMpande observed the silver garment, a fine silk and whalebone bodice meeting lace dress over silk petticoats, purchased from the finest tailor in Port Elizabeth. His goods imported from all corners of the British Empire, whale bone hunted in the Atlantic, lace spun in Nottingham, England, silk purchased from Japan, she was every bit an English lady.

Queen kaMpande called outside the hut and young girls dressed in multi-coloured beads shuffled inside, closing the door behind them.

Upon noting Nkosazane's dress the girls giggled, they'd not witnessed such a sight in all their lives. These colours were unfamiliar to Zulu garb, then its fabrics, they weren't worn by Zulu either. These girls had heard of such strange apparel but never had they thought to witness garb so alien to their senses. Finally Nkosazane's hair, at first they believed it to be a wig; they'd heard tales of white women who balanced hair on their heads. However, on discovering Nkosazane's hair was straightened word got around that the umlungu had used his magic, transforming her African bush into the flowing locks of a white woman.

The giggling continued until Queen kaMpande grew weary, a crushing glare from the Queen and the girls quickly silenced themselves.

"I want my daughter dressed as a Zulu woman ought to be," stated the tall and proper Queen her height similar to her daughter, her stubborn nature equally familiar.

The women were mother and daughter in action as well as look and so Nkosazane believed she might find an ally, "Mother," our springbok dropped to one knee, imploring the Zulu Queen, "I appeal to your kinder nature, my father is stubborn, will you beseech him? Will you beg him for mercy?"

Queen kaMpande crossed her arms as servants stood by her side awaiting the Queen's word, "Mercy? You are to marry one of the bravest warriors in all KwaZulu and you beg for mercy? Child, you have your priorities confounded!"

Our sable springbok clutched her mother's knees, "To be his fourth wife?"

Queen kaMpande sighed, "Come now child it is our custom, there is no shame in becoming his fourth wife."

"That is easy for you to say," stated our African Princess shivering in fear, "you are the first wife, tell me mother, what is to become of me?"

This was true, for once wed to Dabulamanzi she would have to share her husband with three other wives, no doubt jealous of their younger, taller, fairer counterpart.

"I cannot help it, it is the way of things, besides, would you rather be the slave of a white man?" huffed Queen kaMpande.

"I am not his slave mother, I am his betrothed and I will be his only wife not his fourth or fifth or sixth or …"

Queen kaMpande cut her daughter's plea short by taking Nkosazane's forearms and pulling her onto her feet, "I will speak with your father not that I can promise you anything but I shall do my best, is that satisfactory?"

Nkosazane broke into tears as she hugged her mother; the Queen was a woman who understood the trials and tribulations of the Zulu woman. As Norse women had a hard life so did Zulu women, their hardship unmatched on the Cape of Africa. Zulu men met battle with greater ferocity than any other tribe and so their women laboured under a greater burden.

A Zulu woman, by the time she was married, was not only skilled in beadwork and house duties but could build a dwelling, known as an indus. European settlers sometimes refer to them as beehives since they resemble such constructions.

The male carried out the skilled architecture but a woman would execute all of its thatching and weaving. The kraal, where cattle were kept, would be somewhere around the centre of the homestead, and since Zulu had a somewhat nomadic life a Zulu woman would be expected to work hard.

It was not an easy existence being the wife of a Zulu man, added to that if he had enough cattle he might marry another wife. Women accepted their lot, besides, another pair of hands on the kraal was always welcome, but many were against such circumstances since women are naturally protective creatures, of their children first then their husbands.

The hardships of Zulu women were not unfamiliar to Queen kaMpande and so she'd do her best to satisfy her daughter and her husband, for a Zulu woman's life is one of duty to her husband and children dispersed only by back breaking work.

The Queen did envy her daughter and the English women of the Cape Colony, in so much as they'd never be forced to share their husband with another wife, a luxury Zulu women could not afford in today's society.

149

It did annoy many wives that once their husband had proposed and paid the lobola with so many head of cattle she would join him on his kraal and engage in gruelling work.

The arduous labour itself was not cause enough for a Zulu woman to complain, but the fact she was helping her husband rebuild his herd so he may meet the lobola of a second wife was often cause for resentment.

It felt unfair to its core; therefore Nkosazane had an ally in every married woman in KwaZulu; for they felt the pain of a system seemingly designed by men for the pleasure of men. It was they who were forced to participate and support it with their labour yet they'd never complain, a Zulu woman was not a quarrelsome woman, not if she desired marriage which I suppose is the catch.

Nkosazane had seemingly escaped the monotony of a circular existence, designed by Zulu men, and it intrigued them all. Besides, why shouldn't a Zulu woman be permitted a husband of her own?

That is why couples fled KwaZulu to KwaNatal, living a life of monogamous love, in banishment on the Buffalo River. Nkosazane fled there to escape marriage and in doing so stumbled into love. She'd always held an attraction toward the white man close to her heart yet opportunity was never present, not in the confines of Ulundi. The only white men she was familiar with were missionaries with whom she spent every available hour, learning European language and protocol. She might have been at an academy for girls in England for her education was on a par with some of the best boarding schools for girls of wealthy families. Sending daughters to academies in order they be thoroughly schooled on how to impress an English gentleman and hook him for marriage, the objective of all young ladies during these times.

Oddly enough it was not Nkosazane's objective, yet in doing so she'd caught the eye of the most eligible bachelor in the entire Cape Colony. A shockingly pleasant turn of events for our young African Princess; she'd nabbed an English gentleman of the highest social status, a man who possessed more than a single estate, one in England the other in Port Elizabeth. The former worked for him providing surplus income, not that he spent much, the latter being his residence in South Africa.

Then there was the issue of Sarah Hart, Commissioner Bartle's niece, for she'd pursued Lord Chelmsford since the day his wife died. It seemed to Nkosazane that Frederic's wife was barely cold in the ground before Sarah launched her first assault, similar to the siege of Sevastopol. A fruitless endeavour Frederic had described in detail one warm evening, charge after charge to break the Russians, the allied defeat at Balaclava, the Russian defeat at Inkerman, the final assault, the defeat at the Great Redan, the French victory at Malakoff Redoubt.

A victory for the bachelor, defeat for the pretty young thing assaulting his lines, Sarah had been held at a frustrating stand still for years.

Sarah perused this gentleman from India to the Cape of Africa to no avail and then, before her eyes, some African girl materialized from nowhere, at a ball held by her father; a ball which, as far as Sarah was concerned, served but one purpose, not to celebrate victory over the Xhosa or the absorption of KwaNatal into the British Empire, but for the function of Sarah snagging an English gentleman, THE English gentleman; Lord Chelmsford, a man no different than an over-ripe piece of fruit prime for the plucking, a fat hen ready to feed the farmer's family.

Nkosazane's victory left Sarah somewhat afflicted, a doctor diagnosed her with hysteria, a condition thought to only affect the female of the species, since at that time it was believed to originate solely from the vagina. However, on discovering Nkosazane had been kidnapped and returned to Zululand, she would quickly recover from her feminine ordeal.

Chapter Eight: Isandlwana

It was early morning in Africa, Cimmerian sun rose above Zulu dusk, a hot country, a hard country, a country of warrior men and winsome women.

Nkosazane clad in her protective bodice remained a quintessentially defiant Victorian lady. Servants flanked either side of her crossed arms, our springbok's rebellious attitude displayed as a Napoleonic battlefield banner before all but Lord Chelmsford. Nkosazane permitted the young girls to undress her, for fear they might damage her garments. Since the sable springbok intended on wearing them in the future, for she could sense her lion's approach.

It was ironic that she submitted quietly when in his presence, as a fawn to its mother on the plains of Africa, for he was just the sort of authority figure she'd been in conflict with all her life. Yet Frederic's presence did not repel Nkosazane, perhaps he truly was a lion? A real man? No, that couldn't be it, for her intended Zulu husband was certainly a man, he'd tasted battle, felling warriors as an elephant would trees in a mighty stampede, Dabulamanzi's masculinity could not be questioned.

So what set Lord Chelmsford apart from Dabulamanzi? Was it their features? The separation of white and black which altered the attitude of our pugnacious Princess?

No, for Chelmsford was not the only white man in Port Elizabeth, or Cape Town for that matter. On her journeys back and forth she'd noted men of equal charm. Prince Napoleon for one, a dashing man of twenty three years of age, wealthy, cultured, everything a woman might desire yet there was a difference between the pair.

Lord Chelmsford and Nkosazane had a connection, a spark of love, something that cannot be explained without celestial reference. His wealth, success, superior stature and proud features culminated in a flicker of passion as whale oil doth feed a lamp's flame. The purity of said oil betrayed via its flame's hue, the whiter its burn the purer their love and so it burns with increased intensity.

It was more than a simple earth bound matter, for her love of Chelmsford could not be defined by a commodity or facial feature. He was not only a lion he was her lion, her king and hers alone, other men were superfluous, a shadow of masculinity with whom she'd bicker rather than submit.

Today was to be a special day in Ulundi, for all but Nkosazane, the traditional ceremony of wedding a daughter was to begin at a somewhat heightened pace with several shortcuts to be taken.

In the traditional Zulu wedding there are many steps. Requesting the parents' permission being first; this had already been achieved, Dabulamanzi receiving King Cetshwayo's blessing long ago. Next came lobola negotiations where parents, usually the bride's family, would negotiate her bride price in head of cattle.

Now some important factors had been skipped, a Zulu woman has the right to select her husband, usually informing her aunts on both matriarchal and patriarchal sides of the family, known to the Zulu as "malume" and "babakazi".

Yet despite being amongst the highest and most privileged in Zulu society, Nkosazane was not afforded one of the most rudimentary female rights, to select her husband. Rather, her father, the six foot six tyrant of Zululand stripped her of that most basic privilege in an attempt to shore up his grip on power. A practice common amongst European nobility was not absent in KwaZulu.

Lobola negotiations were a mere formality yet Nkosazane received a bride price worthy of a queen, it excited every woman in court, giggling and fussing over the fifty head of cattle paid for but a single woman. Nkosazane remained uninterested in Dabulamanzi's generous offer since she wouldn't have willingly considered him for such a position.

Now the bride's family isn't a silent partner in this investment called marriage, for there are gifts offered to the groom's family, this is known as "umbondo" and can take the form of livestock or jewellery.

After all of this has taken place the bride makes two necklaces, one for her and one for the groom, announcing to the village that they're a couple. Once this has been done, in tradition, the older women of the village will permit her a few nights alone with her fiancé.

Another step skipped, for Nkosazane refused to make those necklaces. Her mother had a pair strung together, much like the unhappy couple, yet Nkosazane refused to wear hers despite the fact Dabulamanzi wore his.

This brought open humiliation upon the impi commander, he'd paid a kingly sum for his bride yet she refused to acknowledge him as her fiancé. Nkosazane raised a bonfire of exasperation in Dabulamanzi's heart; his passion became acrimony, a rankling rhino ready to charge the first human foolish enough to provoke his patience.

The final ritual is when the bride's family prepare goat meat for the bride and burn incense otherwise known as "impepho", for the purpose of informing their ancestors of the impending wedding and the fact that the bride will soon become part of the groom's ancestors.

This step could not be skipped, for the Zulu are a spiritual people who worship their ancestors and without the ancestors' blessing, a marriage was certain to fail.

Nevertheless this was being done as quickly as one might imagine, while incense burnt creating a natural earthy scent that filled the hut Nkosazane glared at a plate of goat meat, refusing even a morsel. In fact she hadn't eaten since returning to Ulundi three days ago.

Her lightly tanned lace dress, purchased in Port Elizabeth by her white fiancé, was removed along with its blouse and silver bodice, and replace by traditional Zulu wedding garb.

An "isiwaba", a leather or animal skin skirt covered her lower half, with an "isicwaya", a similar skin covering her breasts; then there was the "inkehli", a large head band. All of this was brightly decorated with beads in typical Zulu fashion. The bride's face is also obscured with a traditional beaded veil called an "isicholo".

Next, family sat around decorating Nkosazane's arms and legs with red paint, outside music could be heard in celebration of a wedding ... for Dabulamanzi ... for Nkosazane ... an execution.

Pieces of oxtail were tied to Nkosazane's knees and elbows as she gazed at her goat meat, completely disinterested in the hullabaloo while her mother directed family members who painted the bride as an ornament. Nkosazane felt akin to a lamb being prepared for slaughter.

A piece of goat hair was tied around her neck, it could have been a noose, it might as well of been, for she felt as if she were a condemned woman looking through iron bars from a cold damp cell, observing her fate as tribesmen construct gallows for the purpose of stretching her neck until she were dead. Nkosazane's punishment for being born the daughter of a Zulu king, every other amenity the Zulu tribe could provide was afforded her, good food, good living, the best education, the finest clothes, servants to wait on her every desire, yet freedom and choice eluded her.

For as a sable springbok she wished to roam free, leaping here, bounding there, twisting and turning in the air, both body and spirit unchained entities, this was her nature yet she'd been incarcerated, trapped inside a pen named tradition.

Our sable springbok wished for nothing more than to leap across the savannah for all to see, rendezvousing with her white lion, before both creatures pair bond for life on the plains of Africa. For a short time she'd possessed everything she'd ever desired, the amenities of being a Zulu princess and the benefits of an English lady, it was heaven.

Yet all was lost, captured by a vile hunter and dragged back to Ulundi, Nkosazane was to be traded in for the benefit of her father, handed over to a vile animal of which the very thought repulsed her.

Inside the house incense smouldered and women scurried around Nkosazane, preparing her for the greatest wedding in many years. King Cetshwayo entered the premises via a thick wooden door. As it opened light flooded inside, the massive six foot six frame of the Zulu leader, a man with no equal in size or power not just in Zululand but the entire continent of Africa, cast a long shadow within. Every woman inside dropped to one knee as he entered, save Nkosazane, she sat defiant, throwing a rebellious frown in his direction.

The old hippo passed the threshold, now don't misunderstand me, to those who do not live on the Dark Continent a hippo seems to be a somewhat passive creature, happy to wallow in waters all day, something children might pat and feed.

Well there's a reason they don't pat and feed hippos at the zoo, for every man and woman in Africa, be they white or black, understands the hippo is one of the most dangerous beasts inhabiting the dark kingdom.

The hippopotamus is a 2-3 ton, heavily armoured, killing machine. He appears passive and friendly in water but should he sense danger his instinct is to attack. The hippo can charge at a great pace, a terrifying sight and only the most experienced hunters dare antagonise one.

The rhino and the bull elephant are lords of the animal world yet when the hippo displays the slightest disdain they flee. The lion, king of the jungle, overlord to every other creature on the planet will give this swamp dwelling tank a wide berth. For at the moment he senses a hippo's irritation the lion breaks for his life.

To the westerner this seems to be a preposterous notion, at least, to the westerner living outside of Africa, in Africa everything fears and respects the hippo.

Cetshwayo, royal staff in hand, a smooth piece of hard wood hooked at one end, approached his seated daughter. The portly king instructed his subjects to carry on and so servant girls resumed their bustle around Princess Nkosazane.

The Queen greeted her husband with a wide smile, Cetshwayo replied in kind before casting his vision upon his seated daughter. Her ridiculous white woman's attire had been stored away, unbecoming of a Zulu woman in his opinion. Today his daughter presented herself as a proper Zulu woman should before her wedding, how his daughter ought to be, it brought a smile to the old hippo's face.

Our sable springbok scowled and without flinching or even breaking eye contact she flung her veil aside and spat at the hippo's feet ... silence and tension dispelled all other elements from an earthy atmosphere, servant girls froze in whatever task they'd been working.

The Queen, shock filling her face as water might swell the banks of the Buffalo River, snapped at her daughter, "Nkosazane! Beg your father for forgiveness!"

The King towered above his wife, not a short woman herself, it was obvious Nkosazane's genetics were the pick of Africa. He placed his hand upon her shoulder, this time Cetshwayo quelled her heart, "No my Queen, I shall permit this child her last temper tantrum for before the day is out she will be another man's headache."

Nkosazane's visage maintained the most disrespectfully pained expression anyone in this room had ever witnessed. That is, save King Cetshwayo for he'd scrutinized the rebellion of his daughter many times in the past.

"I am thankful," spat Nkosazane in a tone both angered and sardonic, "thankful that the glorious Zulu King, the greatest African glutton," serving girls drew a collective breath, the King steadied his wife while all listened to a royal pre-marital rant, "the most accomplished of the continent in cowardice," another collective breath and the hippo's eyes did open as portholes on a large ocean going steamship, "the fattest fool ever produced by the Zulu people!"

Cetshwayo broke, face afire with anger, his daughter masterful at invoking the Zulu King's temper. The mighty King removed his hand from his wife's shoulder and drew back his royal staff as one might swing a golf club. Yet before splitting his daughter's head open on her wedding day Queen kaMpande clutched his staff with both hands, "NOO!"

Cetshwayo halted in mid swing, Nkosazane glared upwards in utter defiance; she permitted not a single wince to betray her beautiful visage. Rather Nkosazane grinned, raising the giant hippo's fury as a wreck from the seabed.

Our sable springbok mocked the giant hippo, "You are so incompetent you cannot even hit a seated woman with a staff! When my true husband comes for me he will burn Ulundi to the ground! All Zulu will suffer for your pride and foolishness!"

Cetshwayo gathered his faculties after a momentary lapse, had anyone in his kingdom other than Nkosazane addressed him in this manner they'd have met swift correction in the form of execution. But his defiant daughter always managed to get away with it, she was too valuable a commodity to destroy just because she offended his eye or blasphemed his ear, "May the ancestors give me strength enough to end this day without bloodshed, for by sunrise this wayward child with the mouth of a whore shall be in another man's hands, and by the ancestors, I have given him my blessing to see she have the taste of much correction to whatever degree he does deem fit!"

"I will not marry Dabulamanzi, I would rather die than be his harlot!" shouted our sable springbok, while all watched in wonder at this royal rumble.

Her statement brought a combination of smile and smirk to the hippo's mien. Nkosazane was taken aback for she recognised every expression that might ascend from her father's soul to surface upon his visage. As wreckage might surface from the bottom of a tranquil ocean displaying testament to the disaster of those foolhardy enough to navigate Cetshwayo's rocks of fury; some hulks were more or less frightening than others yet this oceanic derelict was the most worrisome, for this shipwreck did display victory and satisfaction.

Cetshwayo called to men waiting outside, sure enough three men in animal skins, over six feet and built as great warships, entered the room. These fellows were in their twenties and served as impi, the elite fighting force of the African sub-continent, put together by the mighty Shaka Zulu, a man without match before or since. The impi kept every other tribe in line whether by fear or violence, those who did not fear the impi soon had a change of heart after enduring battle against these young Zulu warriors.

Impi warriors were raised on a Zulu diet packed with fresh meat and regular exercise. Practicing daily battle drills they demonstrated the peak of human physical perfection; added to that they were loyal to a fault, following the word of King Cetshwayo as if it emanated directly from the ancestors themselves.

Two men carried chains, manacles, their purpose blatantly obvious for even if an Englishman without schooling in Zulu language and custom were present he could still fathom the depths of these actions. Preparations for an important ceremony were underway, no doubt a wedding. The lady being prepared was uncooperative and she'd just had a blazing row with this large gentleman, the purpose of young men and manacles was probably to facilitate her compliance.

Cetshwayo bellowed an order; two men with bodies reflecting Greek statues moved in and pulled our African Princess to her feet clamping a set of iron braces on Nkosazane, binding the sable springbok's wrists with great clinking noises. A second set rigidly clamped her ankles in place with thick ferrous chain linking wrists and ankles, restricting the springbok's movement. Finally a rusty brace snapped ominously to encompass her neck, attaching, by thick linked chain, Nkosazane's throat to the shackles binding her wrists.

Queen kaMpande was horrified at the sight, "By the ancestors! What is this?"

Cetshwayo smirked in deep satisfaction yet his daughter remained defiant. The King stepped forward and grasped Nkosazane's chin, the old man revelled in mirth, "I have been a slave to your foul temper and rebellion for years. I have suffered your foolish wants and demands because you are my daughter and I your father, but it ends here. Today you are little more than cattle, a lame ox I will drag to market and give away to the first fool that desires your hide. Fortunately, for both of us, there is such a fool and you should be grateful to that man for if he did not desire your worthless husk I would have it flayed off here and now!"

Queen kaMpande's hands shook in fear for her daughter. Her quivering hand touched her husband's thick shoulder and she whispered in supplication, "My King, please show your daughter mercy, she is young and foolish."

The King's mien displayed discontent at his wife's petition. The towering warrior King bellowed, "You have been her advocate for more than twenty years, yet due to her defiance and degrading desires I am constantly made into the subject of lewd gossip across the whole of KwaZulu and beyond. No, today I will treat her with no greater dignity than she deserves, no matter whose daughter she may be," at that the mighty King, in one move, released his grasp upon her chin and with the same hand delivered a powerful slap to his daughter's cheek, the force of which caused Nkosazane's entire head to turn.

Every woman gasped yet the impi stood expressionless; these men though in their twenties had seen blood and gore fighting on the plains of Africa. They'd disembowelled warriors, screaming in pain for their mothers, young Zulu gods ripping grown men apart with their iklwa.

"Today it is I," stated the hippo in a relaxed mood, "who shall be free, free of what your beloved white man would call the whore of Babylon, yes?"

King Cetshwayo spoke in a mocking tone, humiliating his daughter in front of serving women, impi and his wife. Nkosazane returned her head to its former position her cheek glowing red from the hippo's mighty strike, a blow fuelled by years of pent up frustration. Yet Cetshwayo was unable to dislodge her rebellious visage for she held her father in an iron gaze and stated in the English language, "Evil shall come upon thee, thou shalt not know from whence it riseth; and mischief shall fall upon thee, and thou shalt not be able to put it off; and desolation shall come upon thee suddenly, which thou shalt not know!"

Cetshwayo's face screwed up as torrents of water spiralling down a drain; next the hippo heard an old man's voice. He turned slowly to witness his witch doctor crouched in the doorway with bent back and feathered headdress casting shadows on the floor, face chalk white, brandishing his wand, "Isaiah, Chapter 47, Verse 11!"

The King was further confounded, the witch doctor and his daughter seemed to communicate in a foreign tongue, "Who do you speak of?"

"The ancestors of the white man are powerful, they watch over this one," the witch doctor pointed his wand at Nkosazane, "our ancestors implore you, return this one to the ancestors of the white man, before the buffalo bleeds, before the princely cockerel dies, before the Zulu are crushed like flies!"

"GET THIS OLD FOOL OUT OF MY SIGHT!" roared the mighty King.

Impi peered with apprehension at their King then his magic man, they were loyal to their ruler yet his magic man could cast a curse, not just on them, but on their entire family for generations, they'd seen it done in the past to great effect.

The impi didn't move an inch but stood in fear, for the King may execute them for disobedience yet his magic man could curse an entire lineage.

Xhegu laughed, his terrifyingly white face mocked the most hardened men in Africa, for they feared him before a bloat of hippos. The umthakathi locked eyes with Nkosazane, "I have spoken with the ancestors, you shall be returned to the white lion be it today or at the cost of much blood tomorrow, I have but a single request of you Nkosazane."

"What might that be?" inquired a curious Princess.

"When the white lion is in Ulundi cool his rage … for the benefit of the Zulu … not their foolish leaders."

Nkosazane nodded her head, "I will old man."

Cetshwayo roared in frustration, "LEAVE US!"

Xhegu nodded his head and exited the establishment under his own volition … no-one was prepared to manhandle the old priest not if they knew what was good for them. Xhegu had ancestors looking out for him and every man in his path did stumble and come crashing down to a miserable end.

Queen kaMpande stroked her husband's mighty chest, his rage unabated, "Let us move outside and allow the breeze to cool your pride my King."

The King of Southern Africa took a deep breath, on collecting himself he looked her in the eye and smiled a little, "You are wise, it is time I retire lest this child become the end of me."

The King made a final glance toward his impi, "Keep her in chains," before turning his back on the room and exiting.

The young men remained while servant girls stood motionless, aghast at what'd transpired before their eyes. Queen kaMpande clicked her fingers, "Back to work girls."

Servant girls gathered themselves, recollecting the task at hand before this kerfuffle had broken in like a wild beast invading a kraal.

Impi guards remained, dark sentinels flanking Nkosazane who returned to a seated position amid the echo of clinking iron.

Her mother was most displeased with Nkosazane's behaviour; she pointed toward our sable springbok and sliced earthy atmosphere with an accusing tone, "What do you think you were doing? Antagonising your father? He has enough to deal with without you fomenting his anger … and making plans with that old witch doctor? Why I've never seen such a thing!"

"What does my father have to worry about?" replied our Princess, "He is King, he does as he pleases."

The Queen scoffed at such a naïve notion, only one so young could concoct so idealised a vision of kingship, "What between Zulu traitors plotting to steal his crown and the British poised to plunder his lands, your father can hardly sleep some nights."

Our sable springbok rejected her mother's sermon, "Pah! His lands?" she remarked in an accusing tone, "These lands belong to the Zulu people not some greedy tyrant who confines his own daughter to shackles, beneath a Xhosa slave, and uses her as a bargaining chip with one of his impi."

This assessment could not be denied. The Queen looked down upon her seated daughter; heavy iron shackles bound Nkosazane's wrists and ankles close together, locked into a burdensome neck brace. Our springbok resembled a common slave for transport to the new world, a princess and a prisoner amongst her own people, yet amongst the British she was free. Ironic that the white man provided her independence enough to be the woman she desired whereas her own people enslaved her.

There are many parts to a Zulu wedding ceremony, most of which were neglected out of convenience for this was not a regular wedding. In Nkosazane's opinion it was closer to a ritual sacrifice.

The assagai knife was strapped to the bride and turned upwards, to indicate she was still a virgin, something of questionable nature yet no-one seemed to be concerned.

Nkosazane sat silently on a mat outside in the kraal, as is the custom. The groom's father made a rather hurried speech welcoming her to the family, it was indicative of all tradition observed on that day.

Nkosazane's bridesmaids gave presents to the groom's family, the groom being the last to receive a gift, the women first.

Usually each person would demonstrate their appreciation for their gift by lying down upon a mat then getting up and singing and dancing. This occurred at extra fast speed, so quick it did raise a few eyebrows amongst wedding guests who felt akin to witnesses in a court of law, rather than guests at a marriage ceremony.

Once the husband-to-be receives his present it is time for the bride to make a bed. A path of mats, which the groom uses for the purpose of navigation, is constructed leading to the bed. On reaching safe harbour he sits upon the bed and his bride pretends to wash his feet as he lies upon the bed.

Suffice to say this didn't happen in the traditional manner, the would-be husband did his part yet a rebellious bride refused to act out hers, so the groom's sisters quickly constructed the bed. He lay upon it while the sable springbok glared at her husband-to-be.

Next occurs the strangest part of a Zulu wedding ceremony, a group of women from the bride's family come in with sticks and begin to strike the groom to which he runs away.

Next is an event called the ukulayla in which the bride and groom are advised on the importance of family, following which a large party called a la mntambama takes place.

The next morning the bride and her maids of honour clean her new home, a breakfast is prepared and the bride is officially umalokazana, that is, daughter-in-law.

Well it got as far as the party; everyone was having a grand old time, aside from Nkosazane, when a young impi in animal skins minus heavy weaponry was let through the gates, breathless from much exertion. Dabulamanzi immediately recognised this soldier as a runner.

The fellow shot up to King Cetshwayo and dropped to one knee before taking a minute to gather his breath.

"Why do you disturb my peace?" inquired the King.

The young man gasped for breath, "The Buffalo …. The Buffalo River!"

"What of the Buffalo River that causes interruption at my daughter's wedding?"

"The Buffalo my King, it bleeds!"

King Cetshwayo felt a pair of eyes on him, gleaming with a sinister life bestowed by the devil himself. Crouching at the gateway to his palace was Xhegu grinning with a terrible vitality, the ancestors of the Zulu and the white man both lending him dread to pierce Cetshwayo's soul.

"What nonsense is this, a river cannot bleed!" bellowed the King.

"It bleeds scarlet my King, with the coats of British warriors," yelped the young man.

"Then why didn't you say you fool!" roared the mighty hippo in rebuke. Cetshwayo cast his gaze on Ntshingwayo kaMahole, a man seated at the wedding close to the father of the bride. A warrior in his sixties he was the officer in command of the impi, "Ntshingwayo, assemble the impi, I want that umlungu's head!"

The old fellow, dressed in leopard skins of the impi rose from his seat, "I will return with his head my King," he locked eyes with the groom, "Dabulamanzi, assemble your men, we make for Isandlwana before dusk."

It was mid-day and Isandlwana was 66 miles from Ulundi yet the impi were not just the premier fighting force in Africa due to achievements on the battlefield; one of the key factors to impi success was mobility. The impi moved quickly on foot and unlike the British they required few supplies, free to travel the plains unburdened by a heavy baggage train.

Dabulamanzi rose to instruct impi officers present at his wedding, all men ascended in concert as bees from long grass when disturbed by a snake. Impi were disciplined and prepared to meet the British in battle for they carried another trait, fearlessness.

Before leaving the kraal Dabulamanzi locked eyes with his silent bride, her self-censorship another form of defiance, "I will return for you!"

At that the highest ranking impi disappeared out of the kraal, past Xhegu. Dabulamanzi offered the old witch doctor a disparaging grimace; the magic man returned it to sender with a mocking smirk.

Previously only Nkosazane was miserable but now the entire party was thoroughly depressed. Xhegu approached Cetshwayo much to the hippo's disdain, "So it begins, the herd is set in motion, the buffalo bleeds, the cockerel is killed, the lion shall have his revenge on the thekwane," a bird of Zulu folklore which represents the common folk, "the hippo must return the springbok to her rightful owner before disaster and destiny collide afflicting all as a great plague."

The magic man dressed in feathers waved his lion's mane wand as if decorating a wall with white wash, having splashed the stuff all over his face.

The wedding party chattered beneath their breath, murmurs passed along the table like a fever, quickly infecting servants who waited on men and women populating the floor.

Cetshwayo took umbrage to such activity; such gossip was dangerous should its reach exceed its origin. The King had to consider his position and what affect anything slightly political might have upon it.

Should the King's people become unsettled it would be his task to settle them or suffer the consequences further down the line, "Why do you bring discord to my kingdom old man?"

Xhegu's dark eyes, surrounded by white chalky paint narrowed, "I speak for the ancestors yet you discard their advice as a child would a banana skin."

"Then tell me something worth listening to and I shall heed it!" barked the King, working himself up into one of his notorious rages ... the only people to have survived such a passionate onslaught being Xhegu, Nkosazane and her mother.

Xhegu's vision locked onto the King, he spoke in a low tone, one of irritation at the hippo's ignorance. Murmuring ceased so everyone might listen to his words with clarity, the only other sound audible was that of impi assembling outside the kraal, "Be careful my King for the sweetest fig is often full of worms."

The great hippo rebuked Xhegu's sage counsel quickly, "Riddles again! What is this for advice?"

The sable springbok, silent all day, as is Zulu tradition, spoke, "He means to say that those who are fond of only positive advice will more often than not taste the negative side."

Cetshwayo stomped his mighty foot sending vibrations through the wooden platform that his and his Queen's thrones rested upon, the noise sent a jolt through party members, save Nkosazane and Xhegu, "Why do these pair blight my life? I can see you two would be suited to one another since you are always in agreement on anything which might undermine my throne!

Tell me, why do the ancestors only speak of doom? Never have they informed me of a bountiful harvest, only drought. Never have they informed me of peace but every time they speak of war. Never do they come to aid but only to caution, why is this so?"

Xhegu spoke in a raspy tone while waving his lion's mane, the magic man's eyes rolled into the back of his skull for a few moments before reappearing. It seemed as if his eyeballs had done an entire rotation inside his skull, disappearing up into his forehead before reappearing from within his chalky white cheeks, this ghastly sight invoked screams of terror amongst members of the wedding party, "The ancestors ask; would you rather know of bountiful harvest or drought?"

Nkosazane scoffed at her father and his temper, it'd dragged him into making another foolish statement that with a cooler head he'd never have considered. For a man can prepare for either one, for the bountiful harvest he can build extra storage for grain, if not he must sell it yet he will still benefit from that occurrence whether the ancestors had informed him or not. A drought however, if preparations aren't made, a man will starve or be forced to sell the contents of his kraal so his family may survive. If prepared he will purchase grain to build up a nest egg so his family may eat, dig extra wells or construct a dam so they may drink. He will plant drought tolerant crops and invest in livestock able to eat drought damaged plants, "Pah, you would have your people starve while waiting on good news from the ancestors?"

Again, Cetshwayo's hand began to shake as it clutched his staff, his Queen steadied his forearm, in fear he might unleash further punishment upon his daughter.

Xhegu approached the furious hippo, "Send your daughter with the impi, it is possible you may cool the lion's heart and avert war."

"What do the ancestors say about the upcoming battle?" demanded the King after recovering from his tirade.

"They say the horns of the bull shall wound the lion at Isandlwana. The lion shall retreat into his cave and the bloodthirsty will be in ascendant on the plains of Africa for a single harvest," replied Xhegu much to the delight of Cetshwayo.

"Excellent! Finally the ancestors have some good news!" revelled a jubilant King, his mood shifting from murderous to joyous in a moment.

"Heed your daughter's words my King, that fig may taste sweet but there will be a bitterness you must contend with," rasped the magic man.

"I have a little joy enter my life and sure enough you begrudge it. I am certain you only smile upon darkness, for when the day does dawn in all her splendour you possess a barren heart, filled with spite and hatred for all that is handsome, for all that fills the world with warmth.

You are the desolate, the sterile, the drought that does chase away humidity bringing fruit to the land and smiles to the faces of children. I will show my people that I do not kneel to stories designed to frighten fools and old women. I am King of the Zulu, they kneel before ME, they do MY bidding!"

Unlike the wedding crowd the old witch doctor was not concerned by the King's tirade, Xhegu smiled through his white mask, "So be it … KING! You shall turn your warriors into dust, your women into whores and your children into slaves for generations to come, thanks to your pride."

Cetshwayo was tired of being furious today, he'd reached his limit before someone would have to pay with blood, and deep down, despite his bold façade, he feared the magic man, "Get him out of my sight before I am forced to shed blood on my daughter's wedding day!" roared the mighty hippo.

As usual no-one would move to evict the witch doctor for he controlled the boundary between life and death and if it so pleased him he might send you and your family over it, into the place even kings fail to return from.

Xhegu's old eyes scanned the wedding party, their stillness brought a grin to his face, he chuckled, turned around and exited the kraal under his own volition.

Nkosazane peered up at her father and in a rebellious tone stated, "The Zulu may kneel to you yet they kowtow to their ancestors."

The hippo frowned upon our sable springbok, "I care not provided they fear their King."

Nkosazane replied, "Surely it is better to be loved by your people than feared?"

Cetshwayo thought for a second and said, "Bakuba is far away; so far no person ever reached it."

A Zulu proverb, Bakuba being the Zulu equivalent of utopia, essentially similar to the English proverb "it's no use building castles in the sky", Cetshwayo was stating it would be over ambitious to attempt to rule by the love of his people, folly in fact, it being far more expedient to do so by fear.

Our sable springbok, attired in wedding garb, shook her head in a disappointed manner, "If Bakuba is far away you have distanced the Zulu still further, for today you send young men to die for your pride. Surely you have brought the Zulu closer to Hell than Bakuba?"

Cetshwayo retorted while the gathering listened intently, "These Christians have polluted your mind with strange ideas, heaven and hell, sins, purgatory, but you shall return to the Zulu ways even if your husband has to beat it into you," the King stood up and pointed his staff into the crowd, "Come quickly, we must make sacrifice for our warriors."

Three priests rose and made their way out of the kraal, followed by Cetshwayo. The impi were soon to enter battle and their King was going to ensure every possible wind was to their backs. This sacrifice was as much to bolster impi confidence as to honour the ancestors. For if a Zulu were to enter battle against such a formidable opponent minus proper sacrament there might be nerves, which would undoubtedly manifest in the form of panic and fear, perhaps causing a break in Zulu battle lines.

Cetshwayo was going to make sacrifice before his impi left so every one of them might witness his offering, putting young minds at ease, focusing their full attention upon the task at hand.

Whether Cetshwayo believed in the ancestors or not was superfluous, he was a crafty man and understood what was required. For if the battle was lost and he'd not made sacrifice he'd be blamed and a possible leadership challenge may ensue. Inversely, should the impi win without their King making sacrifice, well, what use is he now? Another weakness his would-be successors would inevitably exploit to usurp him.

No, he must make sacrifice before his warriors leave for Isandlwana. As impi gathered readying themselves outside Ulundi, Cetshwayo and his priests prepared an altar with animal sacrifice in plain sight. Not just to ensure confidence in battle but also the continuation of Cetshwayo as Zulu King upon their return, no matter the outcome.

As preparations were made outside the kraal wedding guests began to disperse. Nkosazane sat in chains, not the wedding she or her mother had envisioned.

Serving girls helped her up as two dark sentinels monitored our wayward springbok. Queen kaMpande approached the young men, "Release my daughter."

The impi warriors were silent for a moment until one of them spoke in a deep commanding African tone, "My Queen, the King has ordered us to guard the Princess."

Queen kaMpande answered in a cool soothing pitch, "Did he order you to keep the Princess chained at all times?"

The fellows looked at one another rather gormlessly, "No, but the King did not permit us to release her, my Queen."

"Good," retorted the Queen in a haughty pitch, "you are not releasing her, I am, now hand over the key to my daughter's chains," she presented her hand palm up in anticipation of the iron key to Nkosazane's manacles.

The young men froze in fear, men walking a tightrope, for if they misjudged their balance death was a certainty, "Perhaps I should ask the King, your Majesty?"

"What is your name?" demanded Queen kaMpande.

Before he answered the soothing sound of Princess kaMpande intervened for she had no animosity toward her sentinels, "Mother, please, allow these men to speak to father, I can wait a little longer. If these chains become too great a burden I shall rest."

Queen kaMpande gathered her daughter's words as a farmer would ears of wheat, turning them into bread to feed these young men's souls.

Rescued by a merciful springbok as a famished supplicant might grab onto a loaf flung into the street from the royal palace; chunks of bread made by their Queen from the wheat of Nkosazane's wisdom, cast from her table to starving men, "As you wish my child," Queen kaMpande pointed at one of the tall lads, "Go, speak to the King."

He darted off leaving his associate to guard Princess Nkosazane, not that it was possible for her to escape Ulundi a second time. Her previous vanishing act didn't involve the burden of thick iron chains to impede her movement or weigh down a sixty mile trek to the Buffalo River.

Nkosazane retired to an indus, the traditional Zulu beehive hut. She waited within for her release while serving girls removed Nkosazane's wedding outfit and her mother bemoaned such terrible luck surrounding her daughter's marriage.

It was quite amusing from an objective standpoint. If Zulu mothers complained about their daughters, concerning difficulty in marriage, it would certainly be in finding a suitable suitor willing to fork out the lobola, as not all young ladies had the looks, poise and desirable frame as Nkosazane.

No, Queen kaMpande's terrible problem was the fact that the two most eligible bachelors ... well perhaps Dabulamanzi wasn't a bachelor yet he was eligible by Zulu standards. Anyway, the root of her headache was that two of the most eligible suitors in Africa were fighting for her daughter's hand in marriage and when I say fight, this wasn't fisticuffs or even pistols at dawn.

Two armies were about clash at a place relatively unimportant, a hill in the Zulu Empire, a recurring theme in so many of history's greatest victories ... and defeats. Who'd heard of Waterloo before the final battle between The Duke of Wellington and Napoleon? Agincourt before Henry routed the French? The Cape of Trafalgar until Nelson accomplished the most decisive naval victory in history?

So Isandlwana was about to enter the history books, 1,400 British and 2,500 African infantry soldiers were to engage 12,000 Zulu impi. An insane proposition you say? For how could the British hope to win with such a deficit in numbers?

The British Royal Army was the premier fighting force in Africa, perhaps the world at that time. They were armed with the Martini-Henry rifle, a sturdy breech loading, single shot rifle using a lever action which first entered service in 1871.

The Martini-Henry MK IV saw extensive use throughout the British Empire up until the end of the First World War.

In fact it was used by Afghan tribesman against the Soviet invasion. In 2011 Americans recovered three of these rifles from a Taliban weapons cache, it is one of the most reliable and durable weapons of war ever to be issued.

With a high rate of fire and disciplined men behind them they might cut down an oncoming assault of impi warriors, carrying traditional spears and shields, with ease. Besides, every other army of African origin had been annihilated in their attempts to overcome the British with numbers and spears. British redcoats had good reason to be confident.

The Zulu were armed primarily with the iklwa, a short spear or blade named for the sucking sound it generates when drawn from the victim's body. Its shaft is about four feet long and its blade is about two to three feet long.

They also carried a club known as an iwisa, a brutal weapon that the British pith helmet was ill constructed to deflect.

The impi also carried conventional rifles acquired in trading, though untrained in their use; added to that these rifles were often of poorer quality when compared to the British Martini-Henry.

The impi weren't a professional fighting force yet they made up for this with extensive knowledge of local terrain, high mobility and an unbreakable will in defending their families.

The Zulu understood the British well enough, they realised they could not defeat them in a rifle engagement. So Zulu commanders decided on closing distance as quickly as possible, absorbing horrifying losses until close enough to engage with the short spear, at which point they possessed the advantage.

Using a tactic known as the buffalo's horns they'd flank the British and engage in a bloody melee. Isandlwana was to go down in history, glory to the Zulu and infamy for the British, for it would be the worst defeat the British Royal Army had suffered in its history, routed into retreat and chased out of Zululand by impi warriors, a humiliation.

Chapter Nine: Negotiations

Several days later a runner appeared in Ulundi conveying favourable news regarding the battle of Isandlwana … on the surface.

Like a calm sea, good news can feign placidity above yet beneath rests a mighty undercurrent, capable of dragging a man deep into the bowels of Poseidon's kingdom and swallowing him whole; a serene, glistening skin which obscures the turbulence of a terrible storm, until it's too late.

The British had been broken, routed in fact, a mere fifty five men returned alive to KwaNatal.

Thousands of soldiers lost in a single battle, to date it was the most humiliating defeat of a British colonial force. A loss to French or Russians is one thing but to be routed by a band of African tribesman, well, it just wasn't cricket.

Every soldier on the forward firing line was cut down to a man, overwhelmed by wave after wave of impi until they eventually surcame. The horns of the bull closed on the flanks of the British lion as a pair of hands squeezing a man's throat, his neck splitting apart to the tremendous assault brought to bear simultaneously on every side, encapsulating his doom.

Lines crumbled before Lord Chelmsford's eyes forcing him to sound the retreat, with cavalry fighting a rear guard action the British were hounded until they crossed the Buffalo River into home territory.

When word reached the Houses of Parliament there was uproar, Benjamin Disraeli, the British Prime Minister, noted in Parliament, "A very remarkable people the Zulu: they defeat our Generals, they convert our bishops, they have settled the fate of a great European Dynasty."

An unmitigated catastrophe, fifty five returned from an expedition of thousands, escaping over the Buffalo's back. British dead would lay exposed to sun for months, until Frederic returned to bury them in graves of more than one body.

This defeat would bring on the loss of the next British General Election in 1880; the Zulu victory at Isandlwana sent shock waves throughout the Empire on all levels of society.

Colonial military tactics were reviewed; no longer would they face the Zulu with a line of soldiers, also known as the thin red line. In future the British would entrench themselves or form thick squares, heavy artillery and extra Gatling guns would be employed with large numbers of redcoats. Already they journeyed aboard a steam ship soon to arrive on the Cape, for the pride of a nation had been wounded and the British did crave revenge.

Celebrations had been underway for nearly two weeks before impi returned, heroes of all Africa. For on the battlefield they claimed their kleos and now on the homecoming they were to receive nostos. That is glory on the battlefield and glory on the homecoming. Kleos is related to the English word for loud, on further examination it means "what others hear about you". Nostos on the other hand being the roots of nostalgia in the English language.

Drums beat and women danced shrieking to the heavens in joy, for the ancestors returned husbands to families ... for the most part.

The impi had taken heavy losses themselves, 3,000 of their bravest warriors were buried, ten per cent of all Cetshwayo's forces had been cut down in a single battle, so they might repulse these tea stained demons come to steal their lands.

Dabulamanzi marched at the head of his troops behind General Ntshingwayo kaMahole, women lined up forming a procession. Zulu girls squealed in delight at the sight of young warriors, heads held high in victory, a dark procession of African Spartans made its way to the palace.

King Cetshwayo waited inside his palatial kraal, resting on his courtyard throne, wife by his side, his daughter dutifully to the side and behind, all upon a thick wooden dais set in place for such occasions.

Impi officers moved inside while regular troops and the people of Ulundi gazed from outside the kraal. Ntshingwayo approached his King; a long object gleamed in his hands, afternoon sun reflecting on its silver surface.

The Zulu General took a knee before the dais, bowed his head and presented his gift, a cavalry sabre. Its brass guard and handle both brightly polished along with steel sheath, its former owner obviously took great pride in this item.

Nkosazane's heart leapt, beating hard on the door at the base of her throat. Our Zulu Princess had witnessed such weapons whilst living with her betrothed in Port Elizabeth. Yet she was not so familiar with the cutlery of battle as to identify a butter knife from a steak knife for they all appeared similar. Cavalry sabres did not pique her interest to such a degree she wished to study them.

If only Nkosazane had taken a greater interest, for now the worst case scenario did inhabit her mind as a ghoul in a graveyard. Perhaps the man she loved had died near some rocky escarpment no-one had ever heard of? Slowly bleeding onto parched earth, dust and smoke filling its air as fearful Zulu war cries preceded formidable speared charges.

Cetshwayo rose from his throne, stepping forward he observed the item offered by a victorious General, "What is this you bring before me?"

"The cavalry Sabre of a prince, my King" replied the old General.

"Give it to me," stated Cetshwayo, his tone was morose, it retained an attitude of expectancy far from the celebratory harmonies which flowed and ebbed across Ulundi that day.

Ntshingwayo offered the sabre to his King, Cetshwayo took it, unsheathed the weapon to observe a beautiful design etched upon its blade, the depiction was that of a cockerel. Cetshwayo sheathed the weapon with great force, "A French prince?"

"Yes my King, Prince Louis-Napoleon, Son of French Emperor Napoleon III," replied his proud General.

"Where is this Prince?" demanded Cetshwayo with great urgency.

"Vultures pick his bones on the field of Isandlwana my King," replied a somewhat confused Ntshingwayo for this was not the reaction he'd anticipated. Rather than joy and celebration it was as if a crisis were felt to be at hand.

Cetshwayo closed his eyes for a few moments, long enough for those outside the kraal to understand all was not well in Zululand. The mighty hippo turned his face upwards and as if speaking directly to the ancestors, he whispered, "This is a disaster."

His General was bewildered by Cetshwayo's reaction for at Isandlwana the ant had overwhelmed the elephant, "King?"

Cetshwayo stood in suspense, a withering meditation encompassed his being, for the King recalled his magic man's warning, "When the buffalo bleeds, the princely cockerel is killed, the lion shall have his revenge." A stampede seemed to be in motion, its direction firmly against him, for fate is a machine both decisive and perilous in manoeuvre; its subjects paralyzed before a cold hearted mercy, all because pride did outweigh prophecy in a single moment. In his royal rage he'd forgotten that men, even Zulu impi and British redcoats do die without difference of opinion, "Leave me," stated Cetshwayo.

"King?" replied his General in an incredulous tone for they'd won the greatest African victory of modern times and his monarch was nothing if despondent.

"I SAID LEAVE ME!" bellowed a belligerent beast, sending warriors scurrying from his presence as mice flee a tomcat. Impi warriors exited the royal kraal joining celebrations into the early hours of the morning. Drinking beer, supping wine, listening to music and enjoying man's greatest vice, the cause of thousands rotting on the plains of KwaZulu ... women.

Cetshwayo retreated within his palace, a firm grasp on the gleaming sabre, taken from the bloody corpse of a prophetic prince. The cockerel is the symbol of France and the lion the symbol of England but when Xhegu spoke of the Zulu being crushed did he mean in battle or as a people?

So many scenarios did swirl inside the hippo's head; he struggled to sort what might be fact from that of pure fantasy. Only days ago he dismissed everything his witch doctor had proposed as abstract fiction, however, the princely cockerel's sabre rested in his hand. Its owner carrion for the birds on the field of Isandlwana, the Buffalo River seemed to bleed and the lion would no doubt return.

Now that her moment of strife had concluded Nkosazane felt pity for her father, for Lord Chelmsford had escaped with some fifty five survivors, if not Ntshingwayo would have presented his head rather than Napoleon's sabre.

Our springbok's heart throbbed for her father since the clear victor was in dazed disarray much to the confusion of his people.

Ntshingwayo perceived an historic victory sending shockwaves around the world so all might know the glory of the Zulu people. Cetshwayo understood better. Yes, the Zulu had crushed the British and forced them into a disgraceful rout but bloody constraint was to return across the Buffalo's back, this was certain. It was preposterous to believe the British would leave it at that, a humiliating defeat followed by a demeaning rout, no, these men were as proud as Zulu, they would return and exact harsh revenge.

For Zulu, celebration was on the cards, while British licked their wounds as a battered dog whimpering in a corner, yet that dog did plot against the Chief with much ire in his heart. The British beast imagined in what manner he might tear at that Zulu face, gnash its chest, splitting it open to expose a beating heart.

For despite his Christian ways the white man was not inclined to forgive such transgressions and as for this Lord Chelmsford; Cetshwayo knew little of him as a man yet it was becoming obvious he was one of fierce determination and clearly in love with his daughter.

In that moment the King did respect the Englishman, for he imagined him to be as a lion fighting over a lioness, prepared to risk his life for hers and in the instant between a man's breath he bemoaned Chelmsford was not his son-in-law.

Nkosazane sensed her father's despondency, his psyche pulled in all directions. Our sable springbok placed a comforting hand on his forearm, "What ails thee father?"

He turned to his daughter, "I must contact the white man and discuss matters. Perhaps a compromise can be met before every kraal in KwaZulu is soaked in the blood of its children."

Nkosazane smiled and grasped his strong harm harder, "Thank you father."

"But I will need you to decipher his tongue so I might comprehend his true intent. I must put an end to this foolishness. Nearly ten thousand men have died on a meagre patch of earth for a single woman," the hippo spoke in a melancholy tone as he scrutinized the beautiful sabre in his hands.

At that moment Dabulamanzi marched into the palace, on catching the words of King Cetshwayo he composed an indignant roar, "What is this? You speak of surrender? Even as your people celebrate the greatest victory in their history?"

Nkosazane berated her husband, "Watch your tongue in my father's presence Dabulamanzi."

The impi commander's voice lashed out, cracking as a whip, "Silence woman! You shall not speak in the presence of men, now get to your hut and wait for me."

Nkosazane stood firm, her legs as two trunks of the chestnut tree, the rebellious springbok was resolved, she wouldn't give herself up for him. In fact she'd harboured hope he wouldn't return from the battle of Isandlwana but it was not to be.

"TO YOUR HUT WOMAN!" bellowed the mighty impi.

He would've beaten her into submission yet she stood beside the King and although Dabulamanzi was quite happy to show contempt and coarseness toward Nkosazane, for it was his nature, he wasn't prepared to abuse the springbok when it leaned on the hippo for the hippo might easily crush his frame.

"You have enough women," retorted our sable springbok, "go and molest one of them, I'm sure they anticipate your return … as a hyena does anticipate diarrhoea!"

Dabulamanzi's face ignited as fire from a pit of black tar, his psyche skirted the limits of tolerance for this woman did require a firm hand until she learned her place, yet the hippo's proximity blocked that course of action.

"Enough of this quarrel," stated the King, "why do you disturb me Dabulamanzi?"

Drawing a deep breath the impi steadied his nerves, fixed his vision on Cetshwayo and replied, "I have come for my wife yet I cannot believe my ears. I enter this chamber and bear witness to talk of compromise and the blood of Zulu children even as the drums of victory sound across Ulundi."

Cetshwayo sighed, "There is a reason I am King and you command the impi, when you are as proficient at diplomacy as you are battle it might be possible that you are king too."

"I do not comprehend," replied Dabulamanzi in a confused tone.

"Exactly," stated Cetshwayo, "My daughter must stay with me until this war is concluded. I cannot have the Englishman come here and see you with her."

"WHAT IS THIS!?!" barked a furious hyena.

"Composure and contempt shall find themselves fast bedfellows should he witnesses Nkosazane at another man's side, a new husband even."

"If he sees her by my side he will understand, another man owns this woman and he will return home," retorted Dabulamanzi.

The King remained passive, able to think clearly for the first time in a while thanks to his daughter's company, "If roles were reversed and you witnessed Nkosazane married to another man, would you simply renounce your love for her and return home? Satisfied to send thousands of your men to their graves and suffer the greatest loss in your nation's history, with nothing to show for it?"

Dabulamanzi was silent for a moment, he wouldn't rest until Nkosazane was in his arms, the number of men that had to die in the process was of little consequence, "Of course not," blurted a stubborn savannah wolf.

"Then why is it you expect the white man to do differently?"

It was at this moment Dabulamanzi grasped that his wife wouldn't be his until this troublesome Englishman was seen off, whether by diplomacy or on the battlefield, "As you wish your Majesty, I will wait until this umlungu has given up the chase."

When analysed objectively it was quite obvious that the British lord did pose a greater threat to Cetshwayo's throne than Dabulamanzi. In all logic it made common sense Cetshwayo negotiate a stand down using Nkosazane as the main bargaining chip, perhaps that was his future intent?

The thought warmed Nkosazane's heart, she would soon be in the arms of her British lion and away from that impi hyena yet something was off.

Call it woman's intuition, for despite a path to her lover's side emerging from dusty desert, the road was pock marked with deep pits and razor sharp rocks, many hidden behind a haze only the witch doctor seemed able to peer inside.

As Dabulamanzi finished his sentence a familiar voice echoed from behind, all present halted what they were doing as Xhegu's raspy tone made itself known, "The cockerel is dead, the lion wounded, the buffalo's back shall bleed once more, a river of blood winding its way to Ulundi."

A long silence filled the air as both parties stared at one another; there was nothing to add to the magic man's prophetic pitch. After a few moments that seemed like many minutes a pair of impi led by General Ntshingwayo entered the building escorting a single prisoner, a familiar face. Bastijn Klein Soepenberg, the blonde haired slave trader accompanied them.

Ntshingwayo knelt before his monarch, "Rise," stated the King his voice carrying a tone of curiosity as his eyes scanned the Afrikaner.

"Your Majesty, this man was captured by one of our patrols. He was at the head of an armed band on the Buffalo River."

Nkosazane peered into his sunken eyes; he who had enslaved her twice was now in chains, an object of pity himself for in being forced to keep up with the Zulu he'd collapsed more than once.

Nevertheless our sable springbok held empathy in her heart; after all she was a prisoner too. Nkosazane had been married to a man she despised, all in the name of dynastic stability yet ironically her father discarded marriage to the white man in the same cause.

"Well done Ntshingwayo," said Cetshwayo as he focused on the slave trader, "we meet again Soepenberg, tell me what is your business bringing men and weapons into Zululand?"

The exhausted Afrikaner lifted his dirt smeared face, looking into his captor's eyes he replied in that Afrikaans accent, "I was searching for the exiled, banished and desperate."

Ntshingwayo cut in, "I do not believe him your Majesty. My men say he was part of the militia supporting the British invasion."

"What do you say to that?" inquired the hippo.

"No, that's not true," stated Soepenberg, his voice increasing in desperation with each word as bitter fate passed through his mind, the irony of it all. He'd enslaved Zulu for so many years, capturing them on the Buffalo River and selling them to Boer farmers. Yet here he stood, wrists shackled to one another, before the Zulu King, accused of crimes quite different than those he'd spent so many years perpetrating, and to top it off, captured on the Buffalo River of all places.

The blonde haired slaver protested with what little strength dwelled within his miserable physique. He resembled a faded portrait smeared with dirt, bordered by a decrepit frame, "I was on the river looking for slaves, that's all, honest."

"I'm afraid I do not trust white men especially those who trade in Zulu blood. Your kind are the ntothoviyane," the ntothoviyane being the stripped grasshopper, a creature synonymous with double dealing and untrustworthiness, "I said it would be to your advantage we never cross paths again, and now you know why," Cetshwayo fixed his gaze upon his impi General, "send him to his desert, to die."

Now the King was expressing the manner in which Soepenberg was to die, for in Zululand the death penalty was a common occurrence. Essentially there were three different methods of execution, the first reserved for soldiers who failed in their duties.

Soldiers were impaled to death, via the rectum. The second method of execution befell the soldier's wife who also suffered for his crime, whether it be cowardice or insubordination, she too would be impaled with a spear, via the vagina.

As far as non-military were concerned they would be clubbed until close to death before they were taken out into the savannah and left to die from their wounds, starvation and dehydration or torn to pieces by wild animals; their remains were left exposed as a deterrent to anyone who might encroach upon Zulu territory.

Soepenberg was to suffer a clubbing and slow death in the hot African sun. As he was being moved away Nkosazane spoke out, "Stop," the impi paused, their eyes flicking between her and King Cetshwayo, "Father show him mercy."

"Why should I grant this white rat mercy?"

"He was not with the British. Soepenberg is only interested in the purchase and sale of human beings, as one would trade cattle at a market. He is a coward; he would never put his life at risk for the meagre reward the British Army might offer to invade KwaZulu."

Cetshwayo's eyes narrowed as he re-examined the slave trader, "My daughter speaks out for your wretched life, what do you say?"

"She speaks the truth mighty King, I'd make far more money selling a handful of slaves than fighting for the British Empire, and of course, it's a lot less dangerous," gasped the vile Dutchman in a relieved accent.

"Yet my daughter has given no reason I should let you live," stated Cetshwayo, his voice betraying a resigned tone, resigned to the death of Soepenberg.

"Father," implored Nkosazane, "he could be useful in your up and coming negotiations."

"Yes, yes," yelped the blonde haired slaver, "I have information!"

"What information?" pressed Cetshwayo.

"The British, they're sending reinforcements, they're on a steamship already, it'll be here soon!"

"What else?" inquired the King.

"Do you promise not to execute me?" whined Soepenberg.

"SPEAK MAN! Or you will join your fellow white men at Isandlwana!" roared an impatient King.

"Alright, alright," said the slaver his wrists chained with palms pointed at Cetshwayo, "High Commissioner Bartle, he's being recalled, a man named Field Marshal Wolseley has been sent to replace him but he won't arrive until after the reinforcements. I've heard from contacts that Bartle and Chelmsford are going to launch another invasion before he arrives, something about saving their reputations."

The hippo glanced toward his impi commanders, first his General, Ntshingwayo, "What are your thoughts?"

The old General sneered, "He is umlungu, you cannot trust his word my King."

"Umlungu" being one of the old descriptors for the white man, it means "Those who practice magic", ironic since the white man often accuses the black man of the same vocation.

The origin of the label "Umlungu" originates from when white men first appeared in the Cape region of Africa, they brought many wondrous items which seemed to be magic to its inhabitants, even a pair of spectacles was a supernatural work to Zulu.

Ntshingwayo was an old man entrenched in the old ways and so referred to white men as those who practice magic, despite the fact the Zulu had gained an understanding of those objects to the point they employ them in their day to day lives.

Cetshwayo focused on his second in command, "What is your opinion?"

"I agree," added Dabulamanzi, "the umlungu will say anything to save his miserable hide, he sold our people to Boer's for paper money, do you not think he would lie to you?"

Nkosazane stroked her father's arm and spoke softly, "Father, may I speak?"

Cetshwayo raised an eyebrow, his daughter must have something she wants to say, why else would she act in such an agreeable manner? "Very well, what are your thoughts child?"

"While inserting old prejudice into our current situation we have become forgetful," purred the sable springbok.

"Go on my child," stated the King while tension exuded from Nkosazane's husband, the foremost author of the tragedy soon to besmirch the Zulu nation, flanked by his General and a sorry Soepenberg.

"Lord Chelmsford is not umlungu but ipuma lemile. A single defeat will not discourage such a man nor will he cease until his wife is back in his arms," stated our beautiful Princess, her delicate voice playing in his ear as the music box in Frederic's study.

Dabulamanzi scowled at her statement, not for its content but out of fear that perhaps Cetshwayo saw some of himself in this white man, "This is outrageous, she will defend any white man over her countrymen, even denounce her own husband before the royal court. Her word is not to be trusted."

Now to be clear, the phrase "ipuma lemile" in Zulu means "those who walk upright". The origin of the phrase is probably not what you might suspect, its source emanates from the Zulu hut, an iQukwane.

For the iQukwane has a very low entrance and the owner or guest must stoop, even crawl to enter; it's a sign of respect and no doubt conducive to a good environment within.

Well, the doorway to the white man's home is constructed so he may enter upright and so the name stuck; the white man being a proud individual with little respect for Zulu ways.

Nkosazane had an excellent point; if they were to bandy about prejudice in this manner then they must consider more than a single descriptor of their enemy. Added to that no-one here was more familiar with the white man and his ways than Nkosazane.

Cetshwayo contemplated his daughter's words, it didn't take long for him to come to the conclusion, that this man, Lord Chelmsford, was more ipuma lemile than umlungu and almost certain to launch another assault. Cetshwayo caught the eye of Soepenberg, "When does Field Marshall Wolseley arrive?"

"Six months," replied the desperate slave trader without missing a beat.

"In that case the British are likely to launch a second invasion within the next six months. Dabulamanzi, prepare your impi for a second battle, recover as many British rifles as possible and train your men in their use.

Ntshingwayo, contact the British, inform them King Cetshwayo does wish to settle for peace as soon as possible," ordered the King, his voice betraying a troubled nature which engrossed his thoughts.

Dabulamanzi protested yet was quickly placed in check and sent on his way. The impi General did as always, immediately obeying his King's instruction, Soepenberg was held prisoner in the royal kraal.

Xhegu remained silent for there was nothing he might add, the King knew what he must do yet he'd not come to terms with it, the good of his people in exchange for his daughter's hand in marriage to Lieutenant General Lord Chelmsford, commander of the British forces.

It weren't as if he'd be sacrificing her in anyway, not even her happiness for it is what she desired; but for purely selfish reasons he wished her to stay in Ulundi, fourth wife to his impi commander, and to be crystal clear, for those who don't understand there is a definite ranking when it comes to Zulu wives.

The first wife sat at the top of the totem pole, as chief wife she took pride of place in the umuzi, the homestead. Next the right hand wife, then the left hand wife. Nkosazane would be below the left hand wife and no doubt assigned to the filthiest jobs in the homestead, even mocked by the other wives, and for what? The satisfaction of one man's ambition and securing another's dynasty?

Once the chamber had been cleared Xhegu spoke, "The lion and the hippo are proud yet one must kneel to the other if bloodshed is to be avoided; the ancestors are clear, the hippo will bow to the lion and sacrifice the springbok, if not, the lightning bird shall suffer the white man's fury for one hundred years."

It was too late for King Cetshwayo to draw anger from the witch doctor's words, his white face and dishevelled appearance no longer frightened him, it only served as a reminder of his previous foolishness. Fate lay in ambush, preparing to strike from the shadow of Cetshwayo's pride. The Zulu stood teetering on the precipice, the edge of a mighty abyss swirling as a giant black hole ready to crush them as flies, all for a single woman and her father's pride, he resolved himself to do something about it as quickly as possible.

Letters were sent back and forth, a temporary truce agreed upon and a meeting place designated. Once more at the Buffalo River, a strip of water separating KwaZulu and KwaNatal, men would meet to discuss the fate of East Africa and its inhabitants; for on learning of the inbound British forces, King Cetshwayo realised the lion was dead set not only on defeating the bull in battle, but bringing down the ox and conquering the lightning bird, unless he might offer the white man refreshment, quenching his thirst for revenge.

Unfortunately for Cetshwayo the situation was just as dire for both Bartle and Chelmsford. Despite the British government backing Bartle's plans for confederation of the Southern African Cape, an ignominious defeat followed by an equally inglorious rout were never accounted for. Victory over the savages of Africa was expected of Bartle and Chelmsford, men who'd served the Empire so well in the past.

1st Viscount Wolseley would strike land on the cape in six months, a man sent to form control from chaos, while Bartle was to return to England, an imperial stain scrubbed from a soiled reputation on the African Cape.

The two Brits possessed scant time to defeat the Zulu and recover what little of their esteem remained. Fresh troops would arrive three months before the Viscount, leaving but a thin window to salvage the careers of these otherwise greatly distinguished friends.

On the banks of the Buffalo River where wild chestnuts grew, neutral ground had been designated and so Cetshwayo arrived with his impi, a wagon pulled by a lone horse accompanied them.

Chelmsford rose from a canvas chair, dressed in scarlet uniform, black trousers with thin red line travelling from hip to hem, a white belt crossing his chest suspended a British officers pattern 1853 cavalry sabre on his left side, on his right an Adams MK III revolver. Upon his head a bright white pith helmet with brass badge facing forward, flashing intensely beneath savage sun.

Cetshwayo wondered how the white man tolerated the heat of Africa in such apparel. If the hippo had visited India he'd understand that in comparison Zululand was a walk in Kew Gardens on a breezy spring day!

The Zulu contingent pulled up on their side of the river eyeing a wooden bridge, hastily constructed by British Army Engineers. The hippo didn't trust the white man much less his constructions over bodies of fast moving water.

Bartle wore equally smothering dress, a black suit with tall black hat and walking cane, his bushy grey moustache hiding his top lip from scrutiny. Another mad Englishman, either that or his ancestors protected him from the sun's rays; perhaps that is why they were all a shade of pink?

"You may cross, it's quite safe," yelled Bartle in a rather undignified fashion.

The Zulu paused for a minute, Bartle spoke to Chelmsford who waited by his side, "Do these savages understand the English language?"

"I'm unsure," stated Chelmsford squinting a little as the sun caught his eyes, "though I'm aware of one Zulu who speaks both English and French, yet her presence confounds me."

"In Christ's name will you forget about that Zulu girl, we're to negotiate their surrender not concoct a love poem!" snapped Bartle, thoroughly tired of his old friend's pining for Nkosazane.

Chelmsford removed his vision from the Zulu detachment and fixed it upon the high commissioner's mien, "Henry, we're old friends, please refrain from lecturing my ears as if I were a naughty choir boy."

"I understand Frederic, but you've been drivelling on about her and it does test my patience, why your pining would cause my wife to blush!"

The Lieutenant General smirked, "And do tell me, how would you muzzle Catherine?"

Bartle grumbled, "Puh, I don't suppose you'd be satisfied with a new Sunday dress?"

Chelmsford smiled, "If it were purchased for Nkosazane, I'd certainly consider your offer."

Bartle chuckled, "Perhaps I will, if these savages surrender her today."

On the other side Cetshwayo was mystified by the white men and their demeanour. They'd suffered the worst defeat on any battlefield in the history of the British Empire yet they stood chuckling and joking to one another. The King spoke to his impi General, "Ntshingwayo, have you ever witnessed such madness?"

The old warrior strained to see across the river, its torrents smashing on rocky banks spitting white foam into atmosphere as dolphins leaping out of the ocean, "I have not my King, they jest with one another despite the battle of Isandlwana. Look, the English officer, he barely escaped with but fifty men over this very river yet he is jolly, as if it were the celebration of their messiah's birth."

Cetshwayo shook his head, "Bring forth Soepenberg; he will make sense of this madness."

The impi General sent the order; two men marched to the back of the wagon and drew forth the slave trader escorting him to the hippo's side. The white rat stood a good foot shorter than the mighty hippo.

"Soepenberg, speak to the white man," ordered Cetshwayo.

The blonde Afrikaner placed his hands around his mouth projecting his voice toward its target, "HEY! BARTLE! WHAT DO YOU WANT?" he bellowed.

Bartle broke off his conversation with Chelmsford and simply motioned to the bridge then pointed at a group of star chestnut trees.

"He wants us to come over his side, under those trees," stated the blonde prisoner, talking up to Cetshwayo.

"I don't trust these white men; they laugh and joke in the hot sun as crazed hyenas in the desert. I fear they plan to bite and gnaw my body, satisfying their thirst with my blood," replied a wary King.

Soepenberg reassured Cetshwayo, "They won't do that, these British need something honourable, a formal surrender. They ain't gonna back stab you when they've got thousands of redcoats coming on a steamer. Why assassinate you when they could wait and get an honourable victory?"

"We have little alternative," the King peered at his General, "come, bring a guard for this white rat and bring my daughter. I need someone to supervise these white devils while they communicate with one another."

Two impi flanked Soepenberg, one either side, General Ntshingwayo kaMahole moved to the rear of the wagon, it trembled side to side as Nkosazane took his hand and carefully stepped down, attired in her silver bodice and lace dress.

Cetshwayo wanted this negotiation to go as smoothly as possible, he realised Chelmsford would be eager to know of his daughter's condition and hoped her presence might pacify the British General to some degree.

Her Zulu husband was against this yet he wasn't invited, that man was too hot headed; a fine warrior in the field yet a dismal diplomat. Dabulamanzi had ambitions on the Zulu throne but he wasn't ready to be king, a successful Zulu king must know when to make war and when to settle for peace.

Nkosazane stepped down, one hand grasping that of the Zulu General the other lifting the hem of her dress. The Zulu contingent went quiet at the sight of such beauty, as she rounded the wagon and moved toward the bridge, silence befell the British. Men, young and old alike, gawked at her distant image for she'd become something of a mythical creature in the Cape Colony.

All through British territory her name graced the tongues of women on all levels of society. Even men discussed her in drinking houses, debating how a black woman might capture the heart of an English lord.

Akin to Penthesilea, Daughter to Ares and the Queen of the Amazons. A beautiful princess of the most feared tribe, enough so she did distract Achilles in the heat of battle. Yet her Achilles rested on the other side of the Buffalo River, not a man she wished to kill but join in matrimony for the rest of her life.

Five Zulu and one Afrikaner crossed the wooden bridge, Nkosazane's eyes never leaving her love, his vision fixed upon her image. The sable springbok's heart began to beat as if for the first time in months, her lord and master waited in anticipation, every fibre of her sable body desired to leap into his, merging for all eternity.

An apprehensive contingent crossed a sturdy bridge before being led to the chestnut trees. Cetshwayo was offered a canvass chair barely capable of supporting his bulk. Chelmsford approached his love, impi drew short spears and redcoats took aim.

For a few tense moments men watched on, in fear of what might occur for the sake of separating two soul mates. Their distance had already cost so much death and tragedy; surely peace could be maintained for now. And so King Cetshwayo called his men off, they withdrew and Chelmsford took his African Princess in his arms.

"How have they treated you?" he asked, his eyes scrutinized every square centimetre of her face as one who does assess art might examine a great masterpiece, at first to validate its authenticity but on certification he does ponder its canvass, wonderful dark strokes of perfection forming a smooth skin, ogling simply for his own selfish pleasure.

Nkosazane's perfect shade, a rich chocolate that despite its darkness shimmered in the sun as dark African gold, a marvel Lord Chelmsford found both confounding and enticing. Sable eyes, yet bright, amber of the darkest shade sparkling in the light of Zululand; lips so succulent, was he the only Englishman to recognise the superiority of the African bouquet inhabiting her visage? Cheekbones raised high, as flags on a mast flying the colours of radiant beauty for all lonely men to witness, and finally the encore, her nose, the beak of a lightning bird, a bill of esteem and beauty. Its nature alone did excite his senses yet he'd not recognised those feelings until witnessing the masterpiece upon Nkosazane's exquisite African canvass.

"They have not harmed me, my Master," replied his sable springbok in a somewhat subdued tone for she felt overwhelmed in Frederic's presence. Just his proximity electrified her soul, every nerve tingled, trembling with desire and joy, for in his orbit she could let go of her shield and expose her soul in safety. This man would only caress her spirit with his, blending souls as two historic lovers separated by time and location. Their spirits passing down through the ancestors, by the centuries, to reunite by the grace of God on the Buffalo River, no doubt the location they were separated all those hundreds of years ago. Pulled apart by death to be reconciled lifetimes later, a widowed white man and a betrothed black woman colliding in an explosion of sparks to the shock, and even disgust, of an ignorant world.

Chelmsford took her hands in his, scrutinizing ebony fingers, she still displayed her sapphire engagement ring. Cetshwayo had returned it to its rightful place after discovering Soepenberg had failed to deliver it, "I could barely sleep with the thought of you and what you might be suffering."

She smiled, her pillow lips widened, the knowledge that his desire had not waned in their time spent apart filled her heart with glee. As a goblet of wine might be filled at the banquet table, his words of comfort filled a void of doubt. For Nkosazane feared he may have forgotten her, perhaps she was merely some white man's fancy for a few weeks, something he wished to cross off his list of achievements while visiting the continent of Africa, before returning home.

"I did not suffer, though I must tell you, I was made to marry while in Ulundi. Please believe me when I say, I did so only under physical duress. I had no say, quite literally," she decided to drop the bomb before her love went any further; it was only fair he know. The lion could then decide if he wished to continue his pursuit of the springbok.

Chelmsford's cheeks transformed from ivory to meat red, a scarlet hue emerged from an ocean of allegiance to his fiancé. Frederic knew better than to hold her responsible for he'd touched souls with this woman and they were pair bonded, just as they'd been pair bonded on the Buffalo River centuries before and no doubt centuries to come, he couldn't hold her accountable for her father's outrageous behaviour.

Chelmsford clasped her hands, ivory on ebony, masculine protecting feminine, as God intended, "Fear not my love, your father shall be weighed whole, his accounts settled and correction issued on this most grave insult."

The pair kissed, her sable pillows upon his marble steps. Nkosazane feared that not only would her father suffer the taste of Frederic's correction but as the magic man had stated, the Zulu would carry the burden as a generational curse; all because two lovers had been split by a cabal of privileged fools, unable to witness their own downfall in the course of blind pride.

After a tender kiss Chelmsford took the arm of his Juliet and strolled beneath the chestnut trees to face Cetshwayo.

Frederic spoke in a stern tone full of repressed anger, a man who judging by his energies mirrored a warrior in his twenties yet held the authority of a much older gentleman. His reflection the dark backing of this mirror that is death to all those who conspired against his union with Nkosazane, "Sir, I hereby demand the return of my fiancé, I will not take no for answer."

Soepenberg translated for the mighty King, who for the first time in a long time sat in the presence of equals. He looked up at Chelmsford standing stiff and straight, he was ipuma lemile, "He who walks upright", yet the King was reluctant to cede anything so early in a negotiation. It wasn't good practice in his opinion, yet this wasn't just any negotiation, for despite an historic victory at Isandlwana, felt around the world, a single battle on the lips of Presidents, Prime Ministers, Queens, Kings and Emperors in all four corners of the globe, he was at a disadvantage. The Zulu victory had guaranteed a brutal and bloody response, enough perhaps to break his tribe for generations and so today compromise became Cetshwayo's bedfellow.

The mighty King looked up at his prospective son in law, "Today, should we come to a satisfactory settlement; I shall offer my daughter the right to choose her husband. If she so desires, Nkosazane may join you for the journey home."

Before Soepenberg could speak, Nkosazane translated for her love. Frederic was visibly displeased; he was here for his future wife not to quibble over caveats. The lion cared not for peace treaties or the give and take of civil servicemen especially when it came to arguments over the nitty gritty, he was a soldier. Frederic marched forth and conquered his foe then issued an ultimatum or as with the Xhosa chief, defeating him in battle to hunt him down as a pack of hounds might chase a wounded fox through woods.

"Take a chair old boy," stated Bartle in a cool tone for this was his forte. The high commissioner was an old hat at bartering down the price of ancestral real estate until its title rested in the hands of the British Crown.

A scandalous profession if conducted on a private basis yet when done so in the name of Queen Victoria it held the greatest esteem, titles and all sorts of honours bestowed upon its perpetrator.

Negotiations journeyed steadily into the day as a donkey travelling Brighton beach. Bartle demanded that Zululand essentially surrender its sovereignty and agree to become a protectorate of the British Empire.

Cetshwayo refused, he'd be trading his position of ultimate authority in his own land, and for what? So that he wouldn't be required to fight the British a second time?

It was a stark choice, surrender his people to Queen Victoria, now lauded as the Queen of Africa, or fight for freedom.

"Have no fear, as a protectorate you'd have everything you have now, in short you'd be almost complete with but a few minor differences," implored Bartle in the belief he was getting through to the King.

Soepenberg translated, Cetshwayo listened intently before peering toward his daughter. She confirmed the slaver's translation with a single nod of her head.

The hippo sighed and spoke in his native language, "Cishe akudliwa."

An awkward silence was eventually broken by Bartle, "Well? What was his reply?"

Soepenberg spoke through a thick Afrikaans accent, "The King says that almost is not eaten."

The high commissioner returned a puzzled visage, "I'm sorry?"

Nkosazane spoke up, "It is a Zulu proverb Mr Bartle. Tell me, would you eat an almost roasted chicken?"

"Oh, I see what you mean. Then it seems we've reached an impasse," stated Bartle as he stood up.

Nothing was agreed upon that day. Nkosazane returned with her father to Ulundi and Frederic returned to Port Elizabeth, to prepare his troops. Invasion was imminent. Ares was to return to the land of the Zulu, he would ride with his sons Phobos and Deimos, Fear and Terror, pulling his chariot across the savannah, indulging his vile appetite for death, gore, mayhem and misery.

Chapter Ten: Ulundi

Campfires flickered upon the Buffalo River; stars illuminated the Milky Way, betraying tens of thousands of redcoats … on the verge of total war. Large artillery pieces cast in Birmingham, monsters developed from the machine were set in an orderly line on the British bank of the Buffalo, awaiting their master's instruction. Britain and Zululand prepared as lion pitted against bull, scowling at one another from opposite sides of the Buffalo River. More firepower than previously wielded upon any single African tribe occupied but a single space. Gatling guns were lined up and inspected, horrific apparatus of violence, capable of a constant stream of high calibre bullets fired in rapid succession. Several barrels held in a cartwheel of cruelty, rooted to earth via a sturdy base.

From the opposite side, Zulu scouts observed an army of certain doom perceived in a sea of steel and red wool. Younger men held onto the belief of a second Zulu victory, the gusto of youth overcoming the acumen of age. For wiser warriors carried a heavy heart on such matters, nevertheless, they'd fight with no less tenacity than the youth beside them. Today the lion was going to gather its humiliation discharging it into the bull by the force of gunpowder, sucking the oxygen of life from the warriors of Shaka Zulu.

Stars twinkled in sky above; forming a fateful stream of celestial origin which foretold what was to come. Yet mere men remained powerless to influence change, for the white man's God and the Zulu's ancestors had set the outcome in night sky, for eternity. Blood and plunder was to plough a gruesome trough to the city of Ulundi, led by a man who some might say was out of his mind. His love for a Zulu woman causing two great nations to clash and bloody constrain to bathe a beautiful land in the gore of both invader and inhabitant.

In Ulundi King Cetshwayo observed his impi depart the great city, drums beat a melody of war as young women sang raising hearts of warriors, setting off to clash with the white man. A reminder of why they risked their lives, for if man did not fight for woman what did he fight for?

Some would say a man fights for money or property or prestige, this is all true but ask yourself, why does a man covet these things? Is it for the intrinsic value of those items or is there a higher purpose? And if so what is that higher purpose? Well I'll tell you, a man does not covet treasure for the sake of treasure he covets that which treasure might permit him to acquire. That which land or prestige might allow him to possess beyond the item itself and that path has but a single destination, woman. Just as dogs do fight over a bitch in heat, so men will murder one another in great battles, souls consumed by the Devil himself as he moves through the battlefield freely, dragging men down to hell, all for woman. For redcoats fought with the same motivations as impi, and this war, much like that for Helen of Troy thousands of years ago, was for the love of a single woman.

The great King made sacrifice to his ancestors, beseeching them, begging they fight on the side of their children and grant another victory to the people of KwaZulu, yet it was in vain.

The British crossed into Zululand the next morning, their force increased from 15,000 troops to 25,000. Chelmsford, armed with knowledge of Zulu tactics was not inclined to repeat the mistakes of his previous invasion. Frederic wouldn't spread his forces so thinly on this occasion, blinded by his own arrogance to be lured in and butchered by impi, this offensive would be very different.

Added to that the first invasion despite numbering 15,000 only 6,000 of those men were redcoats, 9,000 being African militia, men from opposing tribes and Boer farmers, some out for pillage and plunder others engrossed with thoughts of revenge.

This time around 16,000 red coats were accompanied by 7,000 Natal natives and a 2-3,000 man civilian transport; added to that a rocket artillery battery had been transported from England, its shells filled with quicklime, a deadly caustic substance similar in effect to mustard gas. Once the shell reached its target a timed charge would detonate above enemy lines and a white cloud would expand burning all those caught in its plume, the eyes being particularly vulnerable, quicklime often caused blindness.

This horrific weapon of war was not considered becoming of a gentleman, yet public opinion failed to influence Chelmsford's rather unscrupulous actions, he cared only for his love, kidnapped and held against her will in Ulundi. Besides, quicklime and kidnapping were as ruthless as one another and he'd employ its acid burn to break apart impi lines, forcing them into retreat. An ignominious English stratagem, its origin considered a dastardly trick of war in Napoleonic Europe, was to disgrace the battlefields of Africa and sear the Zulu.

Come morning redcoats marched and Zulu moved to meet them, but rather than the thin red line, Chelmsford and his commanders decided on a totally different tactic.

Instead of a thin line, redcoats took position on high ground, a hill or a cottage with a stone wall surrounding it. Soldiers would form a deep square and dig in, entrenched they repelled every impi assault. Slaughtering warriors who might make it past cannon artillery, then rocket artillery, avoiding plumes of quicklime exploding overhead and into close quarters where redcoats and Gatling gun dropped young man after young man, casting themselves against a thick scarlet barrier of death as black flies dashed upon red granite rock by a hurricane.

Eventually the British army reached Ulundi, having defeated every attempt to halt it. King Cetshwayo witnessed nought but doom and so immediately set about negotiations, he was desperate, 20,000 troops were poised before the royal kraal on a hill outside Ulundi. He sent a gift of oxen, elephant tusk and a promise of guns, but it was too late. Chelmsford refused his offer and with 1st Viscount Wolseley dispatching telegrams more than once a day, demanding he halt his advance on Ulundi and wait for his arrival, Chelmsford had little time to take action before being relieved of command.

Frederic returned the Zulu King's offer demanding he surrender at least one regiment of his impi today before peace could be negotiated.

Cetshwayo stood in his royal kraal staring stoically at a scarlet heap on a hill overlooking Ulundi, for he did comprehend that he examined not only his destruction, but that of a nation.

Nkosazane comforted the troubled ruler, "Father, do you hear me?"

Cetshwayo's mind seemed to have drifted so far from the ground it did wander in a desert of isolation, a sailor adrift on a flimsy raft as salt waves buffeted him one way or the other, this cruel sea possessed a terrible vitality. Miserable fate was fed by ocean waves and gusts of powerful wind pushing the King toward rocks of doom.

"Father?" she squeezed his formerly vigorous arm, an arm which had thrown many spears in its time and brought down many a warrior, for Cetshwayo was no stranger to battle, he understood the back breaking gravity he and his people laboured beneath.

Cetshwayo awoke from his trance and with nought but glumness in his eye peered down at his daughter, "Yes my child?" he said in a solemn tone, one which caused Nkosazane concern.

"Describe these thoughts which cause such a troublesome expression on your exterior? For I see your face silently twist as a woman giving birth and your frame does struggle to maintain stability."

He sighed, "I see resting upon that hill not only a man who loves my daughter but the last days of the Zulu as a free people. Tell me my child to whom would you deliver victory today, if it were in your power?"

Nkosazane pulled a wry smile, partly in answer to his question and the other part to comfort a troubled King, "Father, such matters are decided by men not women."

"Yet it is for a woman that they are waged, remittance demanded and duly paid by one party or the other, the price, once measured in total, being a sacrifice of blood and freedom."

She tugged her father's arm in an attempt to abate a stoic sorrow consuming his person, "Perhaps the Zulu will prevail? Your impi may defeat the British redcoats."

He sensed her concern and it brought a tiny smile to his face lasting but a moment before being swallowed by an abyss of doom, "My child, should the impi attain victory our punishment would only be postponed, and upon arrival it would carry a greater burden than the one you see today."

She squeezed as a washer woman draining a rag yet his arm remained tense and firm. Nkosazane's heart went out to her father and the troubled times he endured, "Then surrender father, in the least Zulu lives will be saved."

"I have offered the Englishman tribute yet he refuses my supplication."

"Father, I have heard from the serving girls that you denied Frederic's request? Is that true?"

Cetshwayo peered down with a grim visage for he despised palace gossip, not that it mattered much now, "He demands I surrender an entire regiment and disarm the impi."

"Why not meet his request?" stated Nkosazane in a naïve tone, for in matters of social etiquette she was well versed, however, matters of war were not a subject our springbok cared for.

"If I were to order the impi to disarm and surrender I would be overthrown, as quickly as a hungry hyena would consume a carcass, then, they would go to battle anyway. The only difference in outcome would be my death and who knows for your mother?"

Our sable springbok shook her head, "Why are men so thick headed father?"

He narrowed his eyes examining the hill overlooking Ulundi as British forces set Gatling guns into position, "It is a great strength ... and a great failing."

"I do not see how thick headedness might be positive to a man's existence, certainly not that of a woman!"

Her naïveté comforted Cetshwayo as he reminisced of a time when Nkosazane was a small girl playing at her father's knee. In those days everything in the world was new and Nkosazane naïve to all aspects of the masculine with only her father for guidance. Under the old hippo's tutelage he'd unwittingly transferred many facets of his own personality, as alcohol fresh off the still does extract elements from the oak barrel it ages within. Some aspects of the liquor are positive, others negative, yet when analysed on its merits as the sum of its parts the spirit was by far the superior to your average white dog whisky, "Without his thick headedness man would not have made such efforts to civilize the world. The white man would live as we do, in his own land with his own women rather than plunder ours.

Take your white lion for example, were he not so thick headed he would've heeded his friend's advice and never courted you. Once you were returned to Ulundi he would've forgotten you. After his first defeat at Isandlwana he would've given up and if defeated here he would return to his homeland, but he is too thick headed.

This Lord Chelmsford will continue fighting as a wounded lion surrounded by baying hyena, he feels neither pain nor concern for his own life, he thinks of but a single Zulu woman and we shall all pay for it in blood and freedom, for generations to come."

After such a gloomy speech Nkosazane felt her heart sink, thank God he hadn't shared these thoughts with the royal court. Our sable Princess felt a wave of guilt pass over her body, then another feeling, for guilt was sucked out and replaced by a contrasting emotion. The tall Zulu woman struggled to pick it out of her memory for she'd not experienced this mix of emotional states before, and it was a mix, not a single sensation.

She realised guilt hadn't been washed away; instead a separate emotion entered her conscience, blending together as her soul had fused with Frederic's. She sensed her knight in shining armour and his thick headedness, love did mingle with guilt to form an odd black and white soup, then she detected attention, how this was all about her.

Despite or because of the fact, yes, because of the fact, thousands of brave men had died and thousands more would lose their lives, ripped from their wives by the march of war, a war for a single woman, for Princess Nkosazane of Ulundi; because of this she felt satisfaction expand inside her.

An odd category of joy saturated her psyche, and as a woman would fill an animal skin with water at a well during drought, making certain not a drop is wasted, Nkosazane protected its existence beneath her dark skin for fear it be divined by others. Nkosazane remained as stoic as her father while she plumbed the depths of sensation saturating her frame.

As she bathed in this bizarre dark brand of delight, its root being attention, a currency all women trade for as men do gold, Nkosazane's mind flitted between a dominating scarlet hill and terrified men and women cowering within Ulundi.

Due to its gruesome nature few women in history did enjoy such an intense spotlight, men died for her by the thousand, nations clashed, humiliated, subjugated, her name would be heard around the world, echoed in mouths of men and women for years to come. Great scholars would teach students centuries from now about the beautiful Nkosazane of Ulundi and the war waged for her love, it did stimulate Nkosazane's ego in a way only a woman could take joy from such savage slaughter.

A man takes kleos and nostos from war, kleos being honour earned on the battlefield, nostos being glory earned on the homecoming.

For a woman there is little to be gained yet in Nkosazane's case she was the focus of every man, woman and child. Some spat when her name was mentioned, others revered it, for she was at this moment considered not only the most beautiful woman in Africa but the most desirable woman in the world. How many women living today can boast such unchecked beastly carnage unleashed to decide her husband?

The battle of Ulundi took place; redcoats entrenched upon a hill forming a deep scarlet square. Impi perished as they charged again and again. Brave men piled up, as logs fill a canal before being floated down stream to the mill where they're sliced into manageable pieces. Once tall proud beings, higher than all they surveyed, today lay flat and lifeless, one spread beside the other stacked three corpses high.

The scene was one of utter desolation, more than six thousand impi slaughtered before the British as rockets fired from troughs, striking in turn like many concussive hammers, they detonated great clouds of quicklime above the heads of fearless warriors.

It was not a gentlemanly sight yet Lord Chelmsford no longer cared for the courtesies Generals pay one another on the battle field. He was here to destroy the impi, to break the Zulus' back and return his bride, the woman he loved, to Port Elizabeth, 30,000 impi wolves would fail to rein in a single savage lion.

Cetshwayo observed solemnly through a spyglass from his royal kraal, one of the magic items the white man brought with him to the land of the Zulu.

In his mind he prayed to the ancestors, perhaps his impi would mount the hill and burst through that thick square, yet the ancestors had already spoken and he ignored them, his pride obscuring that which a wise man might easily divine.

Only after his victory did Cetshwayo deduce the course this river of blood weaved. Rather than dam up glory, the Zulu victory over the British did add to the ferocity of a growing body of catastrophe culminating in an untamed slaughter of Africa's most elite fighting force. Once the impi were broken the Zulu nation naturally followed as a calf trails a cow, there'd be nothing he could do to negotiate down the white man's demands.

Eventually the carnage became too much and impi fled for high ground so that they might take a defensive position … it was too late. Cavalry chased impi warriors as they withdrew, killing every warrior to a man. Before they might reach safe ground young impi joined their brethren, prostrate between bloodied soil and smoke filled air.

Victory not sufficient in itself, the British lions took revenge for their humiliation at Isandlwana. Cavalrymen doubled back, putting wounded warriors lying amongst lifeless comrades to death, sending fine soldiers to meet their ancestors.

Before the day was out not a single impi who'd taken part in the battle of Ulundi remained in this world to recant its bloody tale to his children. It was a scene of utter ruin. Some redcoats celebrated, others looked on with a morose mien, pity for the fallen. Chelmsford's demeanour hadn't altered, he resembled a man carved from rock, motionless but for directing battlefield manoeuvres, as Alexander at the Battle of Hydaspes, the lion would not be satisfied before retrieving his springbok from the hippo's clutches.

The British camped down for the night, come daybreak they formed up and marched toward the Zulu capital. Crisp earthy morning air carried an acrid tonic of distress as the sound of the Scottish highlands closed upon the gates of Ulundi.

A new African sun peeked above the horizon to observe boots thudding upon earth in time to drums and bagpipes, lesser instruments of war employed to lift a man's soul and remind him of his duty to Queen and country. Pipes played at the forefront of long scarlet streams, rivers of blood descending to wash King Cetshwayo's authority away and bring forth a new dawn of British supremacy.

The tune "All the Blue Bonnets over the Border" played, a ballad regarding Bonnie Prince Charlie's march into England with his jacobite army, their blue bonnets synonymous with the army of scots.

The gates to Ulundi were ordered open and as victorious impi had been welcomed home so many times, a similar display was put on for their victorious foe.

Lieutenant-Colonel Evelyn Wood in command of the 91st Highlanders approached Lord Chelmsford; both men rested on horseback, the Colonel insisted Frederic lead his men into the fallen city.

Chelmsford, never one for such grandstanding, relented on his Colonel's insistence. The lion rode to the front as his men cheered, drums beat louder and bagpipes bloomed.

He rode out front, as Caesar might ride his chariot through Rome to the adoration of the crowd. Zulu women, all cognisant of this man and his motivations sang his praises while young girls bared their breasts kicking so high their ankles did collide with earrings.

In ancient Rome a slave would stand behind the victor and whisper in his ear "memento mori" or "remember you're mortal", though after so much death and destruction Chelmsford was in no danger of believing himself anything but a mortal man.

The Lieutenant-General's only concern was Nkosazane, as he rode at the head of this scarlet and tea snake, stern face, stiff back, accepting Zulu adulation to the beat of drums; a group of dark skinned boys circled his horse jumping up to touch his black boots, stained by Zulu earth and impi blood.

Colonel Wood rode up alongside with the intent of dispatching the Zulu children, Chelmsford quickly halted him, "I'll allow it Colonel."

"As you wish, Sir," stated Evelyn dressed in a similar scarlet tunic with insignia of rank upon pith helmet, his tunic discerning him from lower ranks along with officers' pistol and sabre.

"I don't usually permit such pomp and parade; however the men have earned the right to celebrate. It's good to see them in high spirits."

Colonel Wood smiled, nodded and rode back alongside the column. Booming at the top of his lungs Wood's voice exceeded the drone of bagpipes to reach every set of ears housed beneath a tea stained top, "WHO GAVE THE FUZZY WUZZIES A GOOD HIDING?"

Each man roared in synchrony, a chorus of British lions caused all Ulundi to shake as a man when he first tastes battle, "LORD FREDDIE!"

"WHO'S THE MEANEST BASTARD IN ALL OF AFRICA?" shouted the Colonel.

"LORD FREDDIE!" replied a scarlet army marching toward the royal kraal.

"WHO MADE THE FUZZY WUZZIES RUN?"

"LORD FREDDIE!"

"WHO'S THE HARDEST BASTARD ON THE GO?"

"LORD FREDDIE!"

Cetshwayo didn't understand their tongue yet he divined both foreboding and celebration, as white men roared in victory to strange sombre instruments fashioned at the other end of the globe.

A small detachment of impi remained within the royal kraal, upon Lord Chelmsford's approach, surrounded by playful children, its gates swung open. Boys and girls were shooed away as Chelmsford entered on horseback, Colonel Evelyn Wood by his side and a hundred or so of his finest Highlanders.

First Lord Chelmsford dismounted followed by Colonel Wood; young redcoats took the reins of their stallions. The English gentlemen were strident, dressed in black leather boots and dark trousers with a thin red stripe running the outside leg, a fine line of fury was about meet a Zulu delegation headed by King Cetshwayo.

Despite the fact that Frederic was a man of over six feet himself, the King's mighty frame cast a shadow upon Lord Chelmsford.

The Zulu delegation hid behind Cetshwayo, he was their shield against the leering barbarity of the British Empire.

Soepenberg appeared from behind the King as a child does slip from its parents lead, yet remaining within its father's orbit, for fear the powerful hippo might swat this striped grasshopper down should a desperate escape be attempted.

"You?" snapped Chelmsford as the blonde haired beast made his presence known to the Englishmen.

"That's right m'lord," replied a somewhat nervous Afrikaner who was certain the Zulu King's stomach would meet much distress after swallowing the lion's demands. But should he make a desperate run for the British contingent the chances of Chelmsford arranging a hanging were not beyond the scope of probabilities.

"What is your purpose in this residence?" inquired the British General, distaste occupying the tip of his tongue, since where this rat did nest vipers were to be found.

Blood for money was Soepenberg's trade and Chelmsford held a stern dislike for such business.

"King's translator, m'lord."

"As you wish Mr Soepenberg, inform King Cetshwayo I demand to see Nkosazane immediately."

Soepenberg turned to the King relaying Chelmsford's demand, troubled glances flashed around the Zulu party. The population of Ulundi gathered outside the royal kraal peering above its mud brick walls and pushing through its gates. Their eyes transfixed on the exchange within, a discourse that would settle their destiny ... for generations to come.

The great hippo pondered his reply for some time, it was in fact but a few moments yet in these periods moments are often stretched into minutes by the human mind. Just as a piece of dough might be stretched out by a pair of skilled hands, so bartering over the future of the Zulu tribe does cause the dough which forms time to expand in all directions. Negotiations over a single cow will pass swiftly no matter the length of haggling, but for an entire kingdom time becomes elastic and for a woman, for Nkosazane of Ulundi it did stretch into eternity.

Cetshwayo spoke and Soepenberg translated his message, "The King says his daughter will remain under his protection, until peace terms can be negotiated."

Chelmsford became visibly enraged, his cheeks turning meat red, enough so those observing from outside the kraal did gauge his fury. The white lion growled at Soepenberg, "Inform your sovereign that should Nkosazane not be standing by my side this minute I shall order my men to burn Ulundi to the ground and have every man, woman and child shot!"

Colonel Wood was taken aback by his superior's pledge for they were English gentlemen; there was a code to combat and a code to peace. Once victory had been secured such beastly behaviour was not an option, yet at this moment there was no atrocity so heinous that Lord Chelmsford was not willing to inflict it upon the population of Ulundi. Love had exceeded the constraints of gentlemanly conduct and the innocent would be forced to endure its wrath.

Cetshwayo's eyes widened as Soepenberg updated a defeated monarch on his conqueror's nihilistic vow. The great hippo snorted to his men, two impi departed in haste leaving the parties pitted against one another as rabid hyenas. They were gone some minutes, during which time Dabulamanzi kaMpande walked through the kraal gate, he and five impi were spattered in blood, the blood of Zulu warriors shed miles from Ulundi. He'd refused to clean himself of impi gore; his conscience wouldn't permit it, not until his mind was unburdened of yesterday's tragedy.

He was now General of the impi and all Zulu military forces after Ntshingwayo had been cut down outside Ulundi. The old General's final testament being a co-ordinated spread of Gatling gun fire into a concentration of impi warriors, charging through a cloud of quick lime, up a slope, into a British fortification.

Dabulamanzi had been commanding several thousand impi at Eshowe where he'd laid siege to Colonel Charles Pearson for two months.

Chelmsford was expected to come to his rescue and in doing so the impi, hidden in long grass, planned a massive surprise attack on his main force.

Chelmsford hadn't played their game for in his thick headedness he saw nothing but Nkosazane, she was in Ulundi and so Frederic pressed the Zulu capital, paying no heed to his distressed Colonel.

Dabulamanzi exchanged words with Cetshwayo as Nkosazane appeared, resplendent in her silver and tan gown escorted by the Queen. Queen kaMpande realised the danger her people were in and so did her best to appease a white man in the grips of passionate love with her daughter. For this lion was prepared to burn an entire city and murder its inhabitants for want of Nkosazane, Nkosazane of Ulundi.

Our sable springbok exited women's quarters, stepping beneath mortal scrutiny, and so to a man all fell silent in her presence. Redcoats stopped chattering to observe the woman in whose name they'd risked their lives and spilt so much blood across East Africa. Inhabitants of Ulundi peered within, their eyes captured by bright silver contrasting against perfect sable skin.

As our native Princess moved gracefully in their direction she noticed a sea of scarlet, her heart lifted a little, next Nkosazane witnessed two British officers. A little closer and Nkosazane recognised her love, her white lion, her heart burst with joy. She picked up her dress, lifting its hem the springbok ran toward him with a smile stretching from one cheek to the other.

Our sable springbok thrust herself into the arms of her white warrior, he dutifully squeezed her tight. She a trembling ball of emotion for he'd survived Africa's most feared warriors, nay, defeated them and entered the gates of Ulundi as a conquistador might have rode into Tenochtitlan. A vanquisher of heresy spreading the word of the Lord by any means necessary.

Tears began to form in the eyes of our Zulu Princess as she tucked her head into his chest, she was safe. Waves of calm flowed across her body, the excitement of touching her soul mate caused our African angel's frame to weaken and her heart did flutter as a butterfly bobbing up and down on a warm breeze.

Chelmsford's face nestled atop her head his lips hidden inside her hair, he kissed the top of Nkosazane's skull reminding our sable springbok that her master had come to retrieve his love. Men had travelled thousands of miles from the other end of the Earth to fight to the death on the plains of Africa in a titanic struggle. Gore from England did splash on Zulu dust so a single woman might be returned to the arms of her lord, redcoats watched in wonder to see who or what this woman was. Finally they did scrutinize her in person, the woman who'd pulled them from the arms of their wives so she may be returned to Lord Chelmsford.

As Chelmsford comforted his fiancé, a trembling black butterfly, Dabulamanzi stepped forward, spiteful emotion filled his visage. This was intolerable! Before the whole of Ulundi Dabulamanzi was being demeaned by an umlungu; an evil magic bringer from dark cold lands beyond the ability of any Zulu to reach.

The impi General disrupted the couple's tender greeting with a grievous growl. Chelmsford examined his love's concern as a blood spattered hyena barked.

"What on earth is that fellow shouting about?" Lord Chelmsford asked of Nkosazane.

"He is Dabulamanzi … the man I was forced to marry, he is voicing outrage and claims me as his wife," replied a timid springbock.

The white lion set his Princess aside, "Colonel, take care of Nkosazane."

Colonel Wood dutifully stood beside the Zulu Princess, ready to repulse any attempt to retrieve her from the custody of Lieutenant General Chelmsford.

Chelmsford stepped up, boots kicking dust into air, forming a cloud before settling, as a swarm of bees disturbed in long grass; into the atmosphere for a few moments before descending to feed on nectar of exotic flowers.

Erect, his stiff spine directly opposing Dabulamanzi, the Englishman looked down then over to Soepenberg, "What is it this fellow wants?"

Soepenberg made an uncomfortable expression, frustrating Chelmsford, "Well? Out with it man!" roared the lion.

"He says to get your hands off his wife," replied the foul Dutchman.

Cetshwayo watched on with interest as the slaver relayed Dabulamanzi's words, he could use this fool's uncontrollable rage to his advantage. The devious King waited for Soepenberg to finish before interjecting, Soepenberg turned and spoke to Chelmsford, "King Cetshwayo suggests a duel, to settle the issue of his daughter's owner."

Understanding that both men were far too proud to back down the hippo could lure the umlungu into a one on one duel, and, if the ancestors were willing, kill the British General.

The logic behind his strategy was twofold, he'd get his daughter back and secondly negotiations would go smoother. Cetshwayo understood Viscount Wolseley wasn't far from Ulundi and Chelmsford wished to secure a surrender, lock, stock and barrel as soon as possible, restoring his reputation and that of his friend Bartle.

Chelmsford's death would probably result in Colonel Wood handing his daughter back and waiting for Viscount Wolseley before a peace settlement were drawn up. Unlike Bartle and Chelmsford, Viscount Wolseley had no motivation to humiliate the Zulu.

Chelmsford, never one to back down from a good fight, undid the chinstrap on his pith helmet and removed his revolver from its belt, "Wood, take these," he handed the items to his Colonel who stood aghast.

"Sir, you can't do this," stated the Colonel.

"Do what?" replied Chelmsford.

"Duel with a savage."

Chelmsford paused for a moment looking him dead in the eye, "Then what do you think we were doing yesterday?"

There was no reply as two Generals stepped away to secure a patch of ground in the kraal. Zulu men and women cheered on Dabulamanzi, redcoats urged their General as they squared off. The Zulu King administered, breaking the pair up for a moment as he bellowed something in his language instigating roars of men from outside the royal kraal that did mimic the sound of a mighty tsunami crashing against sea cliffs, much like the crowds of ancient Rome cheering on their favoured gladiator.

Chelmsford drew his Pattern 1853 British Cavalry sabre, the British sabre was very much a thrusting weapon, as were all British military swords, for the British were obsessed with designing the perfect blade and they considered a thrusting weapon superior to a cutting blade.

One good thrust finished a man off, there and then, whereas it may take many cuts to achieve a similar outcome. The 1853 had a brass guard and was a point weapon, demonstrating only the slightest of curves. This blade was intended to snuff out a man's life as quickly as one might extinguish a candle, permitting its owner brisk latitude to tackle his next opponent in similar fashion.

Dabulamanzi was handed an iklwa along with a long cowhide shield, the iklwa being a Zulu short spear. A weapon which had subjugated the East of Africa was now being employed in a desperate duel for the greatest prize the Dark Continent had to offer … Nkosazane of Ulundi.

The crafty King cried out, "QALA!"

Dabulamanzi raised his shield and brought his iklwa to bear. Chelmsford didn't require an understanding of Zulu language; he took his stance, saluted with sword, left hand above his head while pointing the sabre's tip directly at his opponent.

Lord Chelmsford was an arduous student of all disciplines involving combat. He'd studied at the Royal Military Academy in Woolwich paying particular attention to artillery and the blade.

Dabulamanzi moved in, as is the impi method, to draw close using your shield as cover then tear your enemy to pieces with the iklwa. Chelmsford retreated in a fencer's stance, maintaining lunging distance, waiting for an opportunity. The lion understood how thick an impi shield could be, it wouldn't stop a bullet but he couldn't risk his sword not making it through and leaving him open to Dabulamanzi's iklwa.

Nkosazane cried in fear, for her lover was risking his all against the most feared and competent warrior of the Zulu nation. She grasped Colonel Wood's arm as if dangling over a cliff edge, an abyss swirled beneath her feet. Its gaping mouth mocking her precarious position, waiting patiently for her grip to give and consume Nkosazane as a child might a chunk of milk chocolate.

Dabulamanzi became frustrated; his greatest weakness in life being a poverty of patience, today it did beckon peril. The impi General charged at a retreating Englishman and in doing so he pulled his arms back slightly … a small opening presented itself in Dabulamanzi's midsection.

Chelmsford required no further incentive; he was long trained through eye, muscle and mind. Instinct kicked in and the white lion lunged into an oncoming impi … his sabre ran through the dark warrior … arresting him, dead in his tracks.

Dabulamanzi froze in time, his spirit torn between two worlds, vision locked on Chelmsford. Slowly his jaw dropped and his eyes moved downwards to scrutinize a steel blade, forged in a land shrouded in myth a century ago, now made reality it penetrated the space between his belly and heart, sliding amidst his ribcage … poking out of his back.

Blood began to flow from Dabulamanzi's gaping mouth, he choked. Relinquishing shield and spear, his body became limp by degrees. Dabulamanzi grasped at cold steel in an attempt to remove it yet Chelmsford fixed his weapon firmly in place, the master of this impi General's destiny.

Dabulamanzi's life ebbed away as he gradually slumped to the ground; his passing complete the hyena joined its ancestors.

The impi General crumpled into a cloud of dust before Ulundi, along with their hopes of freedom, disintegrating backwards into the afterlife. Chelmsford's sabre remained static, the warrior's body slid over it and into the abyss of hereafter. Frederic called his first officer; Colonel Evelyn Wood handed him a tartan handkerchief, primarily used in the safe consumption of snuff.

The white lion wiped his blade clean of Dabulamanzi's stain before returning the cotton patch and sheathing his sword, "Consider that an annulment!" he stated glaring down at the corpse of a once feared warrior.

Rounding on Zulu royalty and their entourage Chelmsford scowled, "Now you shall agree to MY terms or bloody compulsion shall bring that upstart attitude to smooth agreement!"

Soepenberg translated, Cetshwayo was downcast but he had one last dice to throw, the mighty King turned to his magic man, "Xhegu, it is time."

The old witch doctor replied with hesitation in his breath, "Time your Majesty?"

"Use your magic and kill this umlungu, send him to his afterlife and you will be rewarded beyond your own imagination. You will need but request and your desire shall be delivered. The most luscious wine, the most beautiful women, from wherever you wish in KwaZulu; whether a man's wife or daughter it is unimportant, she will be ripped from his arms to serve whatever need you see fit, you have my word as the descendant of Shaka."

The old man grinned, "It is too late your Majesty, the umlungu's ancestors are powerful, his King, Jesus Christ, does protect him. The time for peace has passed leaving the blood thirsty in the ascendant. You refused your own ancestors counsel and so today you will kneel before the ancestors of the umlungu and beg he not take your skin as an ornament for his Empress."

There is an old African proverb "A speaker of truth has no friends" and so Xhegu was a despised man.

Cetshwayo became infuriated, partly because the old man spoke the truth and part due to his rebellious nature, which were one in the same. Nevertheless there was little he could do but meet the white man's demands.

And so Cetshwayo and Chelmsford agreed on peace, the King was deposed, his daughter the property of Lord Chelmsford. Redcoats sang and played pipes into the night.

Oddly enough the Zulu joined the British in celebration. Perhaps they were relieved now that six months of total war and blood soaked savannah had come to a conclusion?

Nkosazane escorted Chelmsford to a large royal hut. Guarded by redcoats they spent the night in each other's arms. Through a small opening at its apex the lovers observed stars travel the heavens, defining their journey of love, their story reflected above by the constellations of Perseus and Andromeda.

The girl Andromeda, more beautiful than Poseidon's own children or so her father boasted before being punished by the mighty god for making such a claim; his kingdom was destroyed and Andromeda tied to a rock, a sacrifice to appease Poseidon's sea monster.

Perseus, on witnessing Andromeda's beauty, did rescue her and kill the sea monster yet he couldn't marry his love as she was already married to Phineus.

So the demi-god Perseus and the mortal Phineus fought with bloody violence over possession of a beautiful woman, until Perseus emerged victorious.

They were married, living long happy lives and upon their deaths both were immortalized in the night sky, their constellations placed beside one another. Today they are beacons of love and loyalty … and so did the tale of Lord Frederic Chelmsford and Princess Nkosazane kaMpande mirror these historical lovers and in years to come some did rightly compare them to Perseus and Andromeda.

For in the tale of their marriage an entire Kingdom was destroyed, split into many different parts by the new high commissioner. A king was deposed, the most beautiful woman in Africa fought over by a fiancé and husband until the husband lay dead.

A beautiful Princess had been released from her chains into the arms of her rightful husband, a man who would travel any distance, fight any battle, duel any demon be it a single man or 30,000 warriors, to take his bride, by any means necessary.

Love and loyalty did define a powerful bond between the two. Perhaps they were Perseus and Andromeda reborn? Unable to resist the connection of their former lives Perseus was drawn to Africa and on witnessing his soul mate, his twin flame, the British General did snap into action, instinctively he took his historical lover.

Nkosazane, as beautiful as Andromeda, enough to anger even the gods, was to be sacrificed for the sake of dynastic stability but she refused to be chained to a rock for the sake of appeasing an authoritarian monster.

Our sable beauty escaped the inevitable drudgery of becoming Dabulamanzi's fourth wife, something drew her to the Buffalo River, as if in a past existence she'd dwelled there with her lover, Perseus, thousands of years ago, now immortalized in the dark vault above her head at night. Tiny filaments beamed out to onlookers beneath, the beacons of Andromeda and Perseus did transmit a legend of the greatest lovers in history yet her eyes failed to decipher such intense love and loyalty, cryptically displayed in a burning night ballet.

On that river she waited, Nkosazane knew not why yet our springbok was convinced an answer to her puzzle would manifest, it had to, since without her love revealing himself she was but an empty vessel.

Andromeda divined the presence of Perseus, for they are twin flames, having come together they burn as a single entity flickering in the night sky for thousands of years, it was impossible for Nkosazane to dismiss him.

When twin flames have converged for long enough they share a part of themselves with the other, an essence is deposited.

He inserts his essence within her and her essence does fill the empty space within him and so they become one, for eternity. Nothing else is capable of replenishing that aperture of love and loyalty.

So that evening in Ulundi, essence did pass between the pair, their link re-established, the lion and the springbok were pair bonded for life beneath the watchful gaze of Andromeda and Perseus, he inside her, her holding on as if for dear life, surrounded by his protection, until they both ascended to the stars to join one another in the night sky for eternity.

And so ends the tale of Princess Nkosazane of Ulundi, Baroness of Chelmsford, the most beautiful woman in Africa and as some have since claimed, the world.

Dedicated to

Queen Princess Karabo Ngcobo

Printed in Great Britain
by Amazon

19355516R00123